I0764635

A Ford in the River

Also by Charles Rose

In the Midst of Life: A Hospice Volunteer's Story (2004)

A FORD IN THE RIVER

Stories by

CHARLES ROSE

NEWSOUTH BOOKS
Montgomery | Louisville

NewSouth Books
105 S. Court Street
Montgomery, AL 36104

 Published in the United States by NewSouth Books, a division of NewSouth, Inc., Montgomery, Alabama.

Library of Congress Cataloging-in-Publication Data

Rose, Charles Spencer, 1930-
A ford in the river : stories / by Charles Rose.

p. cm.

ISBN-13: 978-1-60306-112-4 (cloth)
ISBN-10: 1-60306-112-6 (cloth)
ISBN-13: 978-1-60306-113-1 (eBook)
ISBN-10: 1-60306-113-4 (eBook)

I. Title.
PS3618.O78296F67 2010
813'.6--dc22

2010015018

Design by Randall Williams
Printed in the United States of America

ACKNOWLEDGMENTS

The author and the publisher gratefully acknowledge the following publications in which stories in this collection first appeared: "The Skater," "Remission," and "White Orchid," in *Shenandoah*; "Photographs," "Island Grove," and "Kelp," in *The Chattahoochee Review*; "Vigil," "A New Roof," and "Mr. Hardcastle," in *Alabama Literary Review*; "Harmonica," in *Crazyhorse*; "Chairs" and "Treasure Hunt," in *Southern Humanities Review*; "A Ford in the River," in *Blackbird*; "Complicity," in *Willow Springs*; "Pagoda," in *Passager*; "The View from My Father's Window," in *Cricket*; "Spink Hotel," in *The Southern Review*.

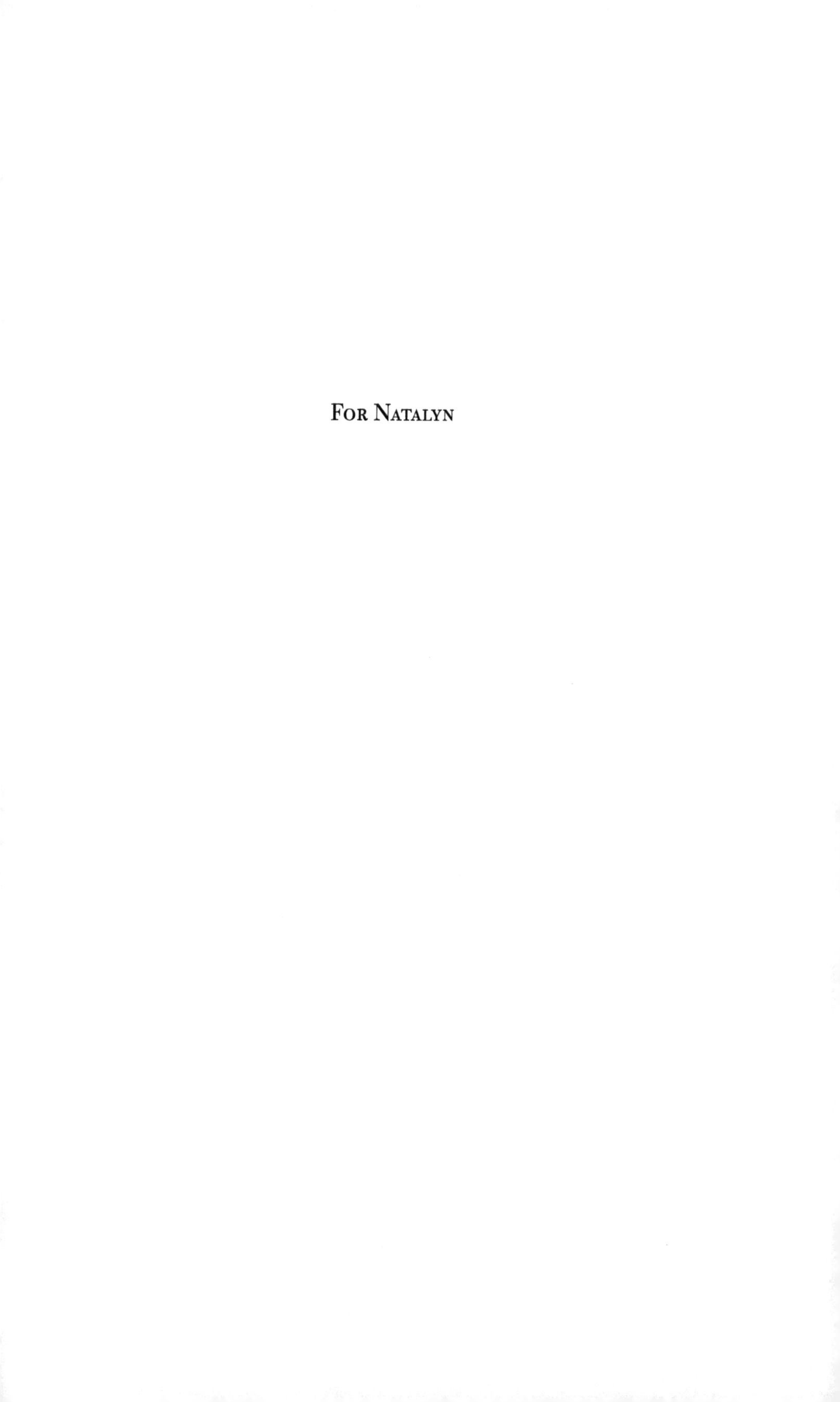

For Natalyn

Contents

Foreword: The Two Raymonds

Marian Carcache and John M. Williams

In late December 2008, after this book was initially scheduled for publication, author Charles Rose suffered a stroke and spent a long time recovering, first in Birmingham and later in Auburn. There were times after the stroke, he says, when his mind could not process what had happened to him. "I didn't know if I was crazy or not. I couldn't tell."

A lifelong reader and writer and piano player, Charlie was unable to read or write or play in the early stages of his recovery. Gradually he became more and more aware of the void the absence of music and literature had left in his life. The music came back first. A baby grand piano was the focal point of the parlor in the facility where he was recovering. As the long winter became spring, Charlie began playing his old beloved jazz standards and hymns for the enjoyment of the other residents.

Then, in May 2009, he picked up two books, one by Raymond Chandler and the other by Raymond Carver. These works sparked something in the dark confusion the stroke had left in his mind, and his love for writing reawakened. He says he had been making his way through Chandler's *The High Window* when he encountered this passage:

> It was a slim tall self-satisfied looking number in a tropical worsted suit of slate blue, black and white shoes, a dull ivory-colored shirt and

> a tie and display handkerchief the color of jacaranda bloom. He was holding a long black cigarette-holder in a peeled back white pigskin glove and he was wrinkling his nose at the dead magazines on the library table and the chairs and the rusty floor covering and the general air of not much money being made.

To the average reader this passage may seem typical Chandler and unremarkable, but for Charlie that was precisely its beauty. Something about that passage made him feel the ache and love of writing again. That feeling was only reinforced when, a few days later, working through Carver's "What's in Alaska?" (from *Will You Please Be Quiet, Please?*), he encountered this exchange:

> Jack and Mary came back. Jack carried a large bag of M&Ms and a bottle of cream soda. Mary sucked on an orange Popsicle.
>
> "Anybody want a sandwich?" Helen said. "We have sandwich stuff."
>
> "Isn't it funny," Mary said. "You start with the desserts first and then you move on to the main course."
>
> "It's funny," Carl said.
>
> "Are you being sarcastic, honey?" Mary said.
>
> "Who wants cream soda?" Jack said. "A round of cream soda coming up."
>
> Carl held his glass out and Jack poured it full. Carl set the glass on the coffee table, but the coffee table smacked it off and the soda poured onto his shoe.
>
> "Goddam it," Carl said. "How do you like that? I spilled it on my shoe."
>
> "Helen, do we have a towel? Get Carl a towel," Jack said.
>
> "Those were new shoes," Mary said. "He just got them."
>
> "They look comfortable," Helen said a long time later and handed Carl a towel.
>
> "That's what I told him," Mary said.

Again, unremarkable. But our laughter as we sat in his room and read this passage again and again, brought delight to the soul in a way too simple and sublime to explain.

MARIAN: *When I first saw Charlie, I was a high school senior who had come to Auburn for a College Day. He was sitting in his office in Haley Center, perhaps the least interesting building that has ever been. I was not very excited at the prospect of leaving my home in rural Russell County, surrounded by a pecan orchard and a ryegrass field, to take up residence in a girls' dorm and attend classes in a brick and metal monstrosity. But there sat Charlie, working behind his desk cluttered with papers and books and coffee cups, wearing a seersucker suit and dark glasses. I knew at that point that Auburn did have something to offer me in spite of the otherwise sterile surroundings I had found there. My overly romantic eighteen-year-old mind named him "the gypsy scholar" when I told family and friends about him upon returning home. Later, when I became a student at Auburn, he was my fiction writing teacher. He also taught me The Short Story and The European Novel. Those who knew him superficially did not always recognize his brilliance as both a literary scholar and a writer. Nor did they always appreciate his unconventionality. He was, and still is, peerlessly brilliant on a plane that many never visit. Years ago, when I was assigned to write an essay loosely based on the Theophrastus Character for advanced composition, I wrote about Charlie—dark-complexioned, small build, soulful brown eyes, a brilliant mind, a quiet man—both larger and smaller than life. Twice in the past few years, I feared losing him, but like the Phoenix, Charlie, the small and quiet man, the larger-than-life man, is back.*

JOHNNY: *I never had Charlie as a teacher. But it doesn't matter: my cousin had him and reported to me about this odd bird (in a flock of them, in those days)—how in discussing* The Confessions of Felix Krull, *for example, cigarette in hand, Jack's coffee cup nearby (those days!), he would sporadically erupt in flashes of searing insight like galaxies from a mumbled continuum of dark matter. I had imagined Coleridge,* *in his "Sage of Highgate" days, doing exactly the same thing, and the analogy has persisted. I've known Charlie maybe thirty years, and our many, many conversations about literature and music and everything else during those years, in numerous locales, will stand out, I know, when I'm looking back over it all. I've been fortunate to know him. Since there is nothing remotely petty, mean, cruel, or nasty in the man, the stroke seemed a really cheap shot. But my God, is he resilient. I've seen him recover from a series of setbacks, and now here he is recovering from something that would have silenced most of us—not only recovering but falling in love again. These two passages brought him some great joy which struck me as profound. The mountains are mountains again. I'm telling you, you just don't find them like him anymore.*

This book, containing some of Charlie's best stories, is a testament to his talent and strength of spirit.

A Ford in the River

Spink Hotel

THE BRAKES WENT OUT AT THE TRAFfic light. My right foot crashed on the brake pedal. We ran the light, doing sixty. The emergency jammed. Mona gasped. Birdbaths, horrendous porch swings, a feed and seed store, a barber pole streamed by like bits of wreckage. I geared down, regained control of the car, felt it glide to a stop like a taxi. Sweat trickled out of my armpits.

I switched off the ignition.

"We are not going to make D.C. tonight," said Mona, lighting a cigarette. She handed over the cigarette.

I took a drag and gave it back to her. Mona was right. We were not going to make D.C. tonight. Or tomorrow. The nation's capital was nearly four hundred miles away. Mona had pushed us along all evening, setting sunup as our ETA. Out of Cincinnati along the Ohio River, doing seventy on the two-lane, eighty on I-64. We were deep into West Virginia when Mona ordered me off the freeway. She said we couldn't go on because a black sedan was tailing us. She clenched her fists.

Arc lights on the courthouse square, one sputtering, stone facades and cornices of drab buildings, a church on the opposite corner—hulking and short-steepled, flaunting its dank red brick. A carillon chimed a hymn. *I walk through the garden alone.*

A neon sign flaked rouge off, sifting down to the sidewalk. The hotel was four stories high, the windows set close together. Beyond the neon, a lobby spilling sour light like bile. Mona looked up at the neon, spelling out Spink Hotel.

"Should be pink, not Spink," Mona said.

I said carefully, "Here there are no pink hotels."

"Okay, it's a Spink." Mona grabbed her loaf-shaped makeup kit after slipping on her cheapo wedding band. Got out of the car. "Remember if anyone stops us, it was your idea to stop here. I wanted to make D.C. tonight."

We had to stay here until I could have the brakes fixed, in this hotel in West Virginia, in a town that looked clean, respectable. Only the church looked ugly, still chiming about the garden. *And the joys I share are beyond compare.* What joys, whose? The carillon stopped with a lurch, an off-pitch, cretinous sound. I hauled the suitcase out of the trunk.

I followed Mona into the lobby. Metal ashtrays, sour green leather wing chairs, rust-flecked, junk cigarette machine. From his cubbyhole behind the registration desk the night clerk wobbled to greet us. He wore a Civitan pin in the left lapel of his iron gray gabardine suit coat. His head was bald as a billiard ball.

Mona sat down in a wing chair, crossed her legs, wiggled her toes in espadrilles, pulled her miniskirt down. She opened a package of Chiclets and popped a wad into her rosy mouth. I asked the desk clerk for a room for two.

He sized us up and shook his head like a deacon seeing his church profaned, then relaxed, realizing a buck was a buck, even at Spink Hotel. "A single is all we have available. I can arrange to put in a cot."

"As you see we're married."

As he saw Mona was jailbait. But he opened up the register. "Sign it mister and missus."

My ball-point signature skittered into illegibility. The night clerk turned to the mail slots and extracted a key with a dull green tab. Room 411 it told me. Mona was out of her chair, hugging her makeup kit as she made for the stairs. The night clerk lit up a Camel. He took a drag and coughed phthistically, spraying ashes on gray gabardine.

"We can't afford to have your kind here. One night will be your limit. Or do you want me to call the law?"

I said we would be leaving tomorrow. Maybe late. We had car trouble.

"Two nights then." He took another drag, closed up the register, turned toward the plate-glass window, the street outside. I turned too. A patrol car idled in front of the church. My car was parked by a meter but we had an out-of-state tag. At this hour worth checking out, along with certain guests at the hotel, who could be taken into custody if such was the night clerk's whim. The night clerk nodded me toward the stairs. The patrol car glided out of view.

I passed the junk cigarette machine. There was a gum machine by the stairs, dispensing Chiclets along with other brands. Mona'd parked her wad on the coin slot. Thumbed it like a kidney. She'd kept on climbing, to the fourth and top floor, I was sure.

I climbed the first flight of stairs. Alone on the darkened landing I tried to clear my mind. For eighteen hours a day I had kept Mona off the streets of Cincinnati. Her sister was three hundred miles away, in Richmond, our real destination. Sally had promised me she would take charge of Mona's care. There Mona might get straightened out, live without me. With me she would only get worse. Yet I knew, as I stood on the landing, mustering strength to keep climbing, that I wouldn't be able to let her go. That was why I'd veered off the I-64 exit ramp, come to Spink Hotel.

MONA WAS STILL asleep. I lit a cigarette and got out of bed. I straddled a rickety chair, rocking with a furry squeak. Our room had a ponderous chiffonier beside a door to a tiny bathroom. On the other side of the bed a window overlooked a funeral home. Dust hung in the sunlight streaming in, lacing the carpet with hieroglyphics. The bed had a low headboard depicting a pastoral scene in low relief—a nymph being enticed by a satyr, in a scratchy, ivory stain. The satyr was playing a flute of some sort and the nymph was shielding her seat of love with both hands, fingers entwined. Smoking, I rocked with the back of the chair.

From a room below I heard hammering, intermittently, yet with what seemed a willed intent. I was now on my second cigarette. Smoke from the first blimped over the bed. In her sleep, Mona's breath mushroomed, lofted smoke toward the scarred plaster ceiling. Rust streaks showed in Mona's frowsy hair. The hammering had given way to the sweeping clip of a carpenter's plane. Next door, beyond the bathroom, the chiffonier, a lachrymose bleat of a radio emitted theme songs from old soaps, "Stella Dallas," "Lorenzo Jones," "Mary Noble Backstage Wife." Must be a geezer next door, over ninety, or were these songs meant for me. *He walks with me and He talks with me*, the carillon chimed, way off key.

Mona slept like she used to once, as if in a sodden sleep of depression. She used to total sixteen hours, waking up to watch Turner Classics, play solitaire, do crossword puzzles. I would come home to find her waiting up for me, with a list of words she was stuck on. Animal waste, *urea*, golden brass, *ormolu*. Oh the blessing of torpor, easy ease as I did my tasks, drove a taxi, worked in a housepainters crew, did whatever it took to keep her happy.

All this before the telephone call from her shadowy lover, Roebuck.

The chiming stopped, the radio stopped, the carpenter planing coffin boards stopped, in sequence, as if on cue. I pictured Roebuck's oblong noggin, his bulging, baleful left eye. A black patch masked his right eye. I had inquired concerning the telephone call—your lover, who might he be? She had touched up a photo of Tom Cruise, inked in an eye patch, blackened in teeth. "This isn't the Roebuck I know. He's the Roebuck you think you know."

She raised her head up to the headboard. Scrutinized me out of a sunny haze, knowing instantly where my mind was, on the Roebuck she, not I, had known. She'd claimed Roebuck was a lobbyist for Harlan County Strip mines. Promoting strip mining in D.C., driving a tan SUV. She had met Roebuck in a Covington, Kentucky, strip club in her last little manic excursion across the Ohio River—where she had been—mistake—a cooperative cocktail waitress. She had run off with Roebuck in his SUV, barreled around D.C. with him for a glorious month while I suffered an agony of worry back home. Dumped, she had come back home. Come back to me on a Greyhound bus.

Roebuck had sent her a postcard, last week, the Washington Monument. He had printed in caps "I need you. Let bygones be bygones," and in lower case "Meet me at the Harrington Hotel. A fleabag on Tenth Street." He'd telephoned her at home. I'd picked up the receiver. Roebuck's baritone had bombarded my ear like amplified Ezio Pinza. Can you connect me with Mona? Connect? A singing telephone call. Unwillingly I had connected him to her. Before she picked up the receiver she had taken a drag from my cigarette. She had stubbed it out, as she was doing now.

"We are going to march on the White House. You were one of us but you finked out."

Said Mona. The loonies, the kooks, the feebs, the nuts and bolts of the nation. Fink out, a Roebuck locution. My Roebuck's, not hers. For only I used words like fink out. Only I had thought of marching on the White House once, so far back in time it seemed primeval.

Mona squinted. She clenched her fists and rolled her eyeballs. She was receiving messages. My gut knotted as I waited for her to get through yet another delusion. Her demons were floating across the room as she motioned them out the window. "Out! No, don't move! Sit!" Sally had to keep her in Richmond. Sally's husband had to pay for the therapy. Alex, a textile engineer.

This D.C. business was a ruse. No march. No Roebuck.

"We don't need you anymore. We're strong. We have each other." From Mona, in a monotone.

I was able to get out of the chair. "I'm going to telephone Roebuck personally."

Extemporize, invent! Get her mind into phase with mine. A bar of Dial and a can of Rise would serve for receiver and mouthpiece. For these I went to the bathroom, pried the Dial off a squash colored stain, grabbed the Rise from the medicine cabinet—our Dial, our Rise. Squirting Rise into my left ear, I put in that call to D.C. Front desk, please. Long distance!

"We can't make it tonight. The goddamned brakes went out last night. We're stuck here, stranded, up shit creek without a paddle."

I lowered the bar of Dial. Felt the seashell pulse in my tympanum, the Rise glob insanely seething. Heard, or thought I heard, a whisper, insidious. *Give Mona up. Put her out of your life.* Or was that Roebuck whispering?

I laid the Dial and the Rise on the bed table. Watched her pick them up, her moving lips.

"Roebuck," said her lips. She clenched her fists, she glared at me. "Please don't try to telephone him. You know he won't listen to you."

"I will listen," I protested passionately, knowing she wouldn't listen, heed, do anything to help me help her. I had to watch her go to the bathroom, I had to sit on the bed while she brushed her teeth. This she did with concentration. Her straggly hair showing rust streaks which she seemed to be trying to lather out. Soapsuds laced her nipples and aureoles, seen through the bathroom mirror. The pipes groaned as she rinsed.

We had a late breakfast in the coffee shop. It adjoined the bar and beauty parlor, these facing away from the lobby, fronting a side street of plum-colored brick. There was a familiar marble-topped counter, a tarnished nickel coffee urn, booths, a tessellated floor, an ornate cash register from times gone by, a glassed-in cigar and candy counter, another with slices of various pies, apple, lemon meringue, pumpkin.

Mona was slumped on her side of the booth. Her eyes were dulled. She was wearing her purple T-shirt, appliqued with a yellow cello. Brown crystals choked up the salt cellar. The plum-colored bricks outside were rippling with maple-leaf shadows.

Suddenly Mona spun something dire for me out. "This town is a good place for you. Your family is here. Your friends. Me, I'll be moving on. On and on," she crooned.

I made myself tune Mona out. The plum-colored brick, the soft maples, the darker green of a tree lawn on the other side of this side street, an embankment, steps, a front porch, green shingles, blazing white imbricated boards. Black Packard, Dad's, in the driveway. Other members of my family in other booths, for the coffee shop was familiar, the cashier had a bow tie, red polka dot, a clip-on, like Dad had on. He had nicotine-stained teeth like Dad.

I thought of E. A. behind the prescription counter of the vanished West Side Drug Store. A laxative is it you need now. Or a ladies aid. Or salted nuts. Is it Sal Hepatica you need.

"It fits," I exclaimed, "it figures."

Mona's rosy lips agreed. "Right, it figures. Your dad is in a back booth. The old fart who balled his fountain girls."

"When he had the chance," I said buoyantly, for we were having a conversation.

I ordered black coffee. The coffee arrived in pea-green mugs that I had once beheld brimming in Ovaltine. "Okay, so my Dad did my Mom dirt."

Mona patted the yellow cello. The conversation was over. "I want soft-boiled eggs," said Mona when the waitress showed for the second time. Her iron-gray hair and beaming face loomed like a No Smoking sign. I stared at—who else—Mom. Right here! Bless her! Love her! It was Mom who'd kept my Ovaltine hot. E. A's Vera C. E. A.'s blood pressure she'd monitored—made him lay off strudel and shortcake. Now she waited to take my order.

"You make his sunny-side up. And lotsa hash browns. Lotsa toast." And then, "Looky there in the back booth." Mona smacked her purple T-shirt, cello reeling, wambling, straightening up. "It's your cousin. Your nutty uncle and aunt."

A chubby lad munching a grilled cheese, slurping a cherry Coke through a straw. Sweet pickle slice, sweet disposition, sitting next to Uncle Dell. Uncle Dell ran a ladies' shoe store. Aunt Flo juggled Indian clubs back in vaudeville days at B. F. Keith's. Uncle Dell chewed on a dead cigar, incessantly working crossword puzzles. *Urea* again. *Ormolu.* Cousin Robert made model airplanes. His fingers were gummed with airplane glue. Hunks of balsa wood in the bathtub. It was a race with hungry white corpuscles that Cousin Robert had run and lost. Yet here he was slurping a cherry Coke, munching grilled cheese. Dell and Flo wolfed down pasta. They were good people living careful lives. They ignored my funk, Mona's mania as they might cripples. Just passing through, I grinned at them. Try not to let on they are sickos, Morse-coded their chinking forks.

Mona blurted with conviction. "Only creeps and weirdos, sickos will be members of Roebuck's family. Every one of us is an only child."

Mistake! I wanted to cry out, shake her into sense. There would be Sally, Alex in Richmond. She wasn't alone. Help was on the way. A fly buzzed in the sun haze, the simmering, down-home apathy. Mona chain-smoked, pecked at her hash browns, cracked a soft-boiled egg, let the yolks ooze out. A Greyhound brayed on the plum-colored brick. The coffee tasted like bitter lye, as if it had pooled in the nickel urn for a month. Nobody was slurping a cherry Coke. Mona eyed the cashier's bow tie. She ground her cigarette into egg yolk.

"Either you get me some chewing gum or I turn you in to the management."

Again the carillon, the chimes. I picked up a fork and a butter knife.

"Hello! Put me through to Roebuck." The fork pricked my earlobe. The blade of the knife nuzzled my lower lip. "No, you're not going to put me on hold. I'm a taxpayer. I won't stand for it. You put me through and I mean now."

A fly was buzzing our eggy plates. I brandished the butter knife, shouting. "You tell Roebuck I don't have a family. I have Mona. Only Mona."

Mona was clenching her fists.

MONA WAS CURLING her big toes. Her feet were propped on the footboard. She was staring out the window. She had taken a Valium willingly in the coffee shop after I bribed her with Chiclets. A police car jarred the plum-colored brick. Temper tantrum, I'd thought of signaling. The all too familiar carillon chimed *A Mighty Fortress Is Our Lord*. All this before noon.

We had taken a tour of the town, up Main Street to the surrounding hills, down a side street, left, then left again, down Oak Street toward the funeral home. A cedar tree in the front yard, a hearse in the porte cochere. Viewed from Oak, straight on, the funeral home—with its ivied brick, its rambling porch, its mansard roof—should have resembled a harmless domicile, not a giant hen laying a bloody egg. We sat down on the curb, rested awhile. Big daddy, little Mona smoked cigarettes, courted a vagrancy rap. As I discoursed, Mona rubbernecked.

"Outside of Xenia, Ohio, there is this data bank. In case of sabotage or malfunction its countless records and dossiers can be shunted off to D.C. My divorces, your abortion, all our sins and errors and our slip-ups are on record, mark my words. The day you ran away from home, your first coke hit, on record. My DUI's, my frantic lust. They have a data bank in Xenia. For the losers *who will go first!* For the oddballs, the peeping toms, the stewbums over fifty. Baby our days are numbered."

A steady stream of traffic flowed past us, like a funeral procession, pickups, sedans, SUV's, a decrepit coupe. The jingle of loose fan belts, the whickering slap of corroded plugs mingled with boom boxes. Finally, only birds and maple leaves delineated a breeze soft and silent like a balm.

"Tell all that shit to Roebuck." Mona stood up, lit a cigarette. She was skywriting big and little R's with smoke from her cigarette. The Roebuck I knew, eye patch, oblong noggin, remained hidden from me, like the birds I heard in the foliage.

"Don't tell me my days are numbered. Yours are. Always have been."

Along with E. A's, Uncle Dell's, Aunt Flo's, Cousin Robert's. Mine too. Me, her husband. Washed up, replaced by Roebuck. Mona's dove-gray eyes were turned on me, quietly scanning me up and down. For a nanosecond she was beautiful.

The Chiclets were on the chiffonier, on one side of an Indian club

I had sized up as a delusion. I turned to the open window. A hearse was still in the porte cochere. A cigar butt stuck on the driveway. Mona crooked her big toes. She sat up and turned to the satyr, thumbing Chiclets into its penis. I gripped the neck of an insubstantial Indian club, screwing its head into my left ear.

"Front desk, please. Long distance. I mean long, the Washington Monument."

I heard a seething inside my left fist. I lowered the Indian club, replaced it on the chiffonier. A useless instrument, this telephone. I rummaged through Mona's loaf-shaped makeup kit. Found the Valium, went to the bathroom. The stain on the basin of the sink took on the shape of a fetus. Running water wouldn't eradicate it—and wouldn't drown out Mona's jubilation.

"Roebuck. Babe, it's Mona. Yes, I reversed the charges. Okay, I won't call you again." The things she was offering him. Exotic patterns of sex, highs I had never dreamed of. My face in the mirror was a guardian's face, jowled and haggard, obsolete. The muffled chimes were back, the planing of coffins, the hammering. I gulped a Valium, steadied my hands.

"Him? He's nothing. He can never be what you are to me. That's why he's trying to trick me."

Slowly, I turned off the water.

I'D HAD A beer in the hotel bar. I'd put in a long-distance call to Mona's sister in Richmond, Virginia. I told Sally about my little problem here, brake failure, Mona going bonkers. I told Sally Mona had taken a sleeping pill. Sally put Alex on the phone.

"Eddie you must be on the sauce."

"Get over here as soon as you can."

"It's three hundred miles. Are you out of your mind?"

I hung up on Alex, why not, what good was he to me? I went out to the lobby and sat down in one of the wing chairs and stared out at the street. I thought of Mona asleep up the stairs in room 411. Several sleeping pills had done the job. I remembered how before she had taken the pills, she had craftily eyed her glass of water.

In the rouge light outside a girl carrying a loaf shaped makeup kit was standing under the neon. She was ambling across the street, toward the arc lights pooling the courthouse square.

The night clerk opened the register. With a ball-point he scratched out my signature. I got up, trudged toward the exit. I left the hotel, breathed in noxious particles of neon like bug spray. Then sweet night air. Mona, a distant figure now, in the last of the arc lights, was running. I would follow her to the edge of town, catch up, we would hitch a ride to D.C. We would make D.C. by tomorrow night, find a hotel, any hotel. Crawl into a bed like a diving bell, sleep, drift on, sink deeper.

She was skipping invisible rope in the headlights of a patrol car. One officer picked up her makeup kit. I had to walk away from Spink Hotel, toward the patrol car, its flashing red and blue lights. What I had done before I would do again. Follow her, try to extricate her. See her as somehow recoverable. Or was I the seen, in a tracking shot still unrolling as the red and blue lights glided farther away, the hotel receding behind me, as I clopped over plum-colored bricks—crying *Mona come back to me Mona*—toward Roebuck, my Roebuck, his oblong noggin swelling, his one good eye drilled into mine.

Harmonica

UNCLE WALTON WAS STILL ON THE telephone. Danny Bledsoe would have to wait awhile before he could talk to his uncle about his car. He had come here right after the accident, to his uncle's paint and body shop. He wouldn't take the car to the trailer, not with the front end bashed in. His stepfather, Slade Futral, would be there. Slade had started in on the bourbon by now; he was engrossed in "The Price is Right." The ladies stroking the new car, the washers and dryers, the console TV's, that was exciting for Slade, not the mangled metal in the front end of Danny's car.

"Just bring me one hundred dollars cash. If you haven't got it, I'll settle for sixty. No I'm not going to make it forty. I'm not that generous, Danny."

Danny fidgeted in the armchair that had been his father's, trying to make up his mind if he could get his uncle to come down to fifty. His father would sit in it watching football games, the springs creaking as he reached for a beer. Danny missed seeing his father's boots, on the carpet beside the footstool. His mother had dumped the footstool. Uncle Walton had gotten the armchair when his mother moved into the trailer with Slade. She wanted new things in the trailer. She had an exercise bike, a little present from Slade Futral. You could stand to lose a few pounds, Lorraine, but his mother never used it. And when Lorraine refused to use it today, when Lorraine refused to get slim and trim, Slade put the exercise bike out with the trash. It sat out for anyone to steal. Slade didn't know Danny had stolen it, taken it away and pawned it. Put money in my pocket, Slade.

Uncle Walton finally hung up. Pursed lips, freckled arms and face and neck, eyes off at something besides Danny, something distant, not worth getting but worth looking at tolerantly to pass the time. What can we do for you, Danny?

Danny had bashed in the front end of his car, rear-ending this lady's station wagon. He couldn't drive with one headlight. He couldn't open the hood of the car. Uncle Walton said he had to get on the telephone, locate a header. Uncle Walton was calling used part shops. No header for that Pontiac, Danny. They stopped making them fifteen years ago. He'd keep trying, come back this afternoon. Uncle Walton could put in a headlight, chop out half the header.

His mother was vacuuming the trailer. Last weekend Slade had beat her up and stomped off to Knott's Tavern. She had a black eye again, puffy lips. She ran the machine up and down the wall-to-wall, pennies clicking along the vacuum tube. The feathered dirt stayed where it was, no matter how many ups and downs she did. Danny had to pick up after her. Her ups and downs moved on—to the shared-with-Slade tiny bedroom, where the action was, where the price was right. Taut cord, forgot to move the plug, just thought she could stretch the cord forever like the fat lady's bulging girdle, the long right arm of Plastic Man. Danny was out on the patio when the police car pulled up. You saw what happened. That I did, sir. Clear case of spouse abuse this time, but his mother had still taken the bastard back. And Slade had come back, dragged his sorry ass back in the rain after lying out drunk in the front yard.

Slade had tracked mud on the carpet, untied his boots in the kitchen. His mother was turning away from the stove, putting one hand on her puffy lips. She did what she'd done for his father, pulled Slade's boots off, set them on newspaper. There wasn't anything Danny could do.

Uncle Walton turned in his swivel chair. He gripped his eyes on you, fixed you in the armchair.

"How's your mama doing?"

Danny felt something go slack in his jaw. "You know how she's doing?"

"Every time I been by to see her she's gone."

"You must not have been by lately. She was working at Piggly Wiggly days. Try coming to see her at night sometime."

"I'm not about to do that. No, Danny. Not as long as Slade's still around. I know Slade's car when I see it."

"You're family. You could help her."

"Lorraine made her own bed, Danny. There's nothing I can do for her."

"She could go to your place if you'd take her."

Uncle Walton looked straight at him. "Dee wouldn't like it. She's got little Ed and Winona and me. That's four. You three would make seven. We couldn't get you all in the trailer. Five's top. Maybe six. We could take you and little Ben, but not Lorraine. Dee won't put up with her drinking."

"She only does it because of Slade."

"She's been doing it for too long now."

The off-in-the distance look was back, Uncle Walton pondering something he would never actually get mixed up in himself. "The only way Lorraine stops drinking is Slade moves out on her. But Slade, he likes it where he is. He isn't about to get out of her life. Not unless he got cut or got shot, and that just isn't going to happen."

Uncle Walton's right hand was swinging out. He let it fall on Danny's shoulder. "Don't you do anything rash, Danny. You go after Slade, you'll regret it." No, kill Slade, you get a medal, but Uncle Walton's right hand stayed where it was. "You got a gun or a knife, I'd stash 'em somewhere. Somewhere you can't get at 'em."

He didn't have any weapon to get at. But he'd be getting one pretty soon now. Uncle Walton didn't know this. Uncle Walton was looking to have his lunch pretty soon. He let his hand slide off Danny's shoulder. It was time for Danny to move on.

"I'll have to charge you for the header. If I find one, which isn't likely. And a headlight will cost you twelve bucks. I won't charge you for labor this time."

"I can pay, Uncle Walton."

"Not this time, Danny."

Out of Uncle Walton's paint and body shop, Danny crossed the road to Golden Acres. He stopped off at number nine. The sign on the door said DISASTER AREA.

Billy Hudmon was cleaning his twelve-gauge, running an oil patch through the barrels. He had parked himself in front of the door, the shotgun canted between his fat knees. Pull out the stock, push in the barrel, cold muzzle kissing his goat beard, pull wires attached to the trigger. Coroner's verdict—suicide Slade. Billy Hudmon pulled out the ramrod. He set ramrod and oil patch between his legs, replaced the oil patch with another.

"This shotgun isn't for sale."

"You sure?"

"I told you it isn't for sale."

"I can pay."

"How much can you pay?"

"Eighty-five, maybe ninety-five."

He had the hundred and fifty for the exercise bike. Cross the state line into Georgia, head on south for the Florida line. He'd have Slade in the trunk, packed in ice. Ice you down, Slade, take you south.

"Come back in two hours. Bring cash," Billy said.

"Why not now? Why wait?"

"Read the sign. I can't let you in here right now."

Another sign in one window—EX-ALCOHOLIC FOR FIFTY-THREE WEEKS. Last week it had read FIFTY-TWO WEEKS. Billy Hudmon was drinking a Budweiser. He hadn't gotten around to taking the sign down yet.

"What kind of disaster are we talking about? Hurricane hit you? Tornado?"

"It's Lou Ann. She's the disaster." Danny heard something crash inside. Billy Hudmon pulled out another Budweiser from a cooler without a top to it. He opened it and drank deep. "Lou Ann's mightily pissed off at me."

"Then why doesn't she leave?"

"She thinks I'm the one who's going to leave. And that I am, for two hours. Soon as I clean this shotgun, I'm going to put this mother in my truck and drive down to my watering hole."

"You got another gun you could sell me?"

"I have a Colt .45 I can sell you."

"How much?"

"How much you willing to pay?"

"How big a thirst you got, Billy?"

Case of Jim Beam worth, but Danny didn't have the money for that. Ninety-nine fifty was the least Billy Hudmon would take.

"You can have it for ninety-nine fifty. You come back I'll have it for you."

Danny moved on up the road, toward the plastic pink flamingo in the front yard of their trailer. His brother Ben's dirt bike was missing. Lorraine was in the bedroom with Slade. She must not have known he was around because he didn't advertise it anymore, his comings and goings, not with Slade there. Danny's guitar case was missing. His *Penthouse Forums* were missing. Where was little Ben, little Ben's dirt bike? Danny picked up the Yamaha, cheapest guitar you can buy, man. The steel strings resisted his efforts to chord. He laid the guitar on the bunk bed, twanged the E string, out of tune. Through the dusty slats of the venetian blinds, he watched a squirrel make a leap for the bird feeder. Lorraine kept on trying to feed the birds, but the squirrels got most of the action. Danny was out in a flash with his BB pistol, in the heat sifting off the pines. He took aim for the left eye, pumped BB's into the eyeball. One spattered, jellied squirrel eye for your dinner tonight, big Slade. Here let me put some on your plate.

Danny dropped the dead squirrel in the garbage can. Its good eye stayed in his mind for a little while. The sparrows were back on the feeder. Cardinals and jays would succeed the sparrows. The big boys, grackles and cow birds, would come later, take over for awhile.

Slade's supersensitive radar had picked up on where the dead squirrel was. Slade paid him a little visit. First thing, Slade picked up the Yamaha and put a boot into the sound box.

"How many times have I told you, you take them squirrels out to the woods?" Slade cuffed him, rattled his jaw. "Your mama she don't want to see dead squirrels. She don't want to know about dead squirrels."

Slade told you how much he hated a goddamned stinking garbage can—bits of slithering fat, spoiled meat, dead putrefying tomcats. The BB pistol was no longer yours. From now on Slade would take care of the squirrels. In two more hours, in two days tops, Slade would be ancient history.

Danny took the squirrel to the woods in a Kmart bag. He followed a path that led to the creek where his father would take him when he was five. They were living in a house then, on the other side of the woods. His father would sit down with him. His father would play the harmonica awhile. They'd sit on one of the rotting logs and look down at the creek awhile. There was a log bridge and they would sit on it, let their feet hang towards the water. His father would play the harmonica, one song, "The Streets of Laredo." That was the song his father liked most. Danny wanted to learn the song on the guitar, but now he didn't have a guitar. He had learned it on the harmonica.

The weight of the squirrel, a dead thing now, made him consider dropping it anywhere. But he thought if he dropped it in the creek it would foul the creek for others. That way they would be kept away. He wished his father had been put in the creek. He would have liked to have had his father cremated. He'd have taken the ashes to the creek, in the helmet his father wore on the line trucks. The bright yellow helmet would be in the garage, with his father's power tools, shotguns, and fishing rods. You ever get hold of a hot line, Danny, you will be blown to kingdom come. Slade had gotten rid of the helmet.

Little Ben was already there. Dirt bikes lay on their sides like some sort of parody of languor. Little Ben sat on the log bridge. His pants were around his ankles. Little Ben's little friends were jerking off. *Penthouse Forums* were still in the guitar case. Jerk-offs! Danny was swinging the squirrel. He heaved the squirrel after the dirt bikes. He groped for the C harmonica. It was buried under a crumbling log, lichened, almost a part of the soil. Light slanted through the tall pines; bright pennies peppered the creek. He had to open his knife and pry loose the dirt that had collected inside the mouth holes. He held it, the harmonica, put it slowly to his mouth. In and out, blow notes and draw notes, bending the draw notes, good sound. He imagined he was his father. His father was playing for him. He was playing "The Streets of Laredo," a certain young cowboy I happened to see.

Uncle Walton hadn't finished repairing the car, but Billy Hudmon had a gun for him. DISASTER AREA had been replaced with a sign that said A MAN'S HOME IS HIS CASTLE.

Colt .45 automatic—you can have it for ninety-nine fifty. The door to the trailer was open once he counted out the money. The welcome mat draped on the concrete block welcomed Danny, a paying guest. Inside, Lou Ann was sprawled on the couch. Billy opened a Budweiser before he showed him the gun.

"This piece weighs a ton when you fire it."

There was another path from Billy's trailer, through the woods to the creek. Danny wasn't willing to go that far and Billy Hudmon wasn't able to. Billy Hudmon handed Danny a clip and showed him how to load the clip. With the heel of his left hand, he shot the bolt, flicked the safety off with the flange of his thumb.

He put the beer bottle in the fork of a tree. Danny gripped the .45 with a two-handed grip. He put pressure on the trigger, but the trigger wouldn't give. He had to use both forefingers to pull the trigger. The kick knocked his hands up, deafening.

"Let me show you how it's done."

Beer breath, Billy's sweat in his face, Billy stepping around behind you, leaning around you to grip your left hand, goat beard scratching the back of your neck, but you could take that, his body, the smell of him, his hands cupping yours like a slimy toad. "You got to keep putting on pressure slow. Keep your elbows locked. Let the recoil bring the weapon back."

Bark spattered off the fork of the tree.

Billy stepped back, let Billy take the .45, let Billy demonstrate his marksmanship. The third shot shattered the bottle.

"Now you see how it's done." Billy held out the .45; he had to get close to take it from him. The box of cartridge clips, he took that too.

After Billy went back to his trailer, Danny followed the path to the creek. He pushed back the log and laid the .45 down without looking at the harmonica. He set the box of clips beside the .45.

He picked up the car a little later. Uncle Walton had done the best he could do. The front end had half a header, the other half twisted metal like someone with half of his face gouged out. The right headlight stared back at him, the signal lights hanging down like an ear. You could put your hand on the radiator. His car was parked all by itself, in back of Uncle Walton's paint and body shop. He had walked all the way from the trailer.

Uncle Walton was on the telephone. He was talking to Dee, yes I'll be there Dee, looking off at the paint on the wall.

How many times do I have to tell you get rid of that goddamned piece of junk? I don't want to see it anymore, Slade had said to him. And you take them dead squirrels out to the woods. He saw Slade coming out of Knott's Tavern. Wait till he's about to get in his car. Put the pressure on slow, squeeze the trigger. Head shot, blow out his goddamned brains. Uncle Walton, still talking to Dee.

Uncle Walton wouldn't have anything to say to him because he wouldn't know he had a gun. Watch where you're driving next time. Don't head south to Florida yet. Don't do it, Danny, I'm telling you! Keep talking, you're just wasting your breath. Danny stared at the blood in the water cooler, blood squirting out into paper cups, Slade's blood, his goddamned stepfather's. Pipe blood in from the bathtub, from Slade's body, knees up, throat slashed big. Little snort out of the cooler, Slade. Count Dracula's premium brew for you.

DANNY WAS PARKED outside of Knott's Tavern. He watched a line crew moving a hot line. There were two bucket trucks, a bucket for each lineman. Rubber hoses sheathed the secondaries, clothespinned rubber blankets encased the insulators. Knock you to kingdom come. The linemen worked deliberately, aloft, aloof in their buckets. They were moving the line to a new pole, numeral plates flush with the secondaries catching bits of unapproachable light.

He waited another hour. The linemen tied in the primaries, came down, the elbowed lifts folding in on themselves, setting the linemen on the pavement again. They peeled off their tool belts and hung them up on a rack in the back of the truck. The ground man taped up a coil of copper wire, rolled up the rubber blankets, stashed the hoses, gathered up pulley lines. One lineman went to the water cooler embedded in one side of the truck. Clear cold water for this good man, for all the good men in the line crew.

That night they got into it about the goddamned squirrel with its throat slit with his mother's carving knife. All they could do now was drink and fight. His mother burned the frozen pizza. Dragging it charred from the oven, she stepped on little Ben's skateboard. She skidded across the linoleum. The pizza sailed up off the cookie sheet, splattered in Slade's pig face, his ape hands thickened with cheese, blackened anchovies, tomato splotches, then Slade's pig face behind the network of hands. Danny was swinging the frying pan, trying to get to Slade's pig face. He felt it wrenched away in Slade's big hands. He heard the frying pan clang against the stove. Something crashed in his head and he went down.

When he came to Slade wasn't there anymore. His mother couldn't get up. Bits of cheese were stuck to his mother's face. She put her hands on pink rollers. Danny breathed in the acrid smoke. He went to the door and opened it, letting warm air in to thin out the smoke. He was running now, down the path to the creek. The creek was overlaid with shadow. He couldn't help his mother anymore. He pushed the log back, picked up the harmonica, puckered his lips on a mouth hole, blowing a sustained, soothing note. The .45 and the box of cartridges were where he'd left them, beside the harmonica now. His fingers touched metal. He would leave the harmonica under the log, where he had kept it all these years.

It was dark when he left the creek. He went to his car first and put the .45 in the glove compartment. Then he went to his room in the trailer. He got a suitcase out of the closet. He emptied his dresser drawers on the bunk, picked out some things to take with him, left other things, including his baseball cards. He was on his way out when his mother came in. She was holding an ice pack against her jaw. She held a bottle of sherry pressed to one of her breasts, about half-full, with a cork in it. She still wore rollers in her hair.

"You're leaving me."

"You can come with me."

"I have to take care of little Ben."

"I'll take both of you to Uncle Walton's. Tonight. He's willing to have you."

"Dee isn't willing, you know that."

"You stop drinking she might have you."

"I can't do that, Danny."

"All right, don't do it. You can stay here, but I'm going."

Her face leaned into the ice pack. She set the ice pack down on Danny's bed. She uncorked the bottle of sherry. "You can't go. You're all I have. I lost your father. Now I'm losing you."

He had lost his mother a long time ago. He remembered her, how she was before Slade, with her hair in rollers then like now. It was that way when the telephone rang, while she put on her uniform, fixed her face. She asked Danny to answer the telephone please. He remembered the telephone on the wall, something brown and thick then, a blotch on the wall like a silverfish against the blistered paint and loose plaster, yet thinking maybe he'd hear something good like winning the lottery, like getting rich, like his mother not having to work anymore but his father maybe he should work, be a lineman, but not in bad weather, he thought, work part-time, not on a hot line, he thought, just be up there in your chariot looking proud and tall and good.

It was Tom Brown, his father's foreman. I would like to speak to your mother, please.

Not his mother but Tom Brown in his mind. A tall man who kept his back straight. His father used to do him but not to his face. Striding in from the kitchen, his father stuck out his Tom Brown jaw. He looked up at the ceiling fixture, the way Tom Brown looked up at a spot where a transformer would be hoisted up, or up at the crossbeam not yet in place, the bright wire not yet tied in to the glossy new spool insulators, or looked down to the spot on the ground where the new pole would go, the hole not dug, the posthole diggers unused yet, the cant hooks not yet clawing the pine, the pikes not biting wood yet. His father would stretch his lips in imitation of Tom Brown's distended grin. Here's where the work is boys, his father would say Tom Brown would say. That's all Tom Brown ever says, his father would say.

His mother was standing close to him. "You'll be hearing from me. I'll be all right," he said.

He leaned out to kiss his mother's lips. She kissed him goodbye, she held him close. This is goodbye, this is it.

Little Ben in the passenger seat, his white face set, was waiting for him in the car. "I'm coming with you, Danny."

"You can't come with me," Danny said. He was going where Ben couldn't follow him, already knowing he would have to pay, already seeing the time he would do like a long road without an end.

The View from My Father's Window

My father, Paul Creel, isn't the man he used to be, hasn't been since he's had the brain tumor. Mama says he's deteriorated, and I have to say I agree with her. In the photograph on their dresser they're in their church clothes, holding hands. He's wearing the double-breasted dark blue suit he used to wear to church. Mama's wearing her favorite church dress, sky-blue silk with white polka dots—a little tight on her now. Too many pounds in the wrong places, she says, but she still wears that dress to church.

Mama's feeding him Gerber's baby food. She dips a spoon into the jar, concentrating her gaze without changing her smile on the spoon sliding over to his open mouth. She wraps the jar in aluminum foil so he won't know it's baby food. One time my wife, Sandy, made the mistake of telling him what he was eating. He wouldn't let Mama feed him that night; he wasn't having any baby food. Mama spoons out chicken and dumplings, coaxing the stuff past his lower lip. We're having chicken and dumplings for dinner, Pauley. That used to be one of his favorite meals. Chicken and dumplings, collard greens, corn on the cob, a quart of iced tea to wash it down, you better believe he could put it away.

Mama has him in a diaper when the Reverend Hatcher comes to pray for him. We can't keep him from pulling the blanket off. The Reverend Hatcher is sitting beside the bed. He takes my father's right hand in his big ham hands patting it like he was patting a dog if he had one but he doesn't. He won't look at the diaper.

My father turns over on one side, that he's able to do. He cups his chin in his hand, stretching toes out on one stretched out foot, his toenails so long they're hooking. Pay no attention, Mama whispers, he's deteriorating, so I try not to. The Reverend Hatcher can't get up out of his chair. The Reverend Hatcher's white shirt, it's stuck to the ladder-back chair.

MY FATHER WAS an enlisted man in World War Two. On the living room wall we have a map of France and western Germany showing his unit's movements, in dotted red ink, a Third Army patch and his unit insignia superimposed, and a photograph of him in summer khakis and garrison cap.

He told me this story about the war, just after I turned sixteen. He had me learning to drive; he took me down the road a ways and made me keep at it until the gears stopped grinding and I got the hang of it. Then we went to the Dairy Delight in town and he bought me a banana split. I saw him filling up his side of the booth and remembered the photograph of him in the living room, a skinny kid like myself then, and that made me ask him about the war. He said you wouldn't want to know about it. Then he said—here's something I think you should know about—and lit up a Camel and started in.

He had a buddy, Denny Maxwell. He told me what had happened to Denny Maxwell. That was in November of 1944, in the fighting in the Hurtgen Forest. It was cold in the Hurtgen Forest. In the mornings they'd have to thaw out their socks, try doing that in a foxhole. He and Denny were on patrol one morning and up ahead they saw a farm house. There weren't any Germans around. Denny Maxwell was freezing his tail off so he decided he was going to go to that farm house and get warm no matter what. The farm house sat in an open field edged with woods, but that didn't bother Denny Maxwell. "He told me the bullet that had his name on it hadn't been made yet." Denny Maxwell wanted my father to go with him, but my father wasn't about to do that. He said he didn't want to be a target. So Denny Maxwell went out there himself and the Germans opened up on him from the woods. He must have had a dozen bullets in him and every one had his name on it.

"You remember Denny Maxwell, Wayne," my father said to me, grinding his Camel out in a Dairy Delight ashtray, "when you're about to do something stupid."

I'VE BEEN MARRIED to Sandy for seventeen years. We've had a pretty good life together. We have a teenage son, Wayne Jr., who so far has stayed out of trouble. We have good jobs, a good income between us. I'm still parts manager at Fuller Ford and Sandy's still teaching English at Beauregard High.

My father worked at Uniroyal for thirty years. Before that he worked at the mill hauling cotton bales on a fork lift. He got laid off when the mill closed down, but lucky for him—lucky for me he'd say—he got on at Uniroyal. At Uniroyal, he had job security, and benefits, a pension, a group medical plan, the only bad thing about his job was, toward the end anyway, before he retired, they kept changing shifts on him. He'd work day shift part of the week, then they'd switch him over to the swing shift. That, he used to tell us, can get old pretty quick. He'd tell Mama he ought to quit, take a little less in his retirement package.

I remember him in his blue suit, Mama unfolding her napkin, laying it primly in her lap, her hair gray even then. There'd be this silence when my father said he wanted to quit, fried chicken, fried catfish in front of us, yams, black-eyed peas put on hold while my father studied Mama's dubious face, knowing always what answer he was going to get yet acting as if he didn't. As soon as Mama got her napkin arranged, stirred sugar into her iced tea, she'd say "I hear what you're saying, Pauley, but what would you do if you did retire?" And my father would say, "I'd go fishing."

AFTER CHURCH MY father used to tell Marleah Willis how much he enjoyed her hymn singing. Marleah was married to Buddy Willis at the time. Buddy used to sell Chevrolets, but after the two of them split up he moved to Columbus and started his own used car business.

Marleah Willis could really sing high and sweet, and when she did a solo for the congregation, my father would lift his head up and close his eyes, her voice taking him where he wanted to go. He'd sit on the end of the pew so he could get out quick when Marleah came our way. When he complimented Marleah on her singing, heads turned, people noticed it. He wasn't tall but he was broad in the shoulders He had a gut on him then. He could put away steak and potatoes and corn on the cob, fried okra, a dozen catfish, so he took up a lot of space in the aisle. He'd be pointed one way, toward the altar, and Marleah she was on her way out of the church, the traffic backed up behind her, Marleah trying to get past him, knowing she had to say something back. She'd say, "It's sweet of you to say that, Mr. Creel."

Every Sunday it's sweet of him, Sandy would say, and Mama she'd snap her pocket book shut and shove her hymnal back in the rack.

Mama had talked to Marleah after church because my father, he wanted Marleah to sing a hymn for him, and Marleah said she would come over in the afternoon. She didn't want to, that was clear. Marleah scooted the piano bench under the piano, closed up the hymnal, and looked the other way from Mama. She looked at me once, me with Sandy, like I'd better be just another married man. Then she went over to Reverend Hatcher. Smoothing out the lumps in her sky blue dress, Mama headed up the aisle toward the pulpit.

That Sunday Mama talked to Marleah in church, I was still thinking about what had happened at Jack Lazenby's annual Fourth of July barbecue. Jack held it behind his house, which was half a mile down the road from the convenience store he owned and ran, The Lazy Bee—Lay-Z and a striped bumblebee Sandy tells me is called a rebus.

We were sitting around Jack's barbecue pit, the chigger patch Sandy called it, digesting barbecued pork—y'all come but bring your own lawn chairs and Chigger-Red—that was Sandy's view of Lazenby hospitality. Marleah was sitting next to me. She was telling me about life without Buddy. They'd been divorced for nearly a year now. She'd had to haul the garbage to the garbage pit down the road, wasn't that fun, and keep the lawn mowed. Buddy wasn't making cigarette runs for her Winston One Hundred Lights and his Marlboro One Hundreds.

Big Jack was shooting off bottle rockets. Fire one, he'd boom out, fire two! I heard them whooshing out in the dark, popping over the pines. Marleah shook her last cigarette out and crumpled the pack. "I'm thinking that's my last Winston, Wayne."

I'd smoked my last panatela, but I wasn't about to be her errand boy. I said I wasn't used to making cigarette runs. She tweaked my shirt below the elbow and said she would go with me. Sandy had gone to the bathroom. We might be back before she missed us.

I decided to stop at the Lazy Bee. Marleah went in with me. We both used the restrooms. Then Marleah bought two packs of Winston One Hundred Lights. I bought a five-pack of Phillies Panatelas.

After I parked at Big Jack's place, Marleah said she didn't want to go back to the party right away. We could hear firecrackers popping and crackling down the road. Marleah moved closer to me, and I heard her catch her breath. I put my arm around her, stroked the back of her neck. She leaned over and kissed me on the mouth, and then she put her head on my shoulder. Having her close to me, I wanted that to last.

We kissed again, this time tonguing, then I was biting her lower lip. She pulled away from me, I knew I'd gone too far. I hadn't known when to put the brakes on.

She smoothed her skirt out. "I hope you didn't get the wrong idea."

Without moving an inch, I pitched my voice into casual. "Far as I'm concerned, nothing happened."

Marleah said we should get back to the party.

When we got back, Marleah went right over to Dottie Lazenby. She listened to Dottie talk about their trip to Disney world and Epcot Center. Sandy said to me, "You missed the bottle rockets."

A week went by. I couldn't get Marleah out of my mind. I even called her house from the parts department, but all I got was her voice on the answering machine. That same day after I got off work Sandy told me she couldn't sit with my father this evening. She asked me if I would sit with him. She was taking Mama to Walmart to stock up on trash and garbage bags, laundry and dishwashing detergent, a long list of household items substantially cheaper at Walmart than they are at Winn-Dixie, Sandy said, when I asked her why go across town to Walmart when Winn-Dixie was two miles down the road. I was wishing Sandy didn't have the summer off from teaching, that way Sandy would have been been at Beauregard High, not here asking me to sit with my father while she took Mama shopping on her day to sit with him. I took six garbage bags out to the car and opened the trunk and stashed them.

I brought the radio to the bedroom and plugged it in. We got a rundown on the ball games that afternoon and some stuff on the Braves game coming up, then some call-ins, then gospel. It wasn't long before we were playing the leg game. My father's left leg would fall off the bed. I'd intercept his foot, taking care to avoid his toenails, catch his ankle, and hoist the leg back up onto the bed. He would lower it and I would raise it again. We played the leg game without saying much. Are you comfortable? I'm okay, Wayne.

Through the bedroom window, across the road, I saw Wyatt Kirkpatrick's wife, Stephanie, come around their house driving a lawn tractor. She was wearing a halter and loose-fitting shorts. She raised her hand once and patted her hair. The next time I tried to lift up my father's leg he wouldn't let me. "Leave it be, Wayne." So I let it be.

On Saturday I drove by Marleah's house. She was outside moving a lawn sprinkler away from the mailbox. She gave me a fluttery hand wave and smiled. I waved back but I didn't stop. I drove on over to the Lazy Bee and picked up a six-pack of Diet Coke. There was a telephone outside the Lazy Bee. I thought of calling up Marleah then and there, why not, hey Marleah it's Wayne, I'm down here at the Lazy Bee and thought you might be out of Winston One Hundred Lights. On another Saturday, I might have done it. But on this one I was scheduled to sit with my father.

Mama was outside weeding her marigold bed, and she looked up when I came up the front steps, my feet crunching down on the welcome mat, and she said Wayne Junior's in there with him, Wayne.

My father was sitting on the side of the bed. He had Wayne Junior's Walkman on. He had his legs spread and his hands on his butt, tapping one foot on the carpet. When Wayne Junior saw me coming, he slipped the earphones off my father's ears, trying not to upset him too much. Wayne Junior put the earphones over his own tender ears, waiting for me to start in on him.

His voice was going, "Gimmee that, Wayne." Wayne Junior looked at me for direction and I told him to turn the damn thing off.

My father's hands weren't on his hips anymore, he was on his feet, he was doing this ballerina twinkle toe step across the bedroom and out the door. We caught up with him in front of the TV set, channel surfing with the remote.

AFTER MAMA TALKED to Marleah after church, Marleah came over to do what she promised she would do, sing a hymn for my father, whatever hymn he wanted to hear. My father wasn't wearing a diaper. He had a T-shirt on, khaki pants. Mama had cut his toenails.

While Mama went on back to the bedroom, to tell my father Marleah was here, I was talking to Mama, in my head—*why does this have to happen, how sad can this get? Don't you understand*, Mama came back in my head, *he just wants to hear her sing.*

Marleah was standing in front of my father's unit map. It was just us, in the living room. "I'm really not sure I should do this."

"Do what?" I chanced it. "See me again?"

"I told your mama I'd sing for your daddy. I didn't think you'd be here, Wayne."

Marleah was smoothing her skirt out again. The skinny soldier my father used to be was where he usually was, tacked to the unit map. Then Mama was back. She said we could see him now.

Mama went in first, Marleah next. My father was sitting up in the bed. His hands were folded over his belly. Mama sat near the foot of the bed, Marleah stood next to the dresser. When Mama called her over, she came. She let herself down in the ladder-back like my father was holding the chair for her. Leaning forward inches away from him, she took his right hand in one of hers. "How you feelin', Mister Creel?"

"He's doing real well," I had to say. Paul Creel in his blue suit, the man in the photograph, what if he were here in his Sunday suit, would his left hand be flopping like a fish? But he couldn't fit into that suit anymore.

"Mister Creel?" Marleah raised her voice. "Mister Creel, I came here to sing a hymn for you. What hymn would you like me to sing, Mister Creel?"

"You sing whatever you feel like singing," Mama said.

My father's left hand flopped like a fish. I couldn't allow him to go on this way. I grabbed his left hand and stopped it. I dragged his right hand loose from Marleah's.

My father gave me a look I'll never forget. He yanked his hands away like I was contaminated. "Leave, Wayne! You hear me? Leave!"

I wish I hadn't but I stayed where I was. My father glared out the window at the front yard, the mimosa out by the mailbox, the birdbath, Marleah's white Honda Civic, Wyatt Kirkpatrick's place across the road. He had his chin in his hand, his feet stretched out like he wanted to float away somewhere with Marleah floating with him. The air came on with a rush. Nobody said anything. Finally Mama signaled us to leave the room.

I walked Marleah on out to Mama's marigold bed. It was hot outside. Marleah's frilly white blouse was damp. Sweat streaked her layer of face powder. A butterfly flickered behind her. I heard a mocking bird going—*joodeejoodeejoodee*. I heard a car down the road somewhere.

Marleah looked at me hard when we got to her car.

"I only came because your mother asked me to. I didn't expect to see you here."

"Next time you come I'll make sure I'm somewhere else."

"There won't be a next time," Marleah said.

Marleah got in her car and drove away. Across the road Wyatt Kirkpatrick's underground lawn sprinklers poked their heads up into

Wyatt's front yard, hissing, squirting out water. I could cross the road, keep going, get wet, plant my feet in Wyatt's water-soaked grass. If I did that, would my father be watching me through the window he had on the world? What would he say if I trekked past Wyatt's barbecue pit, the swing set for his two sons, kept on going, the hissing sprinklers behind me now, along with Wyatt, and Stephanie Kirkpatrick, Mama too, Sandy also, Wayne Junior? What would he say if, climbing over Wyatt's chicken-wire back fence, on my way to the woods, the deep woods, the tall pines that would grow taller as more years ticked off my short life, if I were to do that, and, I told myself, I still might, would I be doing what Denny Maxwell had done, would, in my father's view, I be doing something stupid? Or would I be doing what would please him most?

Chairs

I FELT THE CHAIR SLATS RIBBING MY back, a wedge of hot sun on my feet. I got up and moved my beach chair so it would get more shade from the sun umbrella. Settled back in with my diet drink, I watched my wife pat on more suntan lotion. When Linda leaned over to do her ankles, I saw the lines on her back from the slats of the chairs. The suntan lotion was gritty with sand so I decided I wouldn't put any on.

We were the ones who laid claim to the chairs. There were two of them, close to the water. They were low-backed, legs embedded in sand, a ledge of wood connecting the chairs for our drinks and suntan lotion. The chairs were needing a paint job, and the nail heads in the slats were rusted. You saw chairs like these in front of cheap motels, three pairs, sometimes, instead of one. Here there was only one pair.

We had the sun umbrella from a beach supply store. It had a red stripe and a white stripe, then a dark blue stripe and more white, like one of those paint sample color charts where the colors are clear and bright. We had planted our umbrella in the sand before anyone else caught on to the fact that only two chairs were available here—I mean on the beach, not around the pool or arranged behind the lock link fence, where the chairs were clustered in twos and threes on the sun-soaked concrete apron. We laid claim because we got there first. But that is not to say we monopolized the chairs. We would vacate the chairs when we went out to lunch, when we took a nap late in the afternoon. We let other people use them too for the chairs were for everybody in the motel to share and share alike.

I was watching this man from Birmingham who spent most of his time in the water. His sun umbrella and beach towel—the umbrella had green and yellow stripes—were a few feet away from where we were, in the chairs, drinking our diet drinks. Linda was talking about quitting Lucille's. She had worked for Lucille for too many years. She wanted a business of her own. She tilted her bright green plastic cup with the straw poking out of a hole in the lid. With my separation pay and my retirement we could move down here, get out of Georgia. I could say goodbye to Fort Benning. Linda might open up a florist shop down here.

"We'll use the equity from our house," she said. Linda patted my knee. "We can get a thirty-year mortgage. Don't worry, it will all work out."

It will and it won't, I was thinking. That's the way it had been in the past. For now, we could sit out here in the chairs. Out here close to the water, our financial situation looked good. I watched Linda open her magazine; then I folded my hands on my belly—still firm, not much fat down there. I watched a gull skim by with a fish in its beak.

We went out for dinner that night, and then we went to this country and western place. It had a combo and a singer that sang requests. She had a body on her and she could sing. We had a good time dancing, and when we were back in our room we made love in a way we hadn't done for awhile.

The next day we went out for breakfast, and when we came back the first thing I noticed out on the beach was that the chairs were occupied. Another couple had taken over the chairs. They were young. I hadn't seen them before. The backs had been lowered on the chairs so these people could sun themselves. The girl lay on her stomach, her head turned slightly to the right. She was wearing a red French-cut. From where we were, on the sun deck, those squares of shaded sand out there, those sun umbrellas were signaling me to take Linda back to our room for awhile. But I wasn't about to do that yet.

"I give them another two hours," I said. "Maybe more. Who knows?"

Linda looked up from her magazine. "Why don't we go back to our room," she said. "We'll be cool and comfortable in our room."

"This is no time to hole up in our room. Now is the time for us to get some sun before it gets too hot to sit out in it."

"Well why not sit here and get some sun?"

"Come on. We're going out there," I said. "We're not going to waste the morning up here."

So pretty soon we set up the sun umbrella and lay out on our beach towels. After lunch we took a nap. I kept the drapes closed until we came out. It wasn't us who readjusted the chairs so people could sit on them again. We waited for someone else to. We stayed inside until this was done, watching television after we woke up. Towards evening we went back outside. The chair backs had been readjusted. The chairs were chairs again. This joker and his girl friend must have gotten wind of the attitude here. Hogging the chairs wasn't right—this certainly would have come through in the way other people would have looked at these two. Other people would have been willing to share the chairs. Other people's wives wore one-piece bathing suits. Maybe what I was thinking got through to these people because the next day they were gone.

So the next day went all right. We made sure the chairs were available to whoever wanted to sit in them. We set our umbrella up some distance away, lay out on our towels, got gritty. In a corner of concrete, behind the fence, we kept tabs on who was using the chairs. This man from Birmingham and his wife were stretched out with the chair backs down, very comfortable under their sun umbrella. The wife wore a black and white one-piece. Two old ladies were feeding potato chips to the gulls. After the Birmingham people left we let the old ladies have the chairs for as long as they wanted to sit in them. We spent the day on the beach without sitting in the chairs. Around sunset, making quite a ruckus, more gulls followed the ladies on their walk down the beach.

We watched the sunset sitting in the chairs. The sun was a paint sample red, and the sky, it was really worth seeing. Such a sunset you won't see in Georgia, was how Linda expressed it. We had a nice sea breeze on our faces. The chairs were ours to enjoy for as long as we wanted to sit in them.

The next day it was different, even though we got out on the beach early. What we saw was molded in sand. It was lying on its stomach. It had a head and a gorilla's back. What sort of person would do this thing? The sun took a sudden lurch up, beaming light on the blade of the kitchen knife thrust into this gorilla's back.

"You get all kinds on the beach," I said.

Linda gave me a look. "This guy has a weird sense of humor."

"You said guy."

"I mean guy," Linda said.

"So maybe it wasn't a guy. Supposing a woman did it."

"Put a knife in a man made out of sand?"

"He could have been two-timing her. In this woman's imagination, I mean."

"A woman wouldn't do that," Linda said, sitting up very straight in her chair. "A woman might shoot her lover but she wouldn't make a thing like this."

This was true, but I had to have my say—because of the thing itself, just doing this thing behind our backs, not as a threat, as a joke.

"This woman must be a weirdo," I said. "She must be taking it out on men."

"Is that what you think?"

"That's what I think."

I could feel the sun heating up. It was time for us to set up the umbrella. Linda yanked out the telescoped rod, and began to work it into the sand.

"I know that's not what you really think." Linda said. "What *do* you think? You tell me."

"I'll show you instead," I said.

I pulled the kitchen knife out of the sand thing and threw it into the water. Then I pulverized the sand thing.

We ate lunch out, at a beachside oyster bar. We played goofy golf, did some other things. When we came back there were these people.

There were six of them, three couples. They were standing around a catamaran. It was beached and the sail was furled—not twenty feet from the chairs. Two of the women were wearing one-piece bathing suits. You could tell they were trying to watch their weight, but being middle-aged, they showed fat. These women were with two middle-aged men, big men without much fat on them. The girl in the red French-cut was the first to sit down in one of the chairs. Her boy friend didn't adjust the back. Not this time, not like yesterday. The others took a walk down the beach, disappearing from view for the day.

We spent the day sitting by the pool, which wasn't much, not a whole lot more than postage stamp size. The girl in the red French-cut and her boy friend sat out by themselves in the chairs. Not twenty feet from the chairs the catamaran had its hull and mast in our faces, the mast straight up, the sail furled.

That night we went back to the country and western place, but the singer wasn't there. We didn't dance. We listened. We nursed our drinks for an hour or so; then we drove back to the motel.

The catamaran was on its side, its mast away from the water. I could push it into the water and tow it on down the beach. But I would have had to do that by myself. Linda wouldn't be helping me. We were standing out in front of our room, looking down and out at the catamaran. The catamaran was still twenty feet or so from the chairs, but I wanted to move it still farther.

Linda said nothing doing. "Supposing you got away with it. They'd find their boat. They'd bring it back."

We sat in the chairs in front of our room, in the glare from the overhead light. I talked to Linda about what else I could do. Talk to them maybe, about the chairs. Tell them the chairs were for everybody. The beach, it didn't belong to them.

"I don't want you doing that. Don't lower yourself," Linda said.

The next morning they were all out there. It didn't come as any surprise. The sail was unfurled. The catamaran was ready to launch, on its runners, pointed away from the chairs. The sail, it was pretty to look at, from the window of our motel room. The upper section was sky blue. There were bands of red and yellow and green, then the dark blue bottom section. Already their towels were draped on the chairs. There were lawn chairs stacked nearby. Soon the women were setting the lawn chairs up.

"That's it," I said. "We go down there."

I had already put on my swim trunks. Linda was still in her nightgown.

"We take our umbrella and go," I said. "Or we check out. We go somewhere else."

Linda came up to me in her nightgown. "You're making too big a deal out of this. But if you want to go, we'll go home."

"I'm not going home. I'm going out there," I said. "You coming?" I waited until Linda said yes. I waited for her to put on her suit before I went outside to get the sun umbrella. Linda followed me down to the beach.

But we didn't get to the spot I'd picked without seeing the next thing they did, them starting it, starting to put up the tent. The women laid out this plastic sheet, sky blue like the top of the sail. It was going to be a tent without flaps, what was going up around the chairs. The women bulging in the wrong places stuck tent pegs in the sand. That's what the older women were doing while the girl in the red French-cut looked out at the Gulf. All three men were knocking the tent pegs in, with a hammer, chucking and chunking. Finally, the girl in the red French-cut picked up a tent peg. I watched her push it into the sand. I heard the sea oats rustling, the chucking and chunking. In front of us, the tent was almost up. The women were moving their lawn chairs in.

We wanted to let these people know that we could do what we liked, so we went in the water, right in front of their tent. Coming out, I saw a tent pole go down. It was windy, the plastic was tearing loose. All three women, they got the poles back in place, and the men, they hammered in the pegs. They were doing that when we left.

Linda picked up the beach towels. I followed her with the umbrella.

At the door to our room, Linda laid the beach towels out on the railing to dry. I laid the sun umbrella on the concrete.

From our room we could see what was going on. The women in one-piece bathing suits were sitting in their lawn chairs. Their towels were draped over the beach chairs The men pushed off in the catamaran. The girl in the red French-cut, she sat down in a lawn chair and set her foot on the arm of one of the beach chairs. She bent from the waist like she was touching her toes.

"She's painting her toenails," Linda said.

"So she's painting her toenails on the arm of my chair. If you ask me that's rubbing your nose in it."

"I didn't ask you," Linda came back. "And if you think that's your chair you're mistaken. I'm the one who sat in it last."

"I know you're the one who sat in it last. And I know we didn't each have our own chair, but if I remember correctly, I sat in that chair most of the time, the one that girl's got her foot on."

Linda didn't say anything else to me about the chairs. "I'm ready to leave when you are," she said.

"Anytime," I said, "we'll pack up and leave."

Linda left me sitting at the window. I heard her plop her suitcase on the bed, yank open dresser drawers. We'd go home and pick up where we left off. In a minute or two I'd start packing.

The girl moved her foot on the arm of the chair, just another chair on the beach.

A Ford in the River

I BUZZ THE DOOR AT THE END OF THE corridor, the red light flashes, the door opens, I check in at the nursing station, ask how Susan's doing, the same the nurse says. I don't see her pacing, so I go to her room. Susan's wearing a purple blouse over her nightgown, tan panty hose, one house slipper. She tells me to sit on the edge of her bed while she goes out to get her hourly allotted cigarette. I wait a little while for her to come back before going to the dayroom. I put her dirty clothes in the plastic bag that I brought to take them home in.

Jimmy Ray is in the day room. He's waiting for us to get started. Already he's laid out the Scrabble board, having turned the tiles face down in the box. I'm conscious of Susan close to me, a cigarette ash on a silk scarf, cigarette smoke in my lungs. Then Susan puts out her cigarette. She has smoked it down to the filter. She sets the filter next to the Scrabble board. When I put it in one of the ashtrays, she puts it back next to the Scrabble board.

Jimmy isn't much of a Scrabble player, and sometimes he doesn't follow the rules. He will play contractions and brand name words. I watch him edge in the D tile in FORD. He has already played the O and the R, playing vertically off the F in BUFFS. But Jimmy hasn't a brand name in mind. He has a ford in a river in mind. Susan's holding a glazed doughnut that she hadn't gotten around to eating yet. I play two O's and a D off FORD, carefully putting each tile in its square. I get triple word points off DODO. Jimmy plays HEARTS off the S in BUFFS.

We're getting the weather on Channel Four. The weather woman is forecasting rain. There is this black man, Big Tim, with his coffee, smoking a cigarette. I've been keeping Big Tim in cigarettes. I leave the cigarettes at the nursing station with instructions to give them to Big Tim because I know he would take care of Susan, look out for her in the corridor. Big Tim is in charge of the refreshment room; he hands out coffee and soft drinks. One time I lined up for a soft drink but he shook his head, not for visitors.

I play two tiles vertically, an S and an E, off the A in HEARTS. I do the adding up, write down the score. Susan is back in the dayroom with her uneaten glazed doughnut. I am about to play SHUT off the H. Susan puts her hands on the card table, rocking the tiles loose on the board. Jimmy hooks his thumbs in his belt. I put the tiles back in the box, the tiles first, then the board, trying not to listen to Susan. She wants me to go to her room. She doesn't want me with Jimmy. I tell Jimmy we'll play again next time.

"I said let's go to my room," Susan says.

Susan is tapping her right foot. I have seen her tap her right foot before when she wanted to get money out of me. It would always be her right foot until I say something, yes or no. Today I say yes; we will go to her room.

MY WIFE, PEGGY, turns on the washing machine. She waits for the level of water to rise before putting in the detergent. She has the dial set for warm/cold, for Susan's blouses and washable sweaters. The camisoles, panties, and T-shirts are on high-to-low heat, in the dryer. Water trickles into the washing machine. Peggy waits with a scoop of detergent. I am holding Susan's wash basket, the one she used while she was living with us, in the garage apartment behind the house. Peggy is watching the level rise. She puts in half a cup of detergent. This is my signal to move away so Peggy can put in Susan's clothes.

Peggy lowers the lid and and spreads her arms, palms flattened on the washer. She looks past me at the stairs, through the window across from the washing machine, running up past Susan's window. Neither one of us wants to climb these stairs. We haven't cleaned up

Susan's apartment yet. This is something we will do together, put Susan's apartment in order. Peggy won't do this without me. We will pry loose candles and clotted wax from saucers and paperback books. There are the cigarettes Susan smoked. They are standing in rows on a window sill, on her vanity, in the bathroom. Peggy will leave the cigarettes to me. She will do the dusting and vacuuming.

Peggy moves to the door of the laundry room. She stands in the door, she wants to keep me inside. Then I realize she isn't blocking my way. She is asking me to bring the ironing board, folded up next to the water heater. The iron is in Susan's apartment. One of us will have to get it.

I HAVEN'T SEEN Shirley Ray in the store before. Shirley Ray is wearing the pants suit that she usually wears in the ward. She would watch us sometimes, playing Scrabble, but never for very long. Shirley hands me a prescription, for an antidepressant, Elevil.

"Remember me. I'm Jimmy's mother," she says. "I've seen you two playing Scrabble."

I ask her how Jimmy is doing before I go to fill the prescription. About the same, she tells me. When I come back with the prescription, Shirley touches one teardrop earring with the edge of a painted fingernail. The plastic container she holds up to the light so the capsules show through its apricot haze. Shirley rummages in her pocketbook. She has a checkbook and a ballpoint pen. I tell her we can't take her check because she doesn't have an account here. She asks me if we take credit cards. I tell her to go to the tobacco counter. Someone there will take her credit card. Shirley's eyes narrow like Jimmy's when he is about to make his play. She is moving the checkbook slightly, tapping an edge on the ball of her thumb. Then she comes out with it, about Jimmy.

"There's something I think you should know. My son Jimmy tried to kill me. Jimmy pointed a shotgun at me. I was lucky, my brother was there. Next time he might not be there."

I don't tell Shirley I know about that. I've heard about it, from Big

Tim. I look away from her, at aisle 6-A, toothpaste, dental floss, shaving cream. I know Shirley has things to say to me. I look at my row of prescriptions, lined up in their plastic containers. Witch doctor's mumbo jumbo, voodoo incantations might work better, but I am a pharmacist. I have to stick to what I know.

Shirley pulls out her billfold, spreads it out on the prescription counter. She shows me a family photograph of Jimmy and Shirley together, in the backyard in front of a gas grill. Jimmy is wearing a barbecue apron. He has his arm around Shirley. Beside Jimmy, Shirley looks small and frail.

"That's Jimmy when he was fourteen. Jimmy's Dad took that picture."

I tell Shirley Jimmy looks good, and she shows me a second photograph. Jimmy is riding a bicycle. I think of Susan on her first bicycle, with a nice little smile for her father.

"Jimmy was okay before Jack left. You can tell that in the picture."

"Maybe he'll be okay again."

"That's never going to happen. I can't trust Jimmy anymore. I don't know what he'll do next."

Another customer is approaching, an old man, one of the regulars here. Shirley moves aside to let him in. He waves a prescription at me, and I take it and go to fill it. I measure out the loaf-shaped pills, put the cap on the container. I put the prescription in the computer. Shirley watches me stick the label on. She puts the billfold back in her pocketbook, and I wait for Shirley to leave the store.

SUSAN HAS NOT gotten better. The insurance will pay for thirty days. In eight days we will either have to bring her home or go to the probate judge and petition to have her committed to Stockton. We have to decide what to do next, how long we think we can have Susan here if she isn't better in nine days. Peggy sees no alternative; Susan will have to be taken to Stockton.

Peggy sips on her iced tea, looking up from her pinochle hand. We are sitting out on our screened-in porch. The melds are laid out on the tiles. It is Peggy's turn to lead. She leads a ten of diamonds, trumps. I play the jack from a meld. Then I lead from the melds, king of clubs. Peggy plays the nine of clubs. She draws from the stock and leads from a meld. Susan's window over the garage is shut; the venetian blind is closed. We finish, add up our tricks. Peggy shuffles the cards with authority, riffling the interlocked cards off her thumbs. I have seen her do this at her bridge club, with her friends, without looking down. I've heard her keep up a conversation, shuffling the cards, dealing out bridge hands, seen her do this on my way to Susan's apartment with Susan's meds in a plastic pillbox, pills with different shapes and colors, in each compartment, pills with one shape, one color.

Peggy is wearing the dress she wore to church. She has already been to the psychiatric ward. She has seen Susan in restraints. That hasn't caused Peggy to change her mind. I tell Peggy we should try to keep Susan at home. Peggy stops shuffling the cards. "I won't put up with it," she says. I say nothing. What is there for me to say?

We play pinochle for another hour; then I drive across town to the hospital. The head nurse says they have rules. Susan has to stay in restraints, but they will take one of the wrist straps off. I can hear Susan yelling and cursing. Usually a nurse at the station will tell me to come back tomorrow. But today I can see my daughter. I can sit with her for as long as for ten minutes. I ask the head nurse for a cigarette from her pack at the nursing station. An orderly unbuckles one wrist strap. I light Susan's cigarette and watch her smoke. She complains about being in restraints, and I tell her I'll see what I can do. I tell her I will come back in an hour. I will bring her a cigarette, in an hour.

I leave Susan and go to the dayroom. Jimmy is waiting for me. He is wearing jeans and cowboy boots. Already he's laid out the Scrabble board, having turned the tiles face down in the box. We get started; we draw out tiles. Jimmy looks at his tile rack. His shoulders are hunched as he picks out a tile. He plays ACCEPT. I write down his score. I play my tiles vertically off the E. I play TEE, as in golf tee. That is only good for three points. Jimmy starts cracking his knuckles. He puts his right fist in his cupped left hand. There is something he wants to tell me. He says he tried to call his father today, but all he got was the answering machine. Jimmy picks up a tile and edges it in, an E, off the T in golf tee. "I know why I never see him. He's with this woman who hates me. She doesn't want him to see me."

I play EXIT off of TEE. Jimmy plays BED off of EXIT.

"My mother, she wants to see me. But she doesn't want me in the house."

I wait until his agitation goes, like a hand has passed over his face. I play SPEED off the D in BED, for a double word, write down the score. I can play DEEP, but instead I play SPEED. Big Tim and another black man come in; they go to the Ping-Pong table. I still have thirty minutes to wait before I take Susan her cigarette. The Ping-Pong ball rolls across the room. We can all hear Susan yelling because the room she is in doesn't have a door.

I hold out Susan's cigarette and put it, lighted, between her lips. She waits to blow the smoke out. Susan tells me I have to take her home. The head nurse says Susan will be out of restraints when her behavior becomes acceptable. She says I can take Jimmy outside. She allows us out in the courtyard. Big Tim and some others are going out, have permission to take this smoke break outside.

There is a hoop and backboard outside, but no net, and no basketball. Jimmy's standing with his thumbs in his belt; then he sits down on one of the benches. Big Tim lights up a cigarette. He lets Jimmy take one drag. When Jimmy asks for another drag, Big Tim says he'll have to work for it. He'll have to play him one on one. Streaks of sunset are still in the sky, outside the courtyard gate, in the parking lot. I tell Big Tim he's too tall, over six feet, no contest. I tell Jimmy I'll get him a cigarette on the next break if he can whip me.

Jimmy goes in for a lay-up. He gets by me for the lay-up. I get off a one-handed push shot. Swish, I say to myself, two points. Jimmy cuts to the right, gets by me again. But we can't go on; even Jimmy knows that.

The next day I come home for lunch and see that Susan's window isn't shut. I move out through the screen door and move on to the garage. The door at the top of the stairs is open. I can hear Peggy vacuuming in there. In a paper bag there are cigarettes. And the candles are in the paper bag. Some of the clothes are tied up in a sheet, what was going into the washer. There are skirts and sweaters heaped on the bed.

Peggy turns off the vacuum cleaner. "You can drop these off at the cleaners." I see that Peggy hasn't dusted the window sill. The ashes from Susan's cigarettes, those tiny columns of meaning for her, have been obliterated, are gone.

I say, "I want you to leave it the way it is."

"It's too late for that. I'm cleaning it up."

"I'm not sending Susan to Stockton," I say.

"All right. All right. You say you aren't but I say it's the only way Susan will get better."

Peggy turns on the vacuum cleaner, moving the trolley across the floor. I watch Peggy bear down on Susan's bed. She tries to vacuum under the bed, but she can't get far enough under. She doesn't ask me to help her move the bed, so I leave and go back to the house. The front closet is where we keep the games—Monopoly, Backgammon, Scrabble, a few others that aren't that popular. We keep the games on the top shelf. I pull down the Scrabble game. The box is coated with dust. I go to the kitchen table. I open the box and lay out the board. I think about playing all the tiles to make sure they are all there. But there isn't time to do that today. I soak a handy-wipe in water and wipe the dust off the board.

Susan isn't watching the Scrabble game. Susan is at the window, doing her numbers again. For her, the numbers mean something—one, eleven, three, forty-two. She is out of restraints; she is quiet. There are silences between the numbers. I write down the score. I play my tiles. Naturally, Jimmy is pleased with the score. His hands are gripping his wrists, and he rocks in his chair with glee. I don't intend to finish the game today. I will sit with Susan in her room, accompany her in the corridor, keeping step with her as she paces, alert for the slowdowns, the stops, the shifts in direction mapped in her brain. Will we go to the end, the fire exit, to the showers, the refreshment room? Will we sit down in the alcove, in the love seat, going only part way?

The next day Shirley Ray's there. She tells Jimmy he has to pack tonight because he won't have time to pack tomorrow. She tells him to be ready at six so they can have some time together. A deputy sheriff will be there at seven to take Jimmy to Stockton. When Jimmy asks about his father, she says his father won't be coming. But he will visit Jimmy at Stockton. That is when Jimmy looks at me. I can't say no to that look, but I don't know how to say yes. Peggy wouldn't put up with it. She wouldn't have Jimmy in the house.

Jimmy goes with us to the door. He waits for a nurse to buzz us out. We are leaving the hospital together. We can't see the ward from the parking lot. In the parking lot, standing near my car, Shirley brings up her ex-husband, Jack. Jack is living with Kay Lyn; they are living in a trailer park. It is Kay Lyn who won't have Jimmy. Shirley says she knows this for a fact because she has talked to Kay Lyn herself.

"We had a talk," Shirley says flatly, folding her arms and looking at me. "Kay Lyn said she wouldn't feel safe with Jimmy around." Shirley is standing close to me, a little too close, I'm thinking. I put one hand on the door of the car.

There is a telephone in the paint shop and, sitting next to it, an answering machine. Jack listens to Shirley tell him that I happen to know about Stockton. My daughter has been in Stockton; there are certain things Jack should know. Jack has sideburns and a wavy mustache. For awhile he is looking away from us. Then he gets up and goes to Shirley. He stands over her so I move away.

"I told you I'll visit him at Stockton," Jack says.

"I'll believe that when I see it, Jack."

I go to the door of the paint shop. The body shop is across the yard. There are cars in there being worked on.

The next day I'm back at the ward. Big Tim tells me what happened, how a deputy sheriff took Jimmy out of the ward. Shirley was there. Jack wasn't there. Jimmy's hands were handcuffed in front of him, his legs were chained. That was the way it had to be done, Big Tim tells me.

We are moving along, down the corridor, past the nursing station. Susan might do the numbers next, or ask for a cigarette at the nursing station. Susan might go anywhere, do anything, if she weren't here, having to pace.

Photographs

Snug in the Corvette's bucket seat, a quart of Wild Turkey in a paper sack, he passed a stand of pines, a pair of mailboxes, the mouth of a road yawning out of woods. He thought of stopping right there. He would get out of the car, crack the Turkey. But Jimmy would want him to hold off. Jimmy would break the seal, and they would have their first drink together. That was necessary. That was how it was done. And something else in how they drank together—they used their grandfather's silver drinking cups. The two cups had stood untouched for years, until Richard and Jimmy were men enough to hold their liquor, old enough to buy it legally. They were men enough to serve their country, but the colonel had not insisted on that. Only one thing he would ask of them. *You'll remember me when you drink from these cups.* But Richard didn't want to remember him, not now, not after what he had found in his grandfather's roll-top desk. He had left his silver cup behind. He would drink his liquor out of a jelly glass.

He hadn't written Jimmy a check yet. Jimmy wanted to buy into a marina, get out of the tree business once and for all. Jimmy wanted ten thousand from him, what was left of his share of the inheritance. He knew he could always sell the Corvette. But he wasn't about to do that. Five thousand was as far as he would go.

He had the photographs in the glove compartment. They had been taken on Okinawa—Japanese prisoners of war, in a column of twos, on the double. They had not known they were being photographed, would end up in the colonel's roll-top desk, in the bottom left-hand drawer with Japanese yen and some swizzle sticks. His grandfather had taken the photographs. He was a first lieutenant then; he had fought on Okinawa. He had Japanese yen to prove it, and the photographs, and a samurai sword. *We shot the paymaster and took the yen. Of course, they weren't of any use to us.*

Richard had kept the roll-top desk, and Jimmy had kept the footlocker. It was Jimmy who had the .45, the commendations, the Purple Heart medal. He kept them in the footlocker, in his cabin on the lake. It was time to show Jimmy the photographs because Jimmy thought he might have a future, be somebody for a change. Sooner or later he would have to know. Because for Jimmy the funeral had ended it. What was done in his grandfather's life was done. Jimmy had stared at the coffin, his big hands cupped for the cartridges. The officer in charge of the detail had come to Richard with the folded flag. It would go to the elder brother. Their mother was standing between them, there only for her sons. Their father was missing in action, in Viet Nam, lost, unburied. When the volleys were fired his mother's head twitched, her ash-blond hair brushing his face. Richard lowered his eyes to his grandmother's grave, the tombstones in the family plot. A breeze swept through the canopy. Again he felt the touch of his mother's hair. Jimmy had been close to him then. They were standing shoulder to shoulder. The silence went on spreading.

He passed a trailer, another satellite dish, a row of houses with junked-up yards. Then the pines were on either side of the road, and the branches clawed out at his new Corvette. The next thing the asphalt gave out, around a bend in the road, without warning. He felt the new car shake and bang in the ruts. *Goddamn it you could have told me*—but Jimmy had let him find out for himself. All he had to do was slow down, keep the Corvette crawling for a while. He passed a roadhouse, some cabins behind it, then a bait store selling beer and ice, live minnows, earthworms, catalpas.

He could see one end of the lake now. He took the dirt road to Jimmy's cabin, still driving slow, easing over the ruts. He pulled in next to Jimmy's Land Rover. Inside the cabin he put the Turkey on a table beside an egg-stained plate. Then he went out to find Jimmy.

THEY WERE MOVING along one shoreline. There was a little wind, just enough to blow his line around. He hadn't been fishing for a long time. He didn't want to make a fool of himself. Jimmy had given Richard the boat chair. The boat chair would enable Richard to cast sidearm. *That's why they put this mother in, for guys like yourself who don't know how to fish.* He was able to tie on the jitterbug while Jimmy took the boat out on the lake. They saw ducks flying over a headland. Then Jimmy was raising the motor and letting the anchor slide off the stern. Richard swung the boat chair out to one side of the boat, the jitterbug flying free from the rod, the line swinging out again in the wind. He raised the butt of the rod and pulled back the rod. He hadn't made his first cast yet. It had been that long; he was that bad. Then the line came in and he grabbed it. He flipped the bail, made his first cast, yes sidearm, but that didn't matter. He did an overhead cast when the wind slacked off. Jimmy said nothing, let him fish.

The wind picked up again, rocked the boat, riffling Jimmy's hair in his vented black cap, blowing Richard's line out farther. Richard reached out, pulled the line in. He watched Jimmy pop open a can of beer. Jimmy leaned out and down from the stern of the boat, handed the beer to Richard. He got another beer out of the cooler, opened it, set it between his knees. He turned, flipped the spin reel's bail, did an arching overhead cast. The jitterbug splashed between rotting stumps. Jimmy didn't wait long to reel in his line, drew it in without snagging weeds. Richard had cast in open water, reeling in slowly, methodically. He made sure he was holding the rod straight up. A few drops of water fell on his hand. He felt the sun beat down on the back of his head, squinting out at the glittering shoreline.

"Not much doing," Jimmy said. "You feel like moving on."

"I'll leave that up to you," Richard said. "You know this lake. I don't."

"I think we should move on," Jimmy said. "That is if you want to catch some fish. If you don't we'll sit here and drink our beer."

"Let's sit here then."

"Okay by me."

Richard moved away from the steering wheel. He had to give himself some leg room, one foot was going to sleep. He watched Jimmy take a long swallow of beer. He would nurse his along, take it easy, save the serious drinking for later. He watched Jimmy light a cigarette, cupping a match, taking a drag. Jimmy did a long cast toward the shoreline. He reeled in, threading the stumps. He changed lures, tied on a beetle spin lure, the cigarette hanging from his lips.

Richard laid down his rod and reel, on the sun bleached twill of the carpeting. It had to get said sometime. "You ready to talk?"

"Let's have it."

He was rushing his words, as he knew he would. "I just can't risk it, Jimmy." He pushed more words at his brother's face, at the flat eyes set in an impassive squint. "I'd be willing to lend you something. Hell, I'll give you thirty-five hundred. But that's really all I can handle." He felt the rock and slosh of the boat. "I'll write you a check this afternoon. If that will help, Jimmy, it's yours."

Again Jimmy cast in deep water, without shifting his gaze, moving a muscle in his face Jimmy planted his feet on the carpet, his legs spread, reeling in. "It won't help. I need more than that. I'll go ass deep in debt to get it. But a freebie from you I don't need."

Jimmy pulled the cigarette out of his mouth, let it drop burning into the lake. His brother was turning away from him, facing out from the stern now. Jimmy put one boot on the motor, the other on the thwart in the stern. He did a long cast in deep water. Across the lake, over a mile away, the marina seemed unattainable. Why was Jimmy so goddamned stubborn?

"Okay, you want a loan, that's what you'll get. I'm offering you five thousand."

"Okay, I'll take a loan. I'll take five thousand on a three-year note. I'll use the Land Rover for collateral. How would a Land Rover suit you, Rich?"

"Suits me fine, but you don't need collateral," he said, seeing Jimmy smile, with relief. “I’ll lend you five thousand without collateral.”

“Okay, Rich, you got it. So I say we do some fishing. You can troll from the stern while I look for a spot.”

Richard started to pick up his rod and reel. His brother was lowering the motor. “Leave it. I’ll hand it to you.” Jimmy handed him the rod and reel. He had the motor in the water now and was pulling the anchor up over the stern, his left hand under the anchor, his right on the pulley line. Richard got out from behind the wheel and hauled in the anchor on the bow. He felt the strain on his biceps and wrists. Drops of water lit on the carpeting.

“I’m all set,” he told Jimmy. He crawled back to his place at the wheel, waiting to switch with Jimmy.

Trolling, seeing the shore move by, Richard felt eased, relieved. He would never see the five thousand again, but he had done what he could for his brother. He changed lures, tied on a kangaroo worm. His line trailed out behind the boat. He reeled in a little, slowly, watched the spool rise and fall on the spindle.

He felt the impact, heard the rasp of the drag. Richard got both hands on the rod and held; then his left hand found the reel handle. He knew enough not to reel in yet. He let the bass take the line to the left, swiveled round to keep the line taut. Then he reeled in, fighting the strain in his wrists. The line wouldn’t break; he had set the drag right. Then the largemouth bass was coming up. He was reeling it in toward the side of the boat. Jimmy leaned out with the landing net, stretching to balance the boat. Jimmy netted the bass in one motion, pulled it in over the side of the boat. He stuck two fingers inside its mouth, and pulled the bass out of the net. The hook was caught in a corner of its mouth, torn sideways with the worm hanging out.

He caught the suppressed excitement in Jimmy’s voice. “Not bad. Must weigh at least five pounds.” Jimmy leaned out with the bass on the line, hefted it, let Richard take it. “Maybe five and a half but I wouldn’t say six.” Richard ran his left hand along the dorsal fin. He hooked his thumb under the gaping mouth. The barbed hook came out easily.

Ahead of them bass were feeding. Jimmy picked up his rod and reel. Richard got down from the boat chair, moving one hand along the green twill. The boat drifted into lily pads. Dragonflies skimmed the surface. A bass jumped, thirty feet from the boat. He heard the bass slosh in the net. He would change lures, try a minnow. He found a painted minnow in the tackle box. He took care not to stick himself on a hook. By the time he got the lure tied on, Jimmy had already pulled in a bass. It was small, but Jimmy kept it.

In an hour, they were back at the cabin. There were four bass in the net. Jimmy shook out three of them. They flopped on the sun-bleached concrete steps. Jimmy gripped one bass behind the dorsal fin and the tail. He slapped its head on the concrete. He laid his cigarette on the edge of the step. "You can do it this way, or use a hammer. The toolbox is in the cabin."

The big bass was still in the net when Richard came back with the hammer. The small bass was on the concrete. It was quiet, twitching its tail, the gills spasmodically quivering. Richard laid his left hand behind the gill, raised the hammer and lowered it. His fingertips felt slimy, pressing into the scaly flesh. He raised the hammer again, brought it down. Then he shook the big bass out of the net. It was flopping on the concrete. He would have to put his foot on it. He waited just a little too long, for Jimmy had pinned the bass with his boot. Richard hit it hard below the eye. It was stiff when he picked it up.

They put newspapers under the dead bass. Jimmy cut off the heads, and gutted them, leaving the tails. Richard took charge of the scaling. He used his pocket knife, moving its edge toward the head, in short sweeps, scraping the scales off. Scales stuck to his knuckles. He heard the crunch of Jimmy's fish knife, saw the head with its fringe of blood on the knife-slashed, gut-soaked newspaper. Flies buzzed around the heads and guts. Jimmy waited for Richard to scale the last bass. Fish scales silted the newspaper; the newsprint was unreadable. He read a fragment of a headline. He was getting used to the crunch of the knife, the squishing of guts in the fingers. Then he was cleaning the knife, snapping it shut. Jimmy wrapped up the heads and guts in a section of clean newspaper.

A young woman came out of a trailer. She moved past her maroon Volkswagen. She came across the road to Jimmy's garbage can as soon as Jimmy got there. She watched Jimmy take the lid off and drop the newspaper in like a dead bird before he wiped his hands on his shirt. She let Jimmy have a sip of her beer and put her other hand on the back of his neck. Richard got up and moved toward her. Then her fingers were curling inside his.

"So you're Richard. I'm Paula Smithson." He found it hard to look away from her. Her fingernails on the foam-rubber sleeve were almost the same shade as her lipstick. He watched her take in the Corvette.

"Nice car. It must really move out."

"It gets me there," Richard said to her. Paula walked over to the Corvette, taking long strides in her halter and shorts. She laid her left hand on the side mirror, put her right hand on her hip. Jimmy's big hands made a camera. "Hold it right there," he said to Paula. Paula cocked a hip and smiled at them.

"Never thought I'd get this close to a 'Vette." She did a little kick with her right foot, keeping one hand on the side mirror. "You think you might take me out, Rich?"

"That's up to Jimmy," Richard said. "Ask Jimmy, don't ask me."

Jimmy looked down at his boots. He put his hand on the bill of his cap, and pulled it down over his sunglasses. "We'll all go," Jimmy said. "The three of us. How does that sound?"

Paula Smithson looked at each of them. Richard watched her pull on the beer can, extracting it from the sleeve. She dropped the beer can in Jimmy's garbage can.

"I'm not going out with either of you." Paula fitted the lid on the garbage can. "Not anytime soon anyway."

She touched the side mirror again, clicking fingernails. Then she turned and crossed the dirt road, and climbed into the Volkswagen. She didn't wave at them before she drove off.

It was hot inside the cabin. Jimmy turned on the window unit. He shut the windows on one side of the big front room, with its kitchen and ladder to the loft. He put his breakfast plate and the mug in the sink. There were cold beers in the refrigerator. Jimmy put the bass in the refrigerator without taking them out of the waxed paper. He got an ice tray out of the freezer compartment and went to the sink to pry loose the ice. There were glasses in a dish rack, two large plates, two coffee mugs. Their grandfather's other silver drinking cup, the cup he had given Jimmy, it was also in the dish rack. Jimmy pushed out ice cubes with his thumb.

Jimmy held out his silver cup. "Here, you take this. Or do you want a beer?"

He told Jimmy he would have a drink. He watched Jimmy fill up the ice tray with water from the tap. He'd dumped the ice cubes on one of the plates. He put the tray in the freezer compartment. He put ice cubes into a jelly glass, leaving Richard with the silver cup. Through the vent in Jimmy's black cloth cap, the patch of hair looked darker now, even though it was still late afternoon, the sunlight pooling on the floor, on the table, white on the venetian blinds.

Jimmy turned, moved into the sunlight. "I'm offering you our grandfather's cup because I want you to have a drink with me. If you'd been thinking you would have brought yours."

"I wasn't thinking of it. I left it at home." That wasn't it, but it was what he had said.

"Okay. So you forgot," Jimmy said. "That's okay. Maybe it's better this way. You might forget and leave it out here with me."

"I wouldn't leave it out here with you," Richard said.

"I know you wouldn't," Jimmy said.

He watched Jimmy go to the refrigerator. Jimmy reached in, pulled out baloney, some cellophane-wrapped slices of cheese. There was bread on the table, a bread knife, and an open box of crackers. Jimmy still had his cap on. He set the food down on the kitchen table, took his cap off, and flipped it across the room. He pulled his sunglasses off, along the bridge of his nose, and set them carefully on the table. His hair fell out around his neck. He sliced the seal of the Wild Turkey, poured bourbon into the jelly glass until the glass was half full. He went to the sink for water, then sat down across from Richard.

He watched Jimmy light a cigarette. Jimmy was letting the match burn down. Then he shook out the match and blew out smoke.

"Five thousand isn't enough. You might as well keep your money, Rich."

So it had come up again. Jimmy wouldn't give up. "So what do you need to get started on?"

"I told you. Ten thousand minimum from you."

"And I told you I can't go that far." Ice rattled in Jimmy's jelly glass as he set it down on the table. Jimmy took another drag from his cigarette.

"You could get ten for the Corvette. I wouldn't have to sign a note. You do that, I'll give you the Rover. I'll drive the goddamned truck for awhile. Till I go bust. How's that suit you?"

"That's crap and you know it, Jimmy."

"You do that, I'll see what I can do for you."

There was nothing he could say to that. He wondered which woman Jimmy would ask. Not likely the one before Paula. Jimmy's crowd all knew each other. His women had been with most of his friends, some married, others just live in. Richard poured bourbon into the cup, drank a little, went on holding the cup. He wondered if Paula had drunk from it. He thought of her lips on the rim of the cup.

"I'm not trying to bribe you, Rich. Just saying that if you sold your new car I might let you hang with me."

He felt something loosen, the words upchuck. He wasn't pushing them in Jimmy's face now. "Look, you want me to sell my goddamned car. I want you to have that marina because I know how much it means to you to have some chance of a future." The words spilled out; he couldn't stop them. "Shit, I'd do it just for our grandfather's sake, so he'd know in his grave you were worth something."

Jimmy reached out for the silver cup, his big hands gripping it, shaking. "What he might think doesn't mean anything. He wouldn't care if I turned to shit as long as I remembered him. I mean as long I'm doing my drinking like a goddamned Southern gentleman, it doesn't matter what he thinks of me." Now Jimmy stared straight ahead, with the drinking cup in his hands. "And you, Rich, what would he say about you if you shacked up with one of my women. He wouldn't say it, but he would think it, maybe not my way but his. He'd know if you needed a woman just to keep from whacking off every night, then little brother ought to provide you with one. Which I'm willing to do if you do for me."

There was no way to stop what was happening. Through ridges in the venetian blinds Richard saw the Volkswagen pull up. He watched Paula get out of the Volkswagen with a twelve-pack and go to her trailer. Jimmy put out his cigarette. He was quiet; he didn't say anything. Richard kept his eyes on the trailer, on the venetian blinds in the windows. He tried to calculate how long it would take for Paula to pick up the telephone. Or, forget that, just come over. He might have time to go to the car, get the photographs out of the glove compartment.

"There's something I think you should know. About our grandfather." He would come out with it; he had to do that. Jimmy looked at him; he said nothing. "I have some photographs in the car. I want you to take a look at them."

Jimmy was tilting the bottle, measuring out the next drink until the level was flush with the label. "You can save yourself the trip, Rich. All you have to do is tell me about them."

He wasn't vomiting words this time or shoving them at Jimmy's face. His voice remained flat in its distancing. They were naked or stripped down to loincloths. Their hands were behind their heads, heads low, almost touching the ground. They were squatting or kneeling in front of a ditch. He wasn't able to finish, for Jimmy was out of his chair now, without speaking, without even listening. He moved across the room, his head held high, to the footlocker, its padlock unlocked in the hasp. He didn't come back with the .45, or the commendations, or the Purple Heart. He came back with a photograph. He laid the photograph next to the silver cup.

"The troops had target practice," Jimmy said. "You can see for yourself what the targets were." They were squatting, kneeling in front of the ditch. "He told me himself. He had one too many one night. For once he couldn't handle his liquor. We were sitting out by the pool. He kept his foot locker in the pool house. I found this in his footlocker. The funny thing was he didn't keep it locked."

Richard laid down the photograph. "Why did he keep this thing?"

"He told me it kept him in touch with himself, with what he was capable of doing. When I told him it was the war, he said, yes that's what it was, the war. He hadn't ordered it. But he had seen it. He had even taken photographs."

The glare seeped out of the venetian blinds. A corporal was holding an M-1 with a cigarette hanging from his mouth. In the background was the Pacific, the cargo ships, a destroyer, blasted palm trees on the beach, stacks of boxes and crates, a machine gun emplacement, shell cases. The business of war was being carried on, in the background, beyond the ditch. He was being pulled into the photograph, but Jimmy's flat voice was bringing him back.

"Write me a check for five thousand, Rich. I'll get the rest of the money somehow." Jimmy put one hand on his silver cup. "And you might see how much you can sell this thing for. You can sell yours too, while you're doing it."

Now Jimmy's hands were flat on the photograph, but Richard knew he could never cover it up. "I can never accept what he did." He was looking at Jimmy now, knowing Jimmy had to accept what he'd said.

"I can't either. But I can live with it."

He watched Jimmy roll up the photograph, wedging one end in the silver cup. He moved the cup away from his sunglasses.

"It's yours," Jimmy said to him. "You can do what you want to with it."

Jimmy got up and went to the footlocker. He lowered the lid and snapped it shut.

Complicity

MICHAEL HELD UP HIS SHIRTS ON THE clothesline without taking his eyes from the mower. It was something Eileen had seen him do before, when he was mowing and she had a wash on the line. She watched him push and pull the mower with one hand until the strip of grass was cut. He lowered the clothesline with care. He backed up and pointed the mower into a strip of uncut grass, inches away from her sunflowers. Coming toward her, he didn't look up or move his head. He had half the backyard still to mow.

Eileen had chicken wings, in two skillets. There would be white bread and tomatoes, home-fried potatoes and gravy, and a pitcher of Kool-Aid for dinner. Her children were watching television, in the living room, next to the kitchen. Her son Dennis was stretched out on the floor eating peanuts, the floor she had swept and mopped down today. She ordered Dennis to clean up the peanut shells, take his diet drink and go outside. She told him Michael could use some help with the lawn. Her daughter Melissa sat on a footstool painting her toenails, her big knees raised, her long arms out, intent on the movement of the brush. Bits of polish speckled the floor. From the bedroom Eileen heard baby Marcus cry. So Melissa thought she'd do her toenails while her mama looked after Marcus.

She sent Melissa to the bedroom and went back to turn the chicken wings. She heard Dennis slam the front door. Michael was mowing away from the house. She hurried back to the living room, swept the peanut shells into a dustpan, found a wastebasket to empty the dustpan in. She turned off the television set. Melissa came out of the bedroom with Marcus, one hand supporting his head. Eileen wished Melissa would quit staring at her like it was her mother's fault she had to keep Marcus today. Melissa put her hand on the doorknob, opened the creaky front door, stepped into the heat dazzle outside, and without bothering to close the door she was crossing the front yard, taking long steps, swinging her hips, holding Marcus so his head didn't jiggle. Eileen closed the front door with relief.

Between the polka dot floor-length curtains crinkled apart on the brass rod, she scanned the baked clay road beyond the front yard. She heard the window unit in their bedroom, grease popping in the kitchen, beyond that the whine of the mower somewhere out in the backyard. A light blue Ford Escort was moving up the road. She watched it pull into the front yard, unable to think or move for awhile.

Mr. Green was here, Michael's parole officer. She had to ask Mr. Green to please come in. He was entering her living room. She didn't know yet how to act with him, a thin man, tall, with a long face, wearing seersucker pants, a short-sleeved shirt, a narrow tie with a tie clasp. Mr. Green's thin mouth creased into a smile as if he'd seen something odd or comical.

"You know what I'm here for, Eileen."

It was the shooting at Eddie Nunn's, that was what he was here for. He was looking for Michael's brother Clifford. Eileen looked at Mr. Green's seersucker pants, wrinkled, frayed along the cuffs, then on up to where his smile was creased across his face. "Clifford, he ain't been around for awhile."

"You're sure of that, Eileen." It was Eileen, for him, not Mrs. Reece. She resented it, but said nothing. "Maybe Michael knows what you don't know."

"Maybe. I wouldn't know, Mr. Green."

Mr. Green picked up a photograph of Michael and Clifford together, in a fish camp in North Georgia. She knew the photograph well. Clifford was holding a four-pound bass. He was taller than Michael by half a foot. He wore a T-shirt clipped at the shoulders. Clifford had been out of a job even then. Bad news, that was Clifford.

Mr. Green set down the photograph.

"I told you. Clifford isn't here."

"All right, Eileen, he isn't here. But you know what would happen to Michael if he gets mixed up in this? I mean in any way mixed up in it."

She knew. He'd be violating parole. They would have him back in prison again.

"I wouldn't want that to happen, Eileen. I'd hate to see Michael mess up his life."

She was standing too close to Mr. Green, smelling his sweat, his maleness. She felt something assumed between them, as if she'd allowed him to touch her. The man's voice reached out and covered her; she felt she couldn't shake it off. "You can always get in touch with me. You can always call me at home. If you think that would be the thing to do."

Why wasn't Michael with her? She wanted to go to the front door and open it and rush out. Through the gap in the curtains in the front window, she saw the mower spitting out charred grass, sweat beading Michael's forehead, heard it putt putt down after Michael flipped the switch to off, one hand still tight on the handle. He left the mower where it was. He didn't look at the Escort. Mr. Green turned to the front door. She left him waiting for Michael.

She cleared off the kitchen table so they would have a place to sit down. She poured cherry Kool-Aid into jelly glasses. She could hear them in the living room. They were talking about Michael's pickup truck—Michael had it in the repair shop today, at Buddy Plott's, down the road. This morning Michael had driven off in the pickup. He had left it at Buddy Plott's because he didn't want it sitting in front of the house, and walked back on the dirt road. He'd come in the house to tell her to bring some lunch to the trailer. She had told Melissa to do that because she didn't want to be where Clifford was, didn't want to come in contact with him.

She waited until they were in the kitchen before she took the lid off one of the skillets and turned off the gas on the burners.

Mr. Green pushed back his chair, he was giving himself some leg room. "Sheriff Conroy wants to talk to you, concerning your brother's whereabouts. I said I would have a word with you first."

"How would I know where my brother is?"

"I'd like to believe you, Michael. But the thing is, Sheriff Conroy doesn't. He thinks you know where Clifford is." When Mr. Green set his jelly glass down, it left no trace on the oilcloth. "Okay. So you don't know where he is now. So when did you see him last?"

"I saw him Saturday night, at Eddie Nunn's."

"I thought I told you to stay away from Eddie Nunn's."

She knew Michael had an answer for that. "Eddie Nunn needed an extra man on the door. Eddie Nunn, he gave me this blackjack. I don't even take it out of there. He pays me and I leave it there."

"I told you never to carry a weapon."

"I didn't carry it. I left it at Eddie Nunn's."

She knew Michael carried the blackjack home, left Eddie Nunn's with it in the car because things could happen on the way back. But Mr. Green didn't know that. That Michael could kill a man with his bare hands—Mr. Green knew that, but knowing that didn't scare him at all because he believed Michael trusted him.

"Okay, you left the blackjack there. So you saw Clifford at Eddie Nunn's."

"I saw him last Saturday night."

"You need to tell me about it," Mr. Green said. "Sheriff Conroy, he thinks he'll have to take you in. You have to tell me what I need to know."

"We eat first. Then I'll tell you."

Michael asked Eileen to fix Mr. Green a plate. She'd do it; do what Michael asked her to do. She'd do the chicken wings and tomatoes first, three for Michael, two for Mr. Green, let the chicken wings swim in the gravy, how Michael liked them, not Mr. Green. Mr. Green wouldn't take potatoes, but he would have a slice of light bread. Eileen put light bread on his plate, and set the plate down in front of the man.

Mr. Green looked up from his notebook. "Thank you much, Eileen." He turned in his chair, a chicken wing raised in his skinny hand.

"You're some kind of cook, Eileen."

She had to thank him, he expected it and when she did he put the chicken wing down. He dragged light bread around in the gravy.

She went to the living room and looked out the front window. Between the curtains an edge of the trailer was visible, not the door with its concrete block step, a window with a wall unit. The chrome on the Escort's bumper flashed. Clifford barged through the trailer door. He was glaring out at the woods that seemed to be hemming him in. He moved across the yard to the Escort. He put his hand on one of the side mirrors, tried the door to the driver's seat.

Mr. Green wasn't that big a fool. He would lock his car parked at an ex-con's house. But this was her house; she owned it. Michael had come to live with her. But that wouldn't matter to Mr. Green; he would lock his car in front of her house too. Watching Clifford trying the car door, stupidly thinking he'd steal the car, she was glad Mr. Green had locked his car. She saw Melissa close the trailer door as soon as Clifford disappeared in the woods.

When she came back to the kitchen, she saw Mr. Green had pushed his plate away. He had only eaten one chicken wing. Michael had one chicken wing left on his plate. He set his teeth into the greasy flesh, gravy dripping off his lips. "I tried to talk sense into Clifford. I asked him, is this woman worth it."

"And after that?" Mr. Green said. "What happened then? He didn't tell you what he was going to do?"

"Clifford got in his car and drove off somewhere. That was the last I saw of him."

Clifford hadn't told Michael he would drive back to Eddie Nunn's and put a bullet in Eddie's gut. The man with the tie clasp, Mr. Green, wearing that comical smile on his face, she was listening to him run Clifford down.

"You ever ask yourself how stupid he was. That car of his was about to break down."

"I told you Clifford didn't show up here."

Michael was done with his chicken wing. He set down the bone and gristle.

"You know, that stupid brother of yours must have known that steering belt would bust. Maybe that's why he didn't use your pickup truck. Because he wanted a car he knew would break down, one he could actually run off the road. So he could come here, hide out with you."

"My brother, he ain't that big a fool. He would have headed on out of the county."

"But he needed some way to do it." Mr. Green drank a little Kool-Aid. An inch of pink Kool-Aid was left in his glass. "Clifford won't walk to Atlanta. But he could be driving your pickup truck, if you were stupid enough to let him do it."

She saw Michael's thick neck tensing, the eyes gone hard and flat. For a minute she thought he would hit Mr. Green. She felt pulled away from where she should be, putting chicken wings onto her own plate now, dishing out food for her kids and herself while the men said what they had to say. But she had to say something to calm Michael down. She had to think, break the tension. She heard herself talking to Mr. Green, as if he were someone she really liked, a man she were really trying to please.

"Clifford could take someone else's car. Like yours, Mr. Green, your new car. You want to see if it's still in the yard?"

Mr. Green looked at her, smiling. He pushed his chair back and stretched his legs. "You know I keep my car locked, Eileen."

Michael's eyes were set on her now, but that didn't keep her from saying more. "Locks can be picked, Mr. Green. Maybe you ought to check on your car. See if it's where you think it is."

Mr. Green touched his tie clasp. She made herself keep on looking at him. "I know my car is where I think it is. That's why I keep it locked, Eileen." Mr. Green closed up his notebook. He clipped his ballpoint pen in his shirt pocket. "You have anything else to tell me, Michael?"

Michael pushed his plate away. The two plates on the oilcloth, their rims were hardly an inch apart. "Maybe it's time for you to go."

Mr. Green scooted his chair back and got up from the table. He slid the chair back so the back was close to the table. "I hope you're telling me the truth. I'd hate to see you back in prison."

"You won't. That won't happen."

She followed them out of the kitchen. She knew she shouldn't go to the door; her place was to let Michael do it. At the door, Mr. Green turned and said to her.

"Them chicken wings were mighty fine, Eileen." He didn't say Mrs. Reece; he said Eileen.

She was washing up plates and glasses. She left Michael's shirts on the line outside, but she did sweep up the kitchen floor. She sponged grease stains off the oilcloth, and the circles made by Michael's Kool-Aid glass. Her children had left the house. Melissa was in the trailer, with the baby, keeping to herself. Eileen didn't know where Dennis had gone. She emptied the grease in the skillets, poured in a half-inch of cooking oil. She dropped five chicken wings into the popping grease.

Sheriff Conroy had come by late last night. Michael had pulled on the T-shirt, put the pants on he was wearing today. She hadn't gotten out of the bed last night. She'd waited for Michael to come back to her. He had sat down on the edge of the bed, told her what Clifford had done. She remembered him, in the T-shirt, how she'd run her fingernails down his back, along his shoulder blades, trying to keep him there. But he wouldn't get back into bed with her.

The fog had come in, in the morning. She was up; she had put the coffee on, warmed up the biscuits from last night. Two men were standing in the fog. At first she couldn't really make them out, even though she knew who they were. She saw Michael talking to Clifford, saw her husband gripping Clifford's arm, steering him past his pickup truck, through the fog to the door of the trailer. Melissa would always turn on the trailer lights if a fog set in in the morning. Then Melissa came to the door. She opened it and moved away, and Clifford entered the trailer. Then Michael came back, found her waiting for him. She had a plate of biscuits and gravy for him, but he didn't sit down to eat. He asked her to let Clifford stay in the house. When she told him no, he turned away from her. She followed him into the bathroom. She watched him move a razor along his jaw. Not in my house, she had told him.

Michael's pickup truck was in the repair shop—that's what Michael had told Mr. Green. Mr. Green would have already seen it in front of Buddy Plott's Auto Repairs. He would have passed it in his new Escort, coming out here on the county road. She remembered Mr. Green's final words just as Michael came in the front door. "You give Buddy Plott your business, fine; me, I wouldn't give him a nickel." The pickup was half a mile down the road, sitting out in front of Buddy Plott's.

CLIFFORD WAS SITTING in Mr. Green's place, his legs spread out from her kitchen chair. He had a bottle he kept stashed somewhere out in the woods. Clifford filled half of his jelly glass. He squinted at whisky in the glass; then drank it down. He slammed the glass on the table, moved it slightly on the oilcloth while he went on about his girl friend, things Eileen didn't want to hear about. She was turning chicken wings. Michael was drinking more Kool-Aid.

They would take the pickup truck at Buddy Plott's. They would drive the truck to Atlanta. But first she had to feed Clifford. She had to be here and watch him drink.

She turned the gas down on the burners, she found her way to the back door. They were talking about Atlanta, what Clifford would do when he got there. They wouldn't care whether she left or not as long as she fed Clifford chicken wings. For a little while she stood on the back steps, still feeling the kitchen light on her dress. The yard with its smell of newly mown grass seemed to pull her toward her sunflowers. She didn't see them, but she knew where they were, forty feet or so from the clothesline. She moved away from the kitchen light, raising the clothesline as Michael had, feeling a dry shirt against her skin. She was lowering the clothesline behind her, approaching the row of sunflowers.

She used to spend an hour or so out here thinking of Michael. On the days she would get a letter, after reading it in the morning, she would read it again at night. Her children would be watching television, or off somewhere, did it matter? She would wash the dishes, mop the floor. She would sit at the kitchen table, read Michael's letter in the overhead light, tracing her finger along the page, up and down the snarls in his handwriting. She would come out here to think of him. Stand here, hearing the sunflowers sway, in a nice breeze, absorbing night sounds. What would life be like for her if she lost Michael for a second time?

The letters would come from the prison. It was a medium-security prison; he was up for parole in five years. *You never get used to it,* he said, the last time she went to visit him. She was left with her children to raise. She'd done things she was ashamed of, gone out with men she didn't love. Her life was like it was before Michael came to fill it. She blamed Michael because he'd left her alone.

That was before the letters came. First it was just a line or two. He would write her about the prison food, how he wished she were fixing his dinner. Then he wrote her about wanting to be with her at night, and she stopped going out with other men. She wrote him about things at home; her job waiting tables at Mr. Steak. When she saw him they had little to say; they repeated things in the letters. Michael kept on writing her. He started sending her some of the themes he wrote; he was taking a course in composition. He had written a theme on good and bad guards; that was one of his assignments. One thing Eileen remembered—and only yesterday morning she'd thought of it—he had written this in a letter once, what the warden did when a fog set in. *If a fog sets in he locks us down. Because they know we'd be out of here.*

This morning she'd seen the fog in the road, so thick you couldn't see the pines. The light had been on, in the trailer. These two men out there, in the fog they had looked almost alike. She had hardly been able to tell them apart. She put one hand on a sunflower. She couldn't stay out here by herself. And if Michael went back to prison this time, his letters wouldn't matter. She couldn't wait for him to get out again.

She saw Michael blocking the kitchen light, his hands on the frame of the open door, leaning out with his legs spread.

Returning, she moved toward the kitchen light spilling out of the open window. She felt it seeping into her skirt. In the kitchen, the heat closed in on her, the smell of whisky and male sweat. But she had to stay there, in the kitchen. She had to look after her house. In the living room, there were photographs. There was the overstuffed chair, the throw rug, the floor she had mopped that morning. She watched Clifford pour Michael a drink. The whisky was rising in the glass; then the bottle was back on the table.

For the second time she was feeding another man. She set a plate of her food in front of Clifford, chicken wings, home fried potatoes, the last two slices of light bread. Clifford's hands were moving toward his plate. She watched Clifford pick up a chicken wing, holding it out in front of his mouth. They were talking about Clifford's woman, talking as if she were not around, as if it didn't matter to them what she heard. She emptied grease out of the skillets and set them in the kitchen sink. The burners were clotted with grease. She thought of herself in the kitchen, without Michael, doing these things by rote until she got too old to care anymore. And even then, she would do these things, go on cooking and cleaning alone.

Clifford picked up the bottle. His hand was gripping the bottle. "I'm ready to go when you are."

She said nothing, staring at Michael. The words were locked in her throat. She was backing up, into the gas stove. Michael was on his feet now. Michael's hands were on her shoulders. Michael would move his hands this way when he started to make love to her. He was soothing her, caressing her, because his brother was his brother. "I'm going," he said. "I have to go."

"All right," she said, "you go."

Then Michael was turning away from her because she couldn't

look at him anymore. He was looking at Clifford now. He put his hand on Clifford's shoulder. Clifford set his glass on the oilcloth. Would Eileen make Clifford some coffee? She looked at the smears on the oilcloth. Michael gave her a quick look, and she knew he would not change his mind.

She was out of the kitchen now. She was moving across her own front yard. Their voices were not reaching her. She thought of how they would talk about it, later, in the pickup truck, on the highway to Atlanta. What got into Eileen tonight? There were lights on in the trailer. Mr. Green's car wasn't parked out there, but she could always get in touch with him. When she got to the trailer door, she didn't turn to look at her house. Without Michael there, she couldn't live in it.

She thought of her daughter taking long strides, hurrying to the door to let her in. She would clear away Clifford's mess later, his shaving kit, all the empty beer cans. She found an address book next to the telephone. She sat down next to the telephone, Melissa lounging on the sofa, her knees up, doing her fingernails. Whatever you do, you do. When she took the receiver off the cradle, Melissa got up and went to the bathroom. Eileen heard water splash in the sink.

Through the window, from her place by the telephone, she saw the lights were still on in her house. They were still there, in the kitchen.

"This is Eileen Reece," she was saying, to the walls of the trailer, the walls of her house. "I have to talk to you, Mr. Green."

THE FOG CAME back in the morning. Michael had not come back yet. He could be anywhere in the county, or he could be out there in the woods. All she knew was he would come back, that somehow they would start over.

Mr. Green showed up around noon. She watched the blue Escort pull into the yard, Mr. Green getting out of his car. Through the heat dazzle he ambled to the front door.

Mr. Green put his right hand on his tie, up near the collar of his shirt. "I told you I'd fix it with the sheriff. Michael won't be implicated," he said.

She watched Mr. Green loosen his tie. If she let him in, he wouldn't stay long. He'd sit down where he usually sat, in his place at the kitchen table. He would pull back his chair for some leg room. The door was closed in the trailer. She heard someone off in the woods somewhere, making dove calls, crazy sounds. Or was it a dove, in the woods? Baby Marcus was sleeping behind her, in the crib, in front of the television set. The door of the trailer was open. Her daughter, who knew where Melissa was?

Mr. Green put a hand on his tie clasp. "I thought Michael would be back by this time."

"I don't know when he'll be back."

"I can wait. I need to talk to him." Mr. Green's eyes were set in a squint. Sun flecks jittered in his long face.

His skinny arms in the short sleeved shirt, sun flecked, like his face, his fingers spread, their imprint faint on her shoulders. "You did the right thing, Eileen."

She heard a dove call, far off in the woods.

The Skater

One wing and the fuselage, the clotted tubes of airplane glue, the hobby knife with replaceable blades, all these were still on his desk. Frank Martin ran his fingers along a lateral strut in the fuselage. He tried to visualize rooms downstairs, his mother and father's bedroom where they would let him sleep sometimes, the living room with its fireplace and brass candlesticks on the mantel, its whatnots and foot stools and armchairs, Martha's room at the end of the hall, next to the downstairs bathroom, the dining room with its sideboard, the kitchen with its oven and range. The hired girl's room was upstairs, across the hall from his own.

He no longer saw his wife clearly, not as she'd looked when he'd lost her. He remembered her better when she was young.

After moving the trash bag off his bed, he went to the windows, two of them, looked out at the elm tree in the side yard. He thought about going back downstairs. He would leave the upstairs the way it was. His sister was in the kitchen, packing his mother's china, crumpling newspapers to stuff in coffee cups. Martha wanted him to move in with her. She had already laid claim to the furniture, the china, the silver, almost everything. She might as well have him too. It was what his mother would have wanted.

The door was still open across the hall. so he went in, without much hesitation, stretched out on Dorothy's bed. The springs still creaked from his weight on the bed, but the stains had bleached out on the mattress. The closet door was open. Metal hangers were bunched up on the rod. Above the rod on a narrow ledge was where Dorothy had kept her dress shoes, her one pair of heels for her Saturdays off. Her nightgown had hung on the closet door.

He got up off the bed and moved to the bathroom, at one end of the narrow bedroom, with its window overlooking the roof. He opened the medicine cabinet and took out a can of talcum powder. He shook a little powder out into his hand and put the can back where he'd found it, beside the safety razor, yes left behind, that she'd used to shave her legs. Dorothy had to wash up in the sink. Once a week she could use the bathroom downstairs, take a tub bath, shave her legs. But sometimes she shaved her legs here, then put powder on before she went to bed. He had shaken the powder into her hand. He had sprinkled her shoulders and back with it, in her nightgown with the straps down. Sometimes he gave her a back rub. If she asked him to, he would do that.

There wasn't much powder left in the can. What was left was clotted, unusable. He set the can down and went to the toilet. He would always be sure to shut the door. He went to the toilet and raised the seat. Dorothy would be at her vanity, combing out thick red hair. He would hear her radio going, Guy Lombardo, Ray Anthony. The radio on the bed table, Dorothy had taken it with her. She would let him turn the station band dial. He would sit on the bed and turn the dial.

He would ask Dorothy why she was all dolled up and she'd tell him—I'm going dancing. Dolled up, that was his father's phrase. Sometimes it wasn't dancing but a movie palace downtown. For a month or so the name didn't change; then a new man's name would replace the old. Her men never took her back to her room. She met them outside on the front porch—that's where they must have dropped her off. Sometimes she came back early; other nights she didn't come back until dawn. On those nights she'd take her shoes off before she climbed the stairs to go to her room. He'd hear the water run, the toilet flush.

He was washing his hands in the sink. There wasn't a towel, so he dried his hands on his sweater. He closed the medicine cabinet and looked at his face in the mirror. His mustache needed trimming. He remembered that Martha had told him to make sure that the upstairs windows were locked. He went to the bathroom window, pushed the stiff lock into place, looked out at a patchwork of roofs and trees. He looked at his watch. It was four o'clock. He remembered climbing out on the roof. He would climb out of Dorothy's bathroom, crawl down the shingled roof to the heaven tree by the back porch. Next step, shinny down the trunk of the tree. He might do what he had done as a boy. Suppose he showed up in the kitchen while Dorothy was cooking dinner. He would come in through the back door. He would pull at the strings of her apron, her apron sliding away from her hips. He would embrace her, pull her to him. But first he must see to the windows. Her bedroom window wasn't locked. He quickly pushed the lock into place.

Leaving, crossing the upstairs hall, he felt less hemmed in by his task. Martha was crumpling newspapers below, carefully packing each box and crate. In his room he felt more like himself. He had already filled a trash bag with things his mother would have wanted thrown away. He checked the windows to make sure they were locked. Cold air came through the sashes. He was in no hurry to get started again. He looked down at the side yard, and across the yard at the house next door. How could anyone have ever skated on it?

There was an ice storm that year. The schools closed, things came to a stop. His father couldn't get to his office downtown. His father had put on a suit and tie, for he still thought of catching the bus downtown. After lunch his father decided to skate. He went into the bedroom for the skates, which he must have kept in his closet. Martha was playing with paper dolls. His father came out of the bedroom, wearing corduroys and a sweater. He held the skates looped by the laces. Dorothy helped him put on the skates. Frank had to go to his room to watch. His mother and Martha were downstairs, at the living room bay window. His father was making figure eights on the hissing, clashing skates. Dorothy was standing behind him. At the window, with Dorothy behind him now, he thought of his father on clashing skates. Dorothy's turn now to sneak up on him, put her hands so light on his shoulders. Head up, hands locked behind his waist, knees bent, leaning forward, the skater achieved tremendous speed. The figure eights were getting bigger. How long could this man keep doing this, skate around knotted, cold packed roots? He left the window, went to the closet in which his mother had stored her hats. She had taken over his closet. Frank pulled out and opened hatboxes, emptied them out on the bedroom floor. He picked up a soft felt picture hat with a hat band and a feather. He ran his fingers along the hat band, felt the crisp edge of the feather. There were pillbox hats and picture hats, ribboned, straw-plaited sunbonnets, velours and velveteen cloche hats, fuzzy berets, hats with feathers. He put his cigarette in an ashtray that he had brought up here and put on his desk, without disturbing the model airplane he would leave on his desk, unfinished, without touching the blade of the hobby knife. He picked up his chair, and took it back to the closet. It was necessary to clear out the shelf, but the chair, he knew was rickety. Would it hold his weight? It would have once. He turned on the chain to the overhead light. Coats on hangers, shoeboxes stood out in the glare. Placing one foot on the seat of the chair, he gripped the edge of the shelf, ignoring the smell of mothballs, the glare of the overhead light.

What he pulled out first was the goldfish bowl. Then the Big Little Books, in a shoebox. Crossing the hall, he heard a radio, nothing else, nothing from Martha. Perhaps Martha had taken more trash out. Or had she gone to the downstairs bathroom? He heard a toilet flush, yes that was it. But there was no need for secrecy. Why did it matter where Martha was? He didn't have to close Dorothy's door to put the goldfish bowl on her dresser.

He thought of filling the bowl with water. At one time it had a grotto, a place in the water for a goldfish to go. Watching the goldfish's movements had been a young boy's nightly pastime. Usually Dorothy wore her nightgown. But sometimes it hung in her closet. If the nightgown had hung in her closet, then what had Dorothy been wearing? Perhaps sometimes she wore the nightgown; sometimes she wore a sweater and skirt. Propped up on her thick pillows, an open magazine draped over her knees—*Photoplay*, *Modern Screen*, he remembered, *True Romances*, bedtime reading—she would extend one hand to the radio. He would watch Dorothy turn the station band, her eyes fixed on her magazine. Or sometimes she'd ask Frankie to do it. Easy listening, Guy Lombardo. Sometimes he brought in a chair from his room, but usually she made room for him. Sitting close to her on the edge of her bed, he breathed in her scents, her odors, without yet knowing what they could do—Ray Anthony, Guy Lombardo—no, what Dorothy had already done to him. She would look up from *True Romances* and sing along with the radio.

Then the nights came when he was there by himself. He was turning the bright gold station band. He sat by himself on the mattress, watching the goldfish in the bowl. It would hover awhile, then dart off. It would hide out in the grotto. He would look at the empty closet. Her dresses, all but one of them, had hung evenly spaced on the hangers. The hangers were bunched up after she left.

He opened the medicine cabinet. The safety razor was where he'd left it beside the can of talcum powder. Dorothy had used it to shave her legs. He took out the double-edged blade, tested one edge with one finger. He dropped the blade into the toilet bowl. The hobby knife still had a fairly sharp edge. Or he could put in another blade. He was gripping the bathroom sink. He remembered he'd left the cigarette in an ashtray on his desk. Or had he left it burning on his desk, with the ash hanging over the edge?

Returning, crossing the hall again to his room, he put the cigarette out in the ashtray. If the cigarette had rolled off the desk, it could have started a fire in the wastepaper basket. But he had left it in the ashtray. What if there had been a fire in his room? He would have had time to warn Martha. He would have had time to get down the stairs and call the fire department to put out the fire. Or he could have put out the fire himself. Looking out at the elm tree, where his father had skated when he was twelve, Frank remembered his father skating. But the memory was not as clear now.

The chair was back where he had left it, next to one wall, in the closet. Turning the chair to wall off the coats, the textures of camel hair and fur that might persuade him to stop, he again got up on the seat. The shoebox was where he had left it. He couldn't remember putting it there. His mother must have done that. Climbing down with the shoebox, he decided to leave the chair where it was. The coats he would lay out on the bed, along with his mother's hats. The hobby knife could go in the shoebox. He would carry the shoebox to Dorothy's room. Martha would miss him soon. She would wonder what he was doing up here.

He sat down again on Dorothy's bed. The pencil he used had a soft black point. Dorothy, of course, hadn't known about this, for she hadn't been here to see it. There were things he had written and drawn on the pages of his Big Little Books. The goldfish bowl had been where it was, still sitting on the dresser. A slight bulge in the shoebox should have warned him he'd have to take out the pipe. The pipe stem, with its teeth marks, stood out from the can of tobacco. There was a little tobacco left in the can. He had stolen one of his father's pipes. He used to come in here to smoke it, not at night with his father below but late on a winter afternoon, after school, around four-thirty, about the time it was just getting dark. The tobacco he'd bought at a drugstore. He sucked in on the pipe stem. The pipe stem was clogged so he put the pipe down. He shook dry flakes of tobacco out evenly on the mattress. The tobacco can went into the shoebox too. He laid the hobby knife close, on the mattress. Then he stretched out on the mattress.

The closet door was still open. That was where Dorothy's nightgown had hung. The scuffed toes of his cordovan shoes slowly separated as he spread his legs. He would lie here awhile on Dorothy's bed. What did he have to look forward to? He could visualize the mellow station band. Ray Anthony, Guy Lombardo, Dorothy liked her music mellow. She was with him while his eyes were closed, a shimmer of pink in the closet door. She was putting iodine on a cut. This will sting a little. He shut his eyes.

He heard the wind rattling the windows, the scraping of a branch on glass. The hobby knife was still close to his hand. His father was making figure eights. Frank Martin, Senior was skating while Dorothy was playing the radio, while Dorothy was lying alone in a room, in her nightgown, taken from both of them now. Frank listened to the soft clash of skates.

There was still some light when he opened his eyes. The closet was open but empty. The shoebox with his Big Little Books lay beside him on the mattress. The shoebox would go to the garbage can. The goldfish bowl he would leave where it was. He got up and went to the bathroom. He opened the medicine cabinet. The can of talcum powder was where he'd left it. He unlocked the window with his thumb. With an effort he raised the sash half a foot. He felt the strain on his forearms. Then the sash slipped free and the window was up. The shoebox he held against his chest. He could remember what the next step had been, but he couldn't be sure he could carry it out. He had to let himself down slowly, with his right hand gripping the sill. He felt the toes of his cordovans touch the roof.

He bent his knees with his hand on the sill, then straightened up to try to lower the sash. But he'd raised it too high to pull it down now. Turning, he felt the cold in his face. He moved down the slope of the upper roof. He knew the elm tree was on his left. To the right, he knew, was the heaven tree. He kept himself braced against the cold. He moved on toward the edge of the roof. It was still a long drop to the driveway. He took his father's pipe out before he dropped the box, and laid it out on the roof. He held out the shoebox and dropped it. The lid bounced off the shoebox. He put his hands on the cold, slick bark.

Martha was still packing china, in the restoring warmth of the kitchen. He recognized his mother's engagement ring, on a newspaper, next to a sugar bowl. His sister picked up the diamond ring. He watched her move it along her ring finger. She must have been in his mother's bedroom. Martha got up out of the kitchen chair. She put her hands on her hips and shuffled her feet. He was watching his sister dancing She must have wanted someone to dance with her then. But his father had skated in the yard instead of dancing with Martha in the house.

Martha looked at him; she stopped dancing. She didn't take off their mother's ring. Before telling her he wouldn't move in with her, he would ask her to go back upstairs with him. Martha would know what to do with his mother's hats, with whatever was still up there.

Island Grove

JULIE HAD ALREADY SEEN THE TAPE, at her gynecologist's ten days ago. This was a special showing for her father. John Robert watched what the Ultrasound shaped, belly dissolving, head ballooned.

He had tried not to think of Julie's mother, but seeing Julie had brought Mary Jean back to him. Mary Jean had died a year ago. It had started, her downhill slide, with hepatitis, followed by a kidney infection that had triggered a fungus in her lungs. For his daughter's sake he felt he should have gone to Mary Jean's funeral. Julie had been there, he hadn't.

It's been years since you were married to her. On another sofa in Gulf Breeze, not Julie's, not here in Gainesville, his wife Barbara had caressed the back of his neck while he stared out through the picture window at the goldfish pond in back, at Barbara's flowering hibiscus plant. Two days before Mary Jean's funeral, Barbara had turned off the answering machine, and the goldfish had cruised through the murky pond, the hibiscus soaking up sunlight. The telephone kept on ringing. He waited three more days before he telephoned Julie. *I tried to call you, Daddy. Where were you?* He had worked out his story, his excuse. *Barbara and I were at Fort Walton Beach. We felt we needed to get away.*

But you could have gone to the beach in Pensacola. You could have gone after the funeral.

Now that Julie was pregnant and wanting to see him again, Barbara had wanted him to see her. He could drive over from Tallahassee, spend Sunday afternoon and Monday here, make the long drive back to Gulf Breeze on Tuesday. He had to go to Tallahassee anyway; it was expected of him at Gulf Breeze High, you showed up with your colleagues no matter how many years of teaching you had put in.

The fetal head was lolling to the left, the arms were away from the feet. He asked Julie what the sex was. Julie said they didn't know yet. She wore a tartan plaid jumper, a short sleeved, lace-trimmed white blouse, her hair in a braid with a rubber band, perhaps to offset, downplay the pregnancy. She was supporting her head with her upper right arm on the Persian rug in the great room, her long, thin pelican legs tucked under her hips. "I could have found out, but I didn't ask. We want that to come as a surprise." She kept her eyes on the shifting shapes on the screen.

"We didn't ask, Julie, remember?" Sitting next to him on the sofa, Julie's husband raised his voice a notch, hoisting an ankle until it came to rest on his kneecap. Harry ran ten miles during his lunch break, on the days he didn't have surgery. It showed in his chest and biceps, in the muscles of his neck, the skin stretched tight from the cheekbones.

"We decided we didn't really want to know in advance."

Julie sat up, raising her knees. "Let's concentrate on the tape," she said. "Look, there's the heartbeat."

What he saw on the screen was still going on—yes a rapid methodical twitch—right in front of him, in his daughter's womb, without numbers, without calibrated vertical lines. The number two showed up on the screen and he asked about the size of the head.

"About five centimeters from ear to ear," Harry said. "Her gynecologist says that's normal."

The heartbeat, size of a buttonhole, blurred into convulsive contours of gray. Julie had the remote, sat up and turned off the tape. Nothing for them to see now.

Harry helped Julie up off the carpet. She went to the windows and opened the drapes. Barbara would be feeding the birds about now. John Robert thought of Barbara filling the bird feeder, shooing off cowbirds and grackles so the smaller birds could get to the seed. She'd have to water her plants on the deck—hibiscus, ferns, the spiky cactus. He remembered watering the plants himself, the wet dirt, shiny leaves. It was something they did together, dangling the sluggish garden hose—it had no nozzle—over the plastic pots. Mary Jean would have stuck the hose in a pot, left it overflowing water.

Julie asked him if she could get him a beer. Or would he rather have a cup of coffee? He said he'd have the coffee. Harry asked her to bring him a Heineken. He watched Julie go to the kitchen, her thin legs moving rapidly. Harry extracted the tape from the VCR in its console deck, a big piece of furniture, with a thirty-one-inch screen television. There was a smaller television set in the kitchen, and one more in the master bedroom. Harry put the tape in its box, fit the box in with other tapes, including sports tapes, all of them labeled. Harry asked him about the big powwow in Tallahassee, did he go to this thing every year? No, not that often anymore, but this year he thought he would do it, go one last time before he retired. The meetings weren't much fun anymore, but he didn't tell Harry why. Too many young people making speeches about teaching methods he would never use. And he hadn't been getting awards lately; the recognition went to those coming up. He'd been teaching for twenty-eight years. In two more years he planned to retire. No more lesson plans, grading papers.

Julie came back with the coffee, a Heineken in a frosted glass. She served her father first, then her husband. It had been like that when she was little; she served him first, then Mary Jean, beside the pool at the apartment complex. Mary Jean had a job in St. Petersburg, keeping the books at the Ford agency. He would sit by the pool with Mary Jean before he took Julie off for the day—Busch Gardens, the Ringling Museum. He had let his daughter bring them their drinks. Now he couldn't believe he had done that. Delight in her eyes once because Daddy was here. He kept his hands on the cup and saucer, watching Julie move to Harry. Harry picked up a bottle and glass from the tray. Julie sat down beside him. She asked him again if he wanted a beer. Or would he rather have a glass of white wine.

"I'll have my glass of wine for dinner."

Julie leaned over and kissed him. A little lipstick stayed on his lower lip. "Daddy, I think you're doing great. Just great. I'm really proud of you."

They didn't go out for dinner. Harry did tuna steaks on the gas grill on the terrace. Harry was looking out through the smoke at his private lake, shared with other members of their gated community only. Julie was slicing a loaf of French bread, not quite slicing through it. She patted butter between the slices. John Robert looked at his glass of red wine. It was still untouched. Mary Jean's spinach casserole, Mary Jean's tomatoes and cucumbers saturated in oil and vinegar. He remembered how Mary Jean made them—long on sugar but not much salt. Julie had them in the refrigerator. She set them out in a cut-glass salad bowl. The salad bowl was once Mary Jean's, was in Mary Jean's mother's family.

"We had tomatoes and cucumbers with fish sticks. Or with hot dogs and tater tots. But never with spinach casserole."

"Your mother wasn't much of a cook. You don't have to remind me of that."

"You did like her spinach casserole. I thought I'd throw in tomatoes and cucumbers." Julie sipped on her chardonnay. She was allowing herself half a glass. Mary Jean's lipstick would smear her highball glass and she usually smoked while she cooked.

"I remember when Mama was pregnant. She even cut down on her drinking, but not enough to do any good."

"I was drinking too much myself in those days. And I kept on doing it for too long, as long as we were married. But that's been over for years."

"I want you to have all you want. I mean have what you think you can have. I know the drinking's been over for you. You're doing fine. I know that." Julie looked at the level of wine in her glass. She sipped a little more wine, set down the glass. "We had tomatoes and cucumbers that Sunday before Mama's miscarriage. The thing was I was still stupid enough to think it was something Mama ate. I thought the fried chicken must have been spoiled. The tomatoes tasted rotten to me. I tried some after I came home from school and Mama told us what happened. I mean her version of what happened. I ate two slices out of the bowl, and then I ate two cucumbers." Julie smiled. "The cucumbers tasted fine. But they were oily. And very sweet."

Instead of the stork a cowbird had come and flown off with Mary Jean's baby girl. That was Mary Jean's story. She had said she was going to have a girl. The kitchen had been a mess, three days of dirty dishes. Julie had not been there. She was in school when it happened, had not known what it was like. He had dipped his hand in water and blood, scooped up this dripping dead thing. He'd taken Mary Jean to the hospital, done what was necessary. Wet tissue slopping in his hand.

"We took turns washing dishes. Then we swept every room and cleaned the bathroom. Mama stayed in bed that night." Julie spooned up a cucumber. "Maybe these are too sweet," she said.

He told her he liked his cucumbers sweet. They couldn't be too sweet for him.

"If they are, I know they won't hurt me. I know now what will hurt and what won't." Julie looked out at her husband turning the steaks on the patio. She watched Harry close the gas grill. The timer buzzed in the oven. "I need to take out the casserole. We'll talk tomorrow, if you want to."

He said he did, trying to mean it.

She must have come in while he was asleep. A mug of hot coffee awaited him on the dresser. He took a sip, went to the bathroom. He had unpacked his shaving kit last night, plugged in his electric razor. He squeezed toothpaste carefully out of the tube, the way Barbara would urge him to do, from the bottom, an eighth of an inch at a time. He made sure he washed out the sink before he put the razor back in his shaving kit. He didn't make the bed or close his suitcase. He'd hung his convention suit in the closet last night. There was a wine stain on the lapel, red wine, two glasses at dinner on Saturday night.

He took his coffee mug out on the terrace. The canvas top was buttoned down on the hot tub. The leaves in the pin oaks had turned, but hardly any of them had fallen yet. Today his daughter was wearing a powder-blue jumper, and brand new Nike running shoes. Mary Jean would have worn khaki pants, a sweatshirt and floppy straw hat. She'd worn flip-flops around the house. She wore brogans if she went out in the groves or went fishing, to guard against snakes. You would not have known she was beautiful if you'd seen her traipsing out for the mail. A stranger passing on the road would have thought she was plain, from the way she was dressed.

Julie looked at their private lake, shaded homes, boat docks, everything right and tidy. She sipped on her coffee and laid it aside. "I thought we might drive to Island Grove. The house we lived in, it's still there. It looks almost like it used to."

"You've seen it?"

"I hadn't for years," she said. "Not long after I knew I was pregnant, I was listening to the radio. There's this program that comes on at nine. You know, lost dogs and cats, and also items for sale. I was cleaning up the breakfast dishes," Julie put a bright voice on, "a little shaky still from morning sickness and I heard this man on the radio, I heard him say a lady from Island Grove had lost a female beagle pup. Island Grove, that's where we used to live, that's what came to me then. And then I wondered whether the house was still there."

"And it was there. You went out to see for yourself."

"Yes, I did. I mean I didn't go in. But I thought of knocking on the door. I thought if someone did live there and answered the door, I'd say my family used to live here once. But I didn't do that. I couldn't be sure who would answer the door. But with you along, I wouldn't worry about it." Her lips went tight, her voice was defensive now. "We can always do something else. There's a bookstore downtown we can go to. We can take a tour of the campus. Or go to where Harry and I used to live, on Sixth Avenue. After that I'll take you out to lunch."

No, he would take her out to lunch, in Island Grove. And after that they would go look at the house.

They stopped off at the apartment house on Sixth Avenue. The two-room apartment was occupied by other students now. New generation, old house, he thought. She and Harry had lived there while Harry was in medical school. He'd seen the live oak in the backyard, climbed the steps, had dinner there. That was while Mary Jean was still alive, in St. Petersburg, still in her condo, only nobody brought them drinks by the pool. The bedroom had casement windows then. It was hot, but he hadn't minded the heat. He remembered the mosquito truck chugging by while Harry was grilling the hamburgers.

Julie took a photograph of him with a compact point-and shoot-camera. It had a telephoto lens, macro-micro capability. She slid the camera into its leather case, both straps looped around her neck. He hadn't offered to take her picture, even though he knew she wanted him to, and again he was thinking of Mary Jean, popping in on him naked in the shower, her Kodak, flashbulb attached, in his face.

They drove south through Micanopy, took the county road to Island Grove. In half an hour they were there. Julie stopped to take a photograph of him in front of the city limits sign. He took another of Julie on the bridge, the leather case for the camera tipped on the mound of her belly. He looked down the creek, toward Lake Lochloosa, the boat dock, a hundred yards from the bridge. It was hard to believe they had fished in that lake. He kept his back turned to their house, on the other side of the bridge to the west.

They had lived here for nearly ten years. He had a job teaching history and government at the high school in Island Grove. He'd made enough for them to live on. Sometimes they could afford to rent a boat. He could remember seeing the sleeping porch, a long way down the creek, on past the bridge and the restaurant, the school building where he'd taught. They would be coming in off the lake. He'd move the boat into the mouth of the creek, the outboard puttering at his back, Mary Jean with her hands on the thwarts, facing him, fish twitching in the net. She wore khakis, the straw hat shading her face, nondescript, nothing special, flecks of red hair around the brim of her hat. As the boat moved slowly up the creek, he watched the sleeping porch jutting out from the house. There was a mattress on the floor. The windows would get larger. On rainy nights Mary Jean would open them, let moths and mosquitoes in with the rain.

They had lunch in an air-conditioned cafe. The restaurant with the Sunday buffet, with its ceiling fans and clean tablecloths—there was a Chevron station where it used to be. He remembered the name, "The 'Loosa Cafe." The sign was hand-painted, not neon.

They had cheeseburgers and iced tea. Julie talked about the Sunday buffet. She ran down the list, corn bread, greens, black eyed peas, mashed potatoes and gravy, corn on the cob, platters of Southern-fried chicken. It wasn't long before she brought up Mary Jean. "We tried to eat there one Sunday. That one time we came back from fishing. Mama really looked like hell. But she refused to go home and change clothes. She wanted us to make an issue of it."

He remembered the men in their starched white shirts, their wives wearing flowered print dresses. A few of the men glanced at Mary Jean, but the women refused to look at her.

"They would have served us, you know that Julie. But we thought it would be best to go."

"She shouldn't have gone in there looking like that. She should have worn something decent."

"Well, she didn't. We didn't fit in." He remembered hearing the electric fans hum; it didn't matter what these crackers were saying, those stony-faced decent country women looking everywhere but at Mary Jean.

"I know. I know we didn't. Sometimes I wish we had. I think about what might have been if we had. But I guess there's no use talking about it. If we'd stayed out here for good, I'd have grown up stupid and country. But Mama, she might have been okay. Out here she could live with herself. She could fish. She could do whatever she liked without anyone knowing what she did."

"People know things in the country," he said. "Your neighbors, even those miles away, they know a lot more than you think. It couldn't have worked out, Julie."

Julie looked at him dubiously. "You don't mean that. If you did, you wouldn't have come with me."

"I came with you because you wanted me to."

"You never wanted to come here yourself? Please, tell me. I want to know."

"All right. There were times when I did want to come here. But since Barbara was with me, I didn't do it."

"You don't have to say anymore. I can understand why you didn't come here."

There were times, on their way to see Julie, that he'd wanted to turn off the freeway, show Barbara where he'd lived once, the house still there with its rambling screened-in porch, the tangelo trees out behind the barn, the creek in front, the rutted road. He could have shown her the school at Island Grove. Barbara wouldn't have had to know how he'd felt in the classroom reliving the nights with Mary Jean. He couldn't pull his eyes away from the sun-creased creek, scummed with shadow under the bridge. Sometimes he'd go home on his lunch break and surprise Mary Jean in the kitchen. He would slowly lift up her corduroy skirt. He couldn't wait to get home and have a drink on the porch. Or they'd be taking back roads to the county line to pick up a week's supply of liquor, and Mary Jean, her skirt hiked up on her thighs, would tongue his right ear and he'd pull over.

He had to take his eyes off the creek. "We should have done this a long time ago. I'm sorry we waited so long."

"It's all right, Daddy. We're here now." He watched Julie collecting napkins, a few fries, bits of hamburger bun, arranging them neatly on her plate. "I'll bet you never knew about this thing we did once. Mama told me she wouldn't tell you." Julie folded her hands on her belly, the powder-blue cloth of her jumper, without putting her hands in the pockets. "I must have been in the third grade. In that crappy country school you taught at. I'd get home before you did, and Mama and I had this thing we did. We cut animals out of cookie dough. Horses and cows and a rabbit, Mama even tried to cut out a raccoon, but she said it looked more like a skunk to her. We lined up all our animals on a cookie sheet and put them in the oven to bake. The next day we painted them. We used my watercolors and Mama's nail polish." Julie lifted an eyebrow. "That was something you didn't know about. We had chickens and pigs, a cat and a dog. Enough for a farm, Mama said. She was drinking, I knew that even then, but what she did then was really wonderful."

"So tell me, what did you do next?"

"What we did was start our own little farm, out back of the house in the tangerine grove. We put all our animals out there, one afternoon you were late getting home. Mama said the foxes would get them someday. Or the 'gators. But they would be all right for awhile. Mama said it was like an Easter egg hunt you can do any day of the year."

"An Easter egg hunt? Here in Island Grove?"

"All right, so it was a cookie hunt. And yes, here in Island Grove."

She set down his glass of iced tea, sliding it on the tablecloth. He was able to signal the waitress. The waitress brought the check and he paid with cash. Julie offered to pay, but he insisted. He wouldn't let Julie get the tip.

The house was beside the bend in the creek, off by itself past the edge of town. There was a number to call on the For Sale sign, but no real estate agency. Julie locked both doors of the van, and made sure the sliding door was locked. She had the camera looped around her neck.

He made out newspapers on the front steps, yellowed, rain-soaked, then dried by the sun. How long had the place been up for sale? The grass hadn't been cut for awhile but it hadn't had time to grow that much. He'd kept it mowed with a power mower, taking turns with Mary Jean. She would mow awhile while he rested or raked. She wore khakis and brogans against the snakes; he wore the cleated boots he went fishing in. It took them all day to do it, backing and angling around the trees, squashing tangelos, pulpy fruit split by the rotary blades. He watched Julie move on ahead of him, up the driveway across the flagstone walk, the camera held out in one hand from the strap, away from her belly. He stopped to look into the mailbox, a magazine sweepstakes, junk mail. Whoever had lived here would never get it. Julie tried the screen door, pulled it open. She waited for him on the front steps. He had chosen his words when he joined her there.

"I don't think we should go inside," he said. "It isn't legal. And I don't think it's right."

"You don't want to?"

"I don't think I want to."

"You're afraid of what it might do to you."

He nudged aside one of the newspapers. "This house, it isn't ours anymore."

"Something of it still is."

He followed her into the screen porch, but that was as far as he would go. There was a porch chair, cobwebbed, corroded, not fit for either of them to sit on. They stood there, looking out at the road, the mailbox, beyond it a stand of pines, a brick bungalow with a satellite dish. Anyone who might see them might think he was with his pregnant wife. Would a man bring his pregnant daughter here? A buyer might bring his daughter. A pickup truck with two men in the cab came by, radio blaring. Julie turned away from the screen door.

"I've come here more than once," she said. "It isn't occupied. And we can get in."

The owner hadn't put in new locks; out here what would be the need? Julie asked him to use her skeleton key, much like the key he'd used before, the same pressure on cold metal. Julie closed the door behind them.

The living room was musty from having been closed in. The place where the carpet had been was directly in front of the fireplace. A chunk of charred wood tipped off a firedog. Newspapers and flattened cartons were packed in the back of the fireplace. Something he hadn't done when they left, dumped trash in the fireplace. But this was for starting someone else's fire. He tested the flue; it was closed. He breathed in the smell of ashes. He watched Julie move toward the dining room. She reached up and touched a chandelier, the teardrops

Mary Jean used to touch in the dining room, before dinner.

"We always had dinner on time," Julie said. "Or almost. Not too long after the six o'clock news." Which the three of them watched in the living room, the television set in one corner.

Julie came back from the kitchen. "I don't want to see anymore," he said. "You can do what you like."

"I've already been upstairs. This time I want you with me. You used to put me to bed. Read me stories. You should be there too."

She was waiting at the foot of the stairs, waiting for him to go ahead of her. Her room was at one end of the upstairs hall, past the bathroom, the sleeping porch. He remembered the medicine cabinet's cracked mirror, where the mattress was on the sleeping porch. And Julie's room, there used to be dolls on the mantel, he couldn't remember how many. Julie's bed was by the window. He used to sit in a chair by her bed and read bedtime stories to her. He'd have a drink nearby, on the mantel. He would read on after she closed her eyes. The space heater that had been there then looked like it still might work. He tried the valve, but failed to move it. One corner of her room was covered with ants, streaming in and out from a heap of chicken bones. Behind the space heater, hunks of melon rind.

Julie ran a finger along the mantel, where she used to have her dolls lined up. She made a crooked streak in the dust. "There's something I think you should know. You told me I didn't need all these dolls. Mama stood up for me. Remember? She said I could keep my dolls."

He could see them clearly now, Raggedy Anne and Barbie, the kewpies, the Southern belles, legs splayed or hanging over the edge of the mantel. *I never had any dolls to speak of. My little Julie can have all the dolls she wants, she can have anything she damn well wants to have and you're not going to stop her.* He pushed a wine bottle with his shoe. It rolled a little, then came to a stop.

It came out—"Why did you bring me here? What is it you want from me, Julie?"

"Don't you know? Can't you see, Daddy? I want you to know how I felt in this room. I heard awful things go on between you. And the drinking, that went on all the time." Julie drew something crooked in the dust on the mantel. "But I had the dolls Mama gave me. I thought they would make everything right."

She blew dust off her fingers. "Did you know sometimes while you were at school, Mama and I would take a nap together? She'd come in here where my bed was and say, Julie we need a little rest. I'd be lying awake while Mama slept and look at my dolls on the mantel. I'd smell the whisky on Mama's breath but that didn't stop me from loving her." She put her fingers around the camera case and lifted the strap up over her head. She set the camera case on the mantel, between Barbie and Raggedy Anne. "And I loved her when she was dying. She said she would get all her ducks in a row so I wouldn't feel bad about losing her. Did you know that, Daddy? Her ducks."

"No I didn't know. I wasn't with her."

"That's right. You were with Barbara. You weren't with us while she was dying and you didn't go to the funeral."

Julie came over to where he was waiting for her. "You weren't there when I telephoned you." The telephone had gone on ringing, goldfish cruising in the seething pond, ants crawling over the chicken bones, Julie too close, too close. She put her hands on his shoulders. "So now I want you to know what it was like for me, knowing what I know now." She pushed his hands, hard, against her belly. He felt the elastic band of her panties through the tight cloth of her jumper. Someone unknown was moving inside her.

"I found out for myself ten days ago. I'm going to have a daughter. Harry doesn't know because I lied to him, I covered it up, because he could never know what it was like for me to be your daughter. And Mama's, how could he know that?"

Her hands were loosening on his wrists. He looked out through the dirt-streaked window at the tangelo grove, spots of fallen fruit, standing close to her but not touching her now, not knowing just when she had released his hands, moved away, gone back to herself. Then she was going back to where her dolls were once. She picked the camera case up off the mantel and slung it around her neck, moving rapidly past him through the bedroom door.

She stopped and turned around, facing him. She got the camera out of the case, took photographs, that way they couldn't deny what had taken place in this room. When she finished, she put the camera back in the case. She pulled her hair back and smoothed out her jumper. "What I said to you, that's between us."

"Yes, between us," he said, "you and me."

She went to him, kissed him on the cheek; then she was walking away from him toward the stairs. They went down the stairs and through the living room, out the front door on to the front porch. A pickup truck heading for Island Grove slowed down before it passed the house. A young woman was driving the pickup truck, a woman like Mary Jean had been once when, together, they had been good.

Vigil

"You do it the way you put a dress on. You fit the cover over the seat and slide it on down like so. That's called dressing the seat." Jo Ann Hathaway lifted her arms and pulled an invisible dress off. "Undressing the seat, you slide the cover up, like you were taking a tight dress off."

Shirley Carmichael looked over Jo Ann's life insurance application. She slipped the application into her briefcase along with Jo Ann's check for the first month's premium. She should be on her way, but Jo Ann wasn't about to stop yakking at her. After Les died, Jo Ann had gotten this part-time job sewing up the covers of school bus seats. Jo Ann had to tell Shirley about dressing and undressing the seats, how she supplemented what she made at Hair Expressions. "Patching them up, that isn't so bad, it's undressing them that gets me down." Jo Ann was back in her kitchen chair, her glass of iced tea dipping down a little. "You have forty or fifty seats to undress, all you want to do is get out of the bus. These kids have no respect for public property. And it's the kids who are well-off that are the worst offenders."

Outside the open kitchen window, Traci, Jo Ann's six-year-old, swinging upside down on a trapeze bar, grabbed the chain on the swaying swing, jiggling Kelli, Jo Ann's four-year-old. Jo Ann called out for Traci to stop what she was doing right now. Traci swung herself right-side-up on the trapeze. Kelli dug her heels into a corduroy patch of exposed clay in the backyard's unmown crabgrass, like Shailah would do when she was that age. Shayne, Shirley's ex-husband, had repainted their swing set a soothing pink. Their backyard, Shayne had kept it mowed.

She'd go straight home, not to the office. She'd mail the app off tomorrow morning. Driving back, Shirley looked forward to showing Wiley the check. "You got it, then show it to me, Shirl?" "I got it right here for you, hon'" she'd say, "but first I'm going to give you a big kiss." She had brought home a check last night, but Shayne had called before she could give Wiley his kiss. Shayne had asked her to keep Shailah for two weeks. She'd said no, then said she would think about it. She'd told Wiley that too, she would think about it.

Having Shailah in the house for the first two weeks in November, two weeks, she could manage that without Wiley. Wiley used to take off when Shailah came. He'd say she's your daughter, not mine, and head south for the Gulf Coast.

The road ahead dipped as she passed the millrace frothing on her right, pond pooling out on her left, how nice it would be to get your feet wet, take your clothes off, merge with the water. Nice, but it would never happen.

When she got to the house she lit a cigarette. It was a frame house sitting back from the road, paint scaling off the window frames, with a front porch Wiley never sat out on, a big backyard that ran back to the creek.

She found Wiley cane-pole fishing down by the creek, on the near bank, a purple worm lure in his bait can. His head was all that was big about him now. The rest of him was all skin and bone. "I got a bite Shirl." Wiley yanked the line out, a worm lure jittering past her nose, plopped the worm lure back in the creek. "So how'd your day go?"

"It went as well as can be expected." Wiley should be talking to her, not the creek. "Actually, I had a pretty good day. I took my medication. I watched television. I trimmed my toenails. I turned the sprinkler on as you might have noticed, and as you see now, I did some fishing."

It came to her, what he'd forgotten to ask. "You forgot to ask me if I got the check."

He didn't ask her to show him the check. She didn't say first she would give him a kiss. He shifted the pole so the bobber bobbed, creating bubbles that quickly disappeared. "We're going to need all the checks we can get, so we can satisfy Shailah's wants and needs."

"Two weeks." She tried to keep her voice down. "Is that too long for you? Can't I have my daughter with me for two weeks?"

Wiley yanked up the line, swung the bobber, slapped the worm lure back in the creek.

NONE OF THE things Wiley Peichart had done before was he capable of doing now. Wiley had been a keyboard player in a country-and-western group in a north Nashville honky-tonk, had sold life insurance, had been a post office clerk temporarily, a Catholic Action Bible salesman in New Orleans, been a keyboard player in Biloxi, a dance instructor in Pensacola—fox-trot, waltz, jitterbug, tango, rumba, cha-cha, mambo, he could do them all.

It was the dancing he let go of last. He'd put a tape on, open up his arms, cock a foot out, *come on Shirl let's dance*. She'd feel his hot hand flat on her spine, his fingers pattering up her back, they would waltz and she'd step on his feet. But the cha-cha, that wasn't so difficult, *now remember Shirl you step out on two, like ONE and TWO I taught my baby how to cha-cha cha, cha-cha cha, cha-cha cha so you swing your hips, you shake it Shirl*, that she could get into special for him, and he would turn her, they were doing the waltz, *he was the waltz king, he was dancing with his sweetheart to the Tayyyy . . . naaaseeee Wahhhllllluzzzz!*

THEY HAD MADE this pact, Wiley's idea. When he decided it was time for him to overdose on Halcyon, he would let her know so she could be with him. He wouldn't off himself behind her back.

They kept the bottle in the medicine cabinet, a sturdy sentinel guarding a shelf full of aftershaves Wiley no longer had any use for. The Halcyon caplets had a threaded middle, tiny plastic eggs that you could pull apart.

Shirley called Shayne on a Saturday. She'd keep Shailah for two weeks so Shayne and Betty Jean could go on their November Caribbean cruise. Because she'd said yes to Shayne, Wiley had moved the Halcyon bottle out of the medicine cabinet. He'd taken it out to the creek. He'd put a hook in one of the caplets, used the ruined caplet for bait. She went out to him without making a fuss and told him quietly, "return the bottle please." He pulled the bottle out of his creel and handed it over *no comment Shirl.*

Coming in after work a day later, Shirley went to the fridge to get a beer. The Halcyon bottle was in the crisper. She was sure some caplets were missing because this time Wiley had left her a note. "I hide, you go seek, Shirl." She grabbed the bottle and made for the back door. She found Wiley sitting in front of the bird feeder, arms Xed over his knobby knees, eggy droppings haphazardly mixed in with the seed.

"You want to kill yourself, here be my guest," shaking caplets out of the bottle, shoving them at his nostril hairs, "come on, show me what you're made of."

Maybe he'd hide the shotgun next, and all the knives and razor blades. He'd come in to pee while she was in the shower. He had taken the caplets out of the medicine cabinet. He hadn't flushed the john because *as you know Shirl* that would screw up the water pressure. And don't forget to squirt the shower tiles with shower tile cleaner because you couldn't count on Wiley to do it, get rid of mildew stains, stains on the john, couldn't count on him to do anything that might be a little help to her. Cleaning up after him before she got in the shower, shaving cream blobs in the cheapo pedestal sink, stains rimming the toilet bowl, squinch up the sponge in the scummy water, apply Comet, scrub hard, wipe the bowl free of hairs, she'd done all that but not today, scanning items lined up on the toilet tank lid on each side of the prominently displayed, yes legible note, first his shaving brush sprouting out of his mug, his battery operated nostril hair trimmer, seldom in use, seldom applied to those adorable tufts of nostril hair, yes and the sopping wet bath mat, how did that happen, the slippery tile, how many times had she told him *please Wiley put it back where you found it, just hang it up over the shower curtain like a good boy, all right?*

He had the nerve to lay out her pink chemise on his side of the bed. The missing bottle imprinted his pillow. He still had the set on mute when she got to the living room. He was watching a baseball game in his gunked-up bathrobe.

He had agreed to keep Shailah for one week if she would do the cha-cha for him. In her cherub pink chemise. She had the Halcyon back in the medicine cabinet, had Wiley back in bed, his big head on the pillow. She pulled the bedspread up over his chest. She wouldn't know what he might do with his hands while she was doing the cha-cha. He used to tell her he'd rather lose his legs than his arms or hands. *Does that mean you'd rather play the keyboard than do the cha-cha? I'd rather put my arms around you than do the cha-cha, that you know, Shirl.*

Across the road from the Lazy Bee, pampas grass shimmied in the curlycue wind, needling her shoulder blades, topspinning through her hair. She was trying to pat her hair back into place when Shayne got out of his Buick four-door. The vented coat in his navy blue suit snapping out, he managed to get past the Exxon pumps without swiping his hair down more than once.

He sat down across from her, held his open-in-friendship right hand out, "Great to see you, Shirl, but you could have come to my office."

She felt the fleshy mass at the base of his thumb press deep into her thumb and forefinger vee. "I haven't been out this way for awhile. Not since we were both with Liberty Mutual."

"Well I'm still with Liberty Mutual." *Would you please let go of my hand?*

"And from what I hear you're hanging in there." Shayne was talking to her like she was still married to him. "For me you've always been a winner. And if you ever think about jumping ship, I'll be glad to have you on board at Prudential."

"Thanks Shayne, but I'm satisfied where I am."

Shayne glanced at his manicured fingernails, lifted his hands from the picnic table as if the scuffed paint might be contaminated. One week, not two, she was telling Shayne, she would only have Shailah for one week.

"Shailah can stay at your mother's for one week. You know that as well as I do," she said.

Across the road pampas grass shimmying just for him, for Wiley. *Come on Shirl let's dance. Shayne might as well be talking to a brick wall Shirl.*

But Shayne wasn't, he was talking to her. He wasn't yelling at her; he was reasoning with her, what he did when he wasn't yelling at her.

"I want you to know when Wiley goes—and he will go Shirl—you'll wish you'd spent more time with Shailah. You won't have Wiley for an excuse. You won't have anyone to blame but yourself."

She scrunched her toes up till Shayne finished. Pampas grass shushshushshushing, shimmying pampas grass, *for you, Wiley, I'm doing this for you*, but with Shayne's white teeth in her face she had to get away, just go.

She pulled her hair tight on her scalp, One week, one week only Shayne.

ON THE ROAD, she filed Shayne away with the other bad things in her life. But she couldn't file Shailah away. Shayne was right, she didn't see Shailah enough because of Wiley, the way he was when Shailah was there. She thought of Wiley peeing off the back steps because both bathrooms were in use, how when she took Shailah to church he'd sit out in the car and honk the horn during the service. She'd give Shailah a birthday party and he'd go out to the creek and smoke a joint.

Instead of going home, she drove out of her way to the high school. Shailah wouldn't see her parked down the street from the parking lot. Shailah had dyed her hair a brassy orange. She had on blue-tinted glasses the size of poker chips, hip-huggers showing sickles of bare butt. She was fooling around with a skaggy boy. She plumped her butt down in the passenger seat of a Toyota Camry, swung one leg out of the open window. Shirley could feel the ache in her arms from wanting to hold Shailah close, feel Shailah's heart beating. She wanted to comb out the tangles in Shailah's hair. She wanted Shailah to come back home to her, but already Shailah was too far away.

Wiley had tried to mow the front yard but only ten feet of September grass had been cut. She had to put the mower back in the garage. The keyboard, the amps, the synthesizer, and now the lawn mower he'd never use again.

Wiley was laying out cards on the coffee table. "As you might have observed I tried to mow the lawn today. I gave it my all but I didn't get far."

"We'll pay someone to do it. That won't be any big problem."

She watched Wiley scoop up the cards and shuffle the deck. "Another thing I ought to do around here is move the cable into the bedroom. I'll be spending all my time in bed pretty soon."

They had moved the set two years ago. They'd tried watching TV in the bedroom, but they'd get to fooling around and miss something they really enjoyed watching.

Wiley started dealing. He did it rapidly, one face up, six face down, talking to the cards, not her. "I'm thinking we should get it done soon, while I'm still ambulatory. You'll need me to pull the cable through." He looked at her the way he did when decisions had to be made and he wanted her to do it his way.

"All right. We'll do it this weekend. Is Saturday morning all right with you?"

Saturday morning was good for him.

She had to crawl under the house and move the cable. That used to be Wiley's job. After they'd decided where the set should go, he'd drill a hole in the hardwood floor, put his work gloves on, click the flashlight. It was Wiley who used to crawl under the house. She used to be the one looking down at the hole he had drilled, looking at the beam of Wiley's flashlight, at the cable nut wiggling up through the hole, not under the house wigwagging the damned cable.

On a Saturday morning in October she increased his dosage of morphine from five hundred to eight hundred milligrams a day. She spooned a laxative, made sure Wiley got it down. If his bowels locked he was finished, that his home care nurse made sure Shirley knew. She gave Wiley an enema twice a week. She set a morphine caplet on the tip of his tongue. The bent straw poking out of a paper cup, she lined it up with his jittering lips, kept it steady until he was sucking on it.

She called Shayne, told Shayne Wiley was worse. No way she could keep Shailah for him. Shayne hung up on her. She didn't tell Wiley what she'd done. She wouldn't give Wiley the satisfaction of knowing she'd done what he wanted her to.

ETHEL LEE BAKER had her space heater on. A shutter banged, starting up again when you'd just gotten used to not hearing it. Ethel Lee was spilling bills out of a Crisco can, spreading them out on the coffee table. Shirley was counting out bills, twelve ones, a ten, a five, then fifty-nine cents for her coin changer, smoothing the creases out in the bills and putting them in her money belt, filling out receipts for the premium payment and signing each one, tearing them off her receipt pad.

She couldn't finish the glass of iced tea. She had to move on, get the route covered, she had two more places to go to and already it was a quarter to four. Coming out, moving on to the car, she felt the wind take hold of her hair and pull.

Driving back, she was sure Wiley had taken his life. She could think of his life as over. She could stop off at the office and put the cash in the safe, do her paperwork, make sure he had time to get it done. Make sure, that was a terrible thing to think.

It was dark when she got back to the house. The porch light was on, and a light in the living room window. The TV was on mute. Wiley wouldn't take the Halcyon with the TV on, not Wiley, *I'd rather go quietly Shirl.* She lit a cigarette, unable to go to him yet. She went to the bathroom off the hall, laid her cigarette in the soap dish. No rush, she even had time to comb out her hair, put on lipstick, touch up her eye shadow. She took another drag, opened the medicine cabinet.

He'd scotch taped the note to a shaving cream canister—*I hide you go seek.*

When she got to the bedroom Wiley turned the TV off. Right away she told Wiley Shailah wasn't coming.

Wiley opened and closed his fingers before he folded them across his chest. With his head propped up on pillows, he looked like he might float off the bed and around the bedroom like a sailboat cruising around a lake. But that didn't keep him from bullshitting her.

"We've been through some tough times, Shirl. Shailah would have been another tough time."

"For you, maybe."

"No, for both of us. But if she had come we would have gotten through it. Just like all the other times, we would have found a way, Shirl."

At first she didn't want to get near him. But she had to to pull open the bed table drawer, shake it out, golf tees, package of condoms, dental floss, a cascade of paper clips.

"You and me, we're partners, Shirl. I have a right to know what you're doing."

She had to ask him where he had hidden the Halcyon caplets.

"I didn't hide them, Shirl. I wanted to, but I couldn't. They're right here, under my pillow." He took her hand, patted her knuckles. she felt the force of him pulling her toward the bed. She was sitting on the edge of the bed, looking down at him, poor sick Wiley.

"We'll find a way out, believe me, Shirl. Do you remember that basement room in north Nashville? Remember, you called it the midget room. Two inches of clearance above your head. You had to duck under the furnace pipes to get to the toilet, wasn't that fun? But for two days we got through it."

It was no fun then, and it wasn't now, but if she had to she could play Wiley's game. "After two days we packed up and left. Bye bye Music City."

Hot air was rushing out of the vents. Shirley wanted to turn the thermostat down, but she couldn't pry Wiley's hand loose from hers anymore than she could keep him from running his mouth. "You remember that night in Biloxi. I mean the first night, before I started that gig at The Shores. We checked in at this old hotel on the beach. Remember it said on the marquee, newlyweds could have the bridal suite. And you said we can't check in as newlyweds because neither one of us is wearing a wedding ring."

That hadn't stopped Wiley from wanting to stay there. For Wiley, old beach hotels had class. They could sign a tab for their meals and drinks. Later they had found something cheaper, a rent-by-the-week, beach-view efficiency. It was over, the rumba, the cha-cha, what they did when he came off his gig at the Shores. It was over and done with so why make a face, why are you dragging your mouth down like that, what is it? "What is the matter with you?"

"Nothing."

"You have to tell me."

She saw words floating out of Wiley's big head, what he said, that didn't matter as long as he felt he could say it, say anything, what he had to say to justify what he had done.

"I had a dream while you were gone. In the dream you were thinking I'd offed myself, and then I saw you standing beside me. It felt like I was between two plate-glass sheets. I couldn't move, I couldn't speak, but I was conscious, I knew you were there. I was god damned dead and you weren't. So when I woke up I had to ask myself, how would I feel if you'd come in here and I'd really done it?"

Wiley spread his fingers out flat on the sheet, he raised his head off the pillow, his. She held his head up, pulled the bottle out from under the pillow. It looked like most of the caplets were there but she couldn't be sure how many were gone. She laid dry fingertips on his forehead. *Go to sleep, Wiley, let it all go.* But he wouldn't let go, not Wiley.

Even now he couldn't keep his hands off her. He put his hands on her hips, shake it Shirl, swing your hips like so. They used to do ballroom dancing after Wiley got through at The Shores. We did the cha-cha, we did the fox trot, we did the mambo, we did the cha-cha, she'd have to do it herself, on her feet now, swinging her hips like so, one two, one two three, one two, one two three. She would dance for him, she would stay by his side, but that was all she would do for him.

ON HER WAY back from Jo Ann Hathaway's Shirley stopped at the Lazy Bee for cigarettes. She had delivered Jo Ann's policy, picked up three referral letters, signed by Jo Ann, recommending Liberty Mutual. For what? For paying your spouse off after you died.

She'd left a light on in the living room. Parked in front of their house, hers exclusively now, she lit a cigarette. The ash tray was loaded with cigarette butts. She had scattered Wiley's ashes over the creek, all but a tablespoonful, which she'd kept in a sugar bowl—that's how Wiley wanted it so that's what she'd done. She'd given his keyboard to Goodwill. She'd flushed a handful of Halcyon capsules down the toilet.

She got out of the car, tugged her coat tight about her neck to keep the cold out. She'd left a light on in the living room. The light in her living room window, like the others along her street, kept the same intensity and hue. Wiley had said about lights in windows, they reminded him of fried eggs sunny-side-up. But that wasn't how she saw her windows. Anyone passing by would think of life going on inside her windows. Normal life, not Wiley's kind.

She started walking, hunching her shoulders to keep out the cold. It hadn't quite turned dark yet. When it did, it would get colder. She passed discarded flower pots. She passed a light-tinctured, sodded lawn. She passed windows impacted with TV glows, others curtained, light slivered, walked beneath clicking twigs, bare branches, under streetlights. The lights in Shayne and Betty Jean's front windows were off. Had they gone to the movies, all three of them, or were they eating out at Denny's like she and Shayne and Shailah used to do? Or was Shailah with another skaggy boy, doing what you didn't want to know about?

Shailah had come to the house after the funeral, Shayne too. Sitting across from her—in the love seat in the front parlor—Shayne had clumsily tried to comfort her. Shailah had washed and combed her hair. She had a pretty dress on and high-heeled shoes. Mama I'm so sorry, she'd said—but on the way out she'd slapped on her blue-tinted glasses. Just to show you what she thought of Wiley. And Shailah hadn't been back since. Shayne had. He'd offered her a job at Prudential.

Five trash bags lined up behind the curb. Shayne used to rake the leaves. She'd help out, holding open the mouths of the trash bags. Shailah too. They would take turns, all three of them.

Returning, she passed the same window lights. She shivered, walked faster.

When she got home she would turn the heat up. She would drink a beer, smoke one cigarette. What then? What then? She would make a salad, heat up a frozen dinner in the microwave. Shake lentils into a stock pot, bring eight cups of water to a boil. Sautee diced carrots, a diced onion, sliced mushrooms. She would keep watch over her lentil soup until it was just right, stirring it with a wooden spoon. She would keep it in the fridge. Tomorrow night she would call Shayne, ask to speak to Shailah. What would she say? Not come over and sample my lentil soup. She would say something better than that.

She looked up at the darkening sky. Her house lay ahead of her, waiting.

A New Roof

What Samantha Hall did for Teejay Banks on the morning before her father drove up to visit her in his brown and beige Cadillac Deville, she did biscuits and gravy, cheese grits, three eggs over easy, whole wheat toast. Normally she saw to it he had granola for breakfast. She was worried about his cholesterol even though he was only twenty-five years old. She had to watch hers, for she was thirty-six.

She didn't bring up her father right away. She waited. She spooned up granola and fat-free milk, set her spoon down and asked Teejay to spend the next two days in a Best Western motel.

"Daddy won't understand how we feel about each other. He'll think I'm using you for sex. Since that's just what we don't want him to think it might be better if you were somewhere else."

"So I should care what your old man thinks." Teejay swabbed egg yolk with a piece of toast. "We both know we're not using each other for sex."

"I know we do, but Daddy doesn't. Will you do this for me, just this once, Teejay?"

He said he'd do it one time only. He'd move into a Best Western motel for two days. He saw relief in her pretty blue eyes. She ran her hands through her thick blond hair, her big breasts flattening out a little. "I won't ask you to move out again, Teejay." Then her soft white hands were warming his. "I'm going to tell Daddy I have a wonderful man in my life. You, Teejay, only you."

He held the palm of her soft hand up to his lips. "What you tell your daddy is up to you. You do what you feel like doing."

They made love right away in Samantha's brass bed. Teejay honey! Oh Samantha. She made the bed with Teejay in it, pulling the sheet up past his chest, poking and pinching his arms and legs.

Samantha knew how to make him feel good in bed, but it wasn't just sex they had going for them. There were things that made them feel close, hearing birds sing waking up at dawn, taking long walks, working crossword puzzles together. He would help her set up her still lifes, gladiolas and pussy willows in a long-necked vase, lemons and limes, a Florida orange, oodles, she'd say, of bougainvillea. Sitting quietly in her studio, he would watch her sketch and paint.

On his second day in a motel, a Best Western close to East Pensacola Heights, he got a telephone call from Samantha. He could come back any time, she said, her father had left a day early. Instead of going back to her house he asked her to come to him, get in the minivan her father had purchased for her while he was there and drive to the Best Western. That she did for him, came to his place. She brought an electric razor for him with her, a pair of Levi's, a tank top, mousse for his hair. He waited to ask her what she'd said about him to her father, until just before check-out time.

"When I told him about you, Teejay, he said he hoped it would work out for us." Samantha unsnapped her bulging purse, searched through her many credit cards.

TWO DAYS LATER Teejay got word that his father had died of a heart attack. He'd called his father in Cantonment—the telephone ringing on and on, why didn't his father buy an answering machine—because the next time Samantha's father drove up in his Cadillac, Teejay thought he'd just head back home, spend the time in the house he'd grown up in. He got his old maid aunt on the phone instead; that's how he'd gotten the news. Something quivered, leaped, ran amuck in his brain. The house is mine now. I own it. He put the cordless back in its cradle. *Last time I saw you you were dead drunk, in mama's bedroom in your boxer shorts. You do that one more time I'll whip your sorry ass.*

He didn't ask Samantha to go to the funeral; he wanted to spare her that ordeal. The night before the movers came, Teejay slept in his mother's room. His mother had died two years ago, worn out, riddled with bone cancer. It was raining when he woke up. He had a bucket set at the foot of the bed. The roof had a leak in two places, at the foot of the bed, above his mother's vanity. Something would have to be done about that. He moved the bucket on top of the vanity, seeing his face in the mirror, a surface that once had held his mother's face. His great-grandfather's Bible was still on the dresser, births and marriages written inside. An Olan Mills photograph taken in Biloxi was also there—his father in a rented tuxedo, his mother in her wedding dress and lifted veil. His father was wearing sideburns then. His mother wore her hair in butternut curls. They were holding hands in front of a latticed arch.

He got up and went to the living room, already puddled in several places. He walked out on the front porch and watched the traffic on U.S. 29 nosing through the rain, Gulf beach-bound vehicles with Tennessee license plates or with Ohio or Illinois plates whose occupants stared straight ahead.

The rain stopped before the movers came. Teejay led the moving van back to Pensacola in the pickup truck Samantha had purchased for him. Samantha's house looked good to him, Samantha coming out on the front porch with a paint brush behind her left ear. Teejay got out and went to her right away, while the ramp was coming down from the truck.

What belonged to his father was sold. His mother's dresser and vanity, the television set his mother had watched—game shows, talk shows, sit-coms, day in and day out—Samantha made a place for these things in an upstairs room in the back of the house, with a nice view of the bay. It was somewhere for Teejay to be by himself. He kept the photographs on the dresser. His great-grandfather's Bible he also kept. Sometimes he opened it and read the births and marriages, a sheet of tiny printed inscriptions from before the Civil War on up to his great-grandfather's marriage and his grandfather's name and date of birth. In a broad hand was his father's name and date of birth, William Banks, 1955. No one had ever called his father William. He had always been called Willie.

He stayed in his mother's room while Samantha worked in her studio. Instead of watching her work, he stayed up in this room, watching talk shows on the television set, looking out at the sailboats on the bay. Looking up from the open Bible once, he felt a spear of probing sunlight between his eyes. The letters B . . . A. . . N . . . K . . . S were shimmering, floating away from him. He raised one hand to shut out the voice, Willie talking to him, I'm talking to *you. You can have it all with this woman.* He closed the Bible, let the sailboats go on cutting swaths in the bay. He got out of the room in a hurry. He took a walk down the sandy road. When he got back to her house he went to her studio and put his hand on the doorknob. *You can have it all.* He wanted to tell her it didn't matter what Willie said, but the doorknob, one of his fingers cramped when he grasped it.

In bed with Samantha, it wasn't the same. He would roll over afterwards and go to sleep. He'd be out of bed before Samantha was, making coffee for them in the kitchen just so he could be away from her. Still, he tried not to show what he was feeling. Not much seemed to change in their life together. They went fishing off the bay bridge. He made stretcher bars for her canvases. He drove her paintings to a Gulf Coast art show in the new minivan, and when Samantha didn't win best of show, not even an honorable mention, he did his best to make her feel okay about it. He said the best of show painting made him want to vomit. Samantha shouldn't give up her painting because someday she would be recognized.

He decided he had to put his house up for sale. He listed the house with Deen Real Estate Agency in Cantonment because he felt Hugh Deen should have the listing, not Buddy Purvis, he was telling Samantha, the only other real estate agent in his home town, because everyone knew Buddy drank like a fish.

"He was my daddy's big buddy but he sure isn't mine." He waited for Samantha to set up three long-stemmed calla lilies in the long-necked vase. She ran her pink tongue along her lower lip, looking out at the sailboats speckling the bay.

"Neither one of them sounds very reliable to me. Why don't you let Daddy handle it? He has some good friends in real estate, right here in Pensacola."

I'm talking to you. You can have it all. He had to pull his eyes away from the calla lilies.

Hugh Deen told him over the telephone he was only interested in selling land anymore. Lori Torbert was handling house sales now. Teejay met Lori Torbert at the house. She parked her Nissan Sentra in the driveway. She came up to him on the front porch and sat next to him on the porch swing. Her skirt was a little too tight for her, and there were streaks of orange in her short blond hair, but she was still a nice-looking young woman. He saw she wasn't wearing a wedding ring.

The house needed a lot done to it. A fixer-upper, Lori told him. She thought he could get eighty-five thousand for it if Teejay put in a new roof. Yes, the roof leaked; something had to be done, he thought, but where would he get the money? Not from Samantha, or Samantha's daddy. So he asked Lori to sell the house as-is.

"All right, but that's going to take awhile. At least get someone to clean it up."

"I can do that. I think I can take care of that."

Lori asked him how she could get in touch with him, and he left her Samantha's telephone number. The next day he called Magic Maids in Pensacola and arranged to have the house cleaned. He sat out on the porch swing while the girls did the job. He dropped by the real estate office to leave word that the house was ready to show. Lori Torbert turned in her swivel chair, and gave him the news. "I'm not really sure I can sell your house unless you put in a new roof."

"Try selling it without one. Come down on the price if you have to," he said.

Three weeks later, Lori Torbert called him right before lunch. Samantha picked up the telephone, handed it over without a word, and padded off to the kitchen. Lori Torbert sounded put out with him. She had shown the house on a beautiful day, no likelihood it would rain, she thought, but after she'd shown the house to these people it had rained on the way to the car. "You can imagine how I'd look to my clients if it had rained while they were in your house. That would be one sale I could kiss goodbye."

Samantha was waiting for him in the kitchen. She had a pot of split pea soup simmering, whole wheat toast in the toaster, an endive lettuce green salad already made. She was stirring the soup with a wooden spoon.

"That was my real estate agent on the phone. She wants me to put on a new roof. If I don't it might not sell so quick."

He told Samantha it had started to rain while Lori Torbert was showing the house. "She told me that old roof of mine leaks like a sieve," he said. "She said that was one sale she had to kiss goodbye."

It was the first time he had lied to Samantha. Nothing showed in his voice, nothing showed in her but irritation over the way he was handling the sale. Two slices of toast popped up in the toaster.

"You ask me this woman doesn't know which end is up. I mean she isn't professional. She should have told these people the roof leaked before she had them inside to look at the house."

"So next time she tells them," Teejay said, "and the time after that too."

Samantha set down her wooden spoon. "All right, Teejay. You can have your new roof. My checkbook is in my pocketbook. Would you please go get it for me? You fill out the check. I'll sign it."

"You get it."

"All right, I'll get it," she said, and laid the spoon down on the cook top.

Samantha came back with this bulging leather pocketbook. He couldn't stand to watch her poke through the clutter—change purse, pink tabbed keys to the van, tubes of lipstick, the pink flowered checkbook cover. You can have it all, but not at this price, no goddamned way he would write out the check. Something snapped in him, made him be mean to her.

"You sure your Daddy would want this? If he found out you were paying for my new roof, he'd say you were using me for sex."

Samantha bit down on her lower lip. "He won't find out about your new roof because I don't intend to tell him about it."

"Well, you ask me, you should tell him. Ask him to pay for my roof. That way he'll have to write out the check."

Split pea soup gushed out of the pot, the pot clapped down on the linoleum. "Get out of my house! I mean it! I want you out of here!" Samantha yelled at him.

He got his razor and toothbrush, a change of clothes, his parents' wedding photograph. The Bible he left where it was. He climbed in the pickup truck and drove away to Best Western.

He pawned the pickup truck to pay for the roof. He went down the next day to a pawn shop—we keep the title but you keep the keys—and came out with seventeen hundred dollars in cash. Next he went to a roofer and got a date for getting the job done. He would have to wait a week; he would have to live in a motel until the new roof was on the house. After that he could live in his own house, be there when Lori Torbert showed the house, and when she sold it he could get a decent job and find an affordable place and get his truck out of hock and start living. Samantha called him that evening. She said she had to see him. He watched her pull the minivan into the parking lot. She brought sandwiches in a picnic basket, paper plates and linen napkins. She spread their picnic out on the bed, and opened a bottle of cold beer for him. Her soft plump arms opening out to him made him want her again, like before.

Teejay was sitting out on the porch swing, watching the traffic go by. It was his house now, not Willie Banks's house. Hammers—one after the other, two at once, four at a time—were whacking brads into shingles. Big black men and little white men were laddered against the sloping roof. Their flatbed truck was parked behind his pickup.

Rotten shingles were stacked between the pecan tree and a tall clump of sun-browned pampas grass. Teejay had a mattress in his pickup and a floor lamp and two table lamps, Samantha's kitchen chairs, a small ice chest, a hot plate, his mother's television set. He hadn't turned off the utilities yet even though he hadn't any way of paying for them. He hadn't asked Samantha to pay the bills for him.

He'd gone back to Samantha, slept with her on her brass bed, their love cries echoing in his mind. Teejay honey. Oh Samantha! So why had she come down on him? *You can do what you like with your tacky old house. You can turn it into a museum and live there the rest of your natural life.*

He'd tried to tell her he wasn't doing that. He would live there until the house was sold. He would move back to Pensacola and find a place of his own after that, but that didn't mean they couldn't see each other. But he wasn't about to be a kept man.

Kept, you think I want to keep you. You're the one who asked me for money.

Someone must have let Lori Torbert know he was here because around noon she showed up in her Nissan Sentra.

The roofers were off on their lunch break. Teejay made room for Lori on the porch swing. He had to put his feet on the porch to keep the swing from rocking.

"I see," Lori said, "you're putting on a new roof."

"That's right. That's what I'm doing." He felt Lori's arm brush his elbow. "And that's not all. I'm moving in. I'm going to stay here until you sell the house. I got a mattress and some kitchen chairs in my truck and some other things I need to live here. I'm serious. Here's where I intend to stay until you sell this place."

"You'll have to move your things out when I show the house."

"I can do that," Teejay said. "I can move them out to my truck." He rocked the porch swing just a little, and she put out her feet and stopped it.

"You are actually going to live here?"

"Sure am. I have to live somewhere," he said.

"I know but I may not sell your house for awhile. I think you should be reasonable and find a place to live in Pensacola."

"I had a place in Pensacola," he said, "but that place is no longer available."

He looked away from the stacks of shingles, the ladders, the passing cars and trucks, shutting Samantha out of his mind. He eased his body close to Lori Torbert's, kept his eyes glued to hers.

"Could I ask about you something personal, Lori?"

"Some things I'd rather you didn't ask."

"I'm not prying into your personal life. I just want you to know why I moved out from the place I was in, that's all." He'd been living, he told Lori, with an older woman who was supporting him. He found the words he wanted to say next without looking very hard for them. "What I'm asking you is would you live with an older man if he were your sole means of support?"

"I'm my own sole means of support," she said. "I sell real estate. I get along."

He felt the porch swing move a little, aware that both of them were moving it. "Supposing you met an older man who owned a Cadillac Deville."

He touched Lori's instep with the toe of a boot, and she giggled, rocking the swing. "Who wants a Cadillac Deville?"

"If I stayed with this woman I've been living with I know I might be driving one someday."

"I wouldn't want you to give up a Cadillac."

"I wouldn't want to either but I might."

Lori put out a long leg to stop the swing, looking out at the traffic, controlling her voice so it sounded like how she was on the telephone, her bright blue eyes boring into his. "Why don't you come to my house tonight? I'll cook dinner for you and we'll watch a video."

"I wouldn't want you to cook dinner for me. But I will watch a video with you."

That night they ordered takeout Chinese. He let Lori pay her half of the bill. She poured out Chablis in long-stemmed wine glasses, and when the video started she refilled them. They held hands, watching the video, and then he put his arm around her, dropping his fingers to her breasts. She took his hand and let him fondle her breasts. Her lips fluttered when he kissed her.

Later, still drinking Chablis, she turned on her side and showed him the strawberry birthmark high up on her left buttock. "When I was a little girl my mom told me it would go away. But like a lot of things it didn't go away."

"I won't be going away until you sell my house."

"Well maybe I never will sell your house."

The next night he was back at Lori's place. They drank a pitcher of margaritas. She pointed out the antique furniture she had from her grandmother, really nice things, she said, a tea table with a marble top, a bonnet table with a drawer for gloves, a hall tree in glossy golden oak. She sat up on the carpet, swept one hand toward the hall tree. "That bastard I was married to tried to talk me out of the hall tree."

"What would he want with a hall tree?"

"He's renovating an old house in Pensacola. He says the hall tree is rightfully his because he was the one who refinished it. That's how Bill determines ownership."

There were photographs in her bedroom—she must have a big family, he thought—and a framed Cantonment High School diploma. She showed him her majorette photograph. She was in it with six other girls, kneeling in front of a drum major. He liked Lori as a majorette. He was sorry he hadn't gotten to know her then.

The next time he was with her they drank another pitcher of margaritas. Waking up in the middle of the night, he reached out to the woman beside him. Samantha, he heard himself saying. Lori turned over on her side. She didn't say anything to him, but when he touched her strawberry birthmark she grabbed his hand and shoved it away. He got up and went to the bathroom, and when he came out Lori was asleep. Or faking it, he couldn't tell which. He put his clothes on, and said goodbye to the hall tree.

Lori called him several days later. She was spending the day in

Pensacola; she would come by his place when she got back. "I've got news for you, Teejay," she said. "Someone is interested in buying your house." But by nine o'clock Lori still hadn't shown up. He thought of going to see Lori at her place; then the Nissan pulled into the driveway and Lori was at his front door.

He tried to kiss her but she pushed him away. "I'm showing the house tomorrow at ten. So you need to be out of here. I came over tonight to tell you because you need to clean up the place."

"Out? I live here."

He nudged a beer can with his foot, and went up to her and put his hands out. She took one of his hands in both of hers. "It's not that I don't want to see you, Teejay, but right now isn't a good time. We can see each other after I sell your house."

She let him kiss her before she left him. He stood out on the porch for awhile, watching the traffic go by. He didn't want to go back inside the house right away. Lori Torbert was like the other girls he'd known. She probably would have made life miserable for him. The first girl he'd had sex with, he'd taken her to a high school football game. He'd had her in the back seat of his father's car. When he got back home, there was a light on in the bay window. His mother and Willie were dancing. His mother's hands were locked behind Willie's neck. Teejay had driven around the block several times. They must have heard him pull out of the driveway because when he got back the lights were out all over the house.

He swept up the kitchen and took the garbage out. He loaded his things on the pickup, the floor lamp and table lamps, the kitchen chairs, the hot plate and the ice chest, his mother's television set. The wedding photograph he put in the glove compartment.

He stayed in a motel in Cantonment, across the highway from Kentucky Fried, and the next day he sat in his room until ten, watching game shows and talk shows, as his mother had done for so many years. He got in the pickup at ten-fifteen and headed back to his house. He drove by the brown and beige Cadillac Deville parked behind the Nissan Sentra. Now he knew who was being shown his house. He gassed up at a full-service station, had the oil checked, the windshield cleaned. Returning, he passed his house again. The Cadillac Deville must be on its way back to wherever Samantha's daddy had come from.

Hugh Deen was in his office waiting for him. He was half a foot shorter than Lori Torbert, an old guy she couldn't be interested in. Hugh Deen told him Lori Torbert had gone home early today. She was going on vacation tomorrow and she wanted to get started packing. Hugh Deen had the earnest money for the house. He counted out fifteen crisp one-hundred dollar bills, and handed them over to Teejay.

It started raining when Teejay got to Samantha's. Drops of rain puckered the white sand along the narrow road that led to the bay. He left his earnest money in the glove compartment, put a tarpaulin over his things in the truck. He wiped his shoes off on the throw rug by the door so he wouldn't track up the living room. A still life set up on the coffee table, double-blossomed camellias in the long-necked vase. He moved quietly through the big dining room to the kitchen. Samantha was washing romaine lettuce, patting each beaded leaf dry, folding wet lettuce up in a towel.

It rained on into the afternoon. They made love in Samantha's room, on her brass bed. Teejay honey! Oh Samantha! She had to ask him do you love me? He heard himself saying, "I do, Samantha," rain drumming on their storm-tight roof.

Cutouts

He had driven by an auto graveyard one day and seen the school bus and bought it. He'd put used tires on the rear wheels and had it towed to his daddy's house. He'd taken the seats out, cut a section out of the roof, installed a glass-paneled bubble like the raised glass roof of an observation car so his mother could look up at the sky at night, relive long-ago Union Pacific ads when her mother had been a little girl, move backward in time, not forward, recover people sitting in comfortable chairs, writing letters, reading magazines, the sky overhead, clouds and birds, the sun and the moon and the stars. If they followed a straight line west from the school bus, along the Sno-Cone sign to his daddy's house, it would take them to her hospital bed, the feeding tube in her navel, the drainage machine squatting robot-like on the tasseled, unvacuumed throw rugs, ever ready for sucking mucus out of her throat (to do that he inserted a tube in her mouth, laid his hand carefully over her nose, the machine humming, the level rising in the plastic container Ray would detach, empty out in the toilet, soak in vinegar, replace carefully), the radio on, the tiny school bus cutout he'd made for her on her vanity for her to take comfort in. With the curtains open she could turn her head, see her big bus in the backyard. Day and night she would know she could go there, lie down, look up.

The little buses were set up in his trailer workshop, at one end of the bedroom/kitchen area, a sheet of plywood spanning drain board and stove, his plywood school bus cutouts hand-painted with tiny red lights, a tiny hexagonal stop sign jutting off the driver's side to the left. Ray had laid plywood out, painted in streets, erected shoebox public buildings, schoolhouse, jail, courthouse, bank. His mother, Mabel Rackstraw, his dear mother would be behind the wheel, with a big smile, color in her cheeks, her eyes on the road, not on him. Little Ray would be sitting five seats back from her.

Nothing happened to Ray or his mother while they were inside the bus. The school bus door would stay locked because the key to his daddy's car didn't fit. Hurry up Ray we have to catch the bus. His daddy would pound on the school bus door and his mother held little Ray in her arms until his daddy went back into the house. She'd say your daddy's trying to do better. And when his daddy did do better, Ray still had his hiding place under the steering wheel.

Ray Rackstraw's school bus, his trailer workshop where he made a living as a sign painter, the Sno-Cone sign and his panel truck took up the sixty-by-ninety-foot backyard that his daddy had let him live on free as long as his mother was alive. Lying in bed with Flo Mayfield's hand in his—she had come all the way back from Portland, Oregon, to be with him after his mother died—he would imagine the school bus floating through space. Hang on, Flo, he'd say to Flo, but by this time Flo would be sound asleep. Sleep on, Flo, he would say to her, and lightly kiss her on the forehead.

Sitting out in front of his trailer workshop late one afternoon in September, Ray heard Mason Rackstraw's car in the drive, heard him slam the front door. Mason Rackstraw must have had a bad day selling burial policies, or heard from Chief Cosgrave, or both. A pecan leaf lit on his daddy's bald head; his daddy swatted it like a mosquito. His coin changer still clamped to his belt, his rate books and ballpoint pens hedging the pockets of his shirt, he stood over Ray like he owned him, thumping his fist in his open left hand the way he did when Ray was a little boy.

"I'm going to give it to you straight, Ray. I received another call from Chief Cosgrave today. He's getting complaints from the neighbors about the way you choose to live your life. He wants that bus out of here quick, and you with it, and that woman of yours." The law is the law, his daddy made clear. No vehicle can be used as a dwelling place within the city limits of Ott. Ray got up, looking down at his daddy's bald head. His daddy stopped thumping his fists, his voice lapsing into a whiny surliness. "We could both of us go to jail for what you've taken a notion to do. You find you another place to live, Chief Cosgrave might just cut you some slack."

Ray was picketing. Marching up the long hill to the city building, Ray passed people on their way to lunch. He had left Flo in the school bus. She wanted nothing to do with his picketing. Flo Mayfield wanted no part of it.

Approaching motorists and pedestrians would read the message on Ray's sandwich boards—A MAN'S HOME IS HIS CASTLE. At the top of the hill, the straps cutting into his shoulders, Ray stopped for a drink from the water fountain between the city building and the library. In motion again, he passed police station, library, city building, passing people who looked right past him as if they'd rather he packed up and left town, went back to Portland like Flo wanted him to.

Chief Cosgrave came out of the police station. He gave Ray his Jolly Green Giant grin and laid the law down for Ray to knuckle under to. "I assume you are aware that you need a permit for picketing."

Ray had one, from the city of Ott, signed by the mayor himself. He showed the permit to the chief.

"Picketing's legal. I have a permit."

"Using a school bus for purposes of habitation isn't legal. Not inside the city limits."

"My hearing is set for November fifteenth. I can keep my school bus where it is until Judge Popwell hands down a ruling."

"What you'll get is thirty days minimum. But if you do what I'm asking you to do, I'll see that you don't go to jail. You do it today, you won't even be fined. I'll tell Judge Popwell you made a mistake." Two Brinks guards came out of Eagle Bank, looking warily up and down the street. One was a woman guard. BRINKS showed on the back of her jacket. "Here's what I'm going to tell Judge Popwell, if you're willing to cooperate. 'Your honor, Ray Rackstraw isn't like ordinary folks. He didn't know he was violating the law. He's a weirdo who lives in his own world.'"

Ray couldn't take much more of this. The chief had to hear his side of it. "I'm a sign painter, not a weirdo. Sign painting is my profession. And my world is as good as yours."

The chief had his Jolly Green Giant grin on, and his voice, it wasn't a midget's voice. "Let me tell you something, Rackstraw. I'm willing to let you live your life any way you choose to live it. But not inside the city limits. You get your daddy to buy you some land outside the city limits. You move your school bus out of the city. Is that clear? Do you read me?"

Ray looked past the chief at the jail. He heard a steel door slamming, but he didn't flinch. He said his school bus would stay where it was. And he wasn't about to stop picketing.

Soon Ray was attracting attention. People gathered around the city building to watch Ray do his picketing. A school bus driver put on the brakes. He gawked at Ray in his sandwich boards. The red stop lights blinked, and the arm with the hexagonal STOP shot out from the driver's side.

One morning in early October, just after Ray had gone off to do his picketing, Chief Cosgrave paid Flo Mayfield a visit. Chief Cosgrave took his time getting out of the patrol car. Flo watched the chief move around the Sno-Cone sign. He was coming her way, a big thumb hooked in his thick black belt, and for a minute she thought he might blow his whistle at her.

Chief Cosgrave sat down up front in the bus, across the narrow aisle from Flo's crossed legs. "I thought talking to you might do Ray some good. You're his woman; you must have some influence over him."

"I do, but not about this," Flo said. "Ray's not going to change his mind. He won't do that. That's how he is."

The chief unhooked his thumbs from his gun belt. "Let me tell you something about myself. I've never lived in a school bus. I don't live with a woman who isn't my wife. We have two bathrooms in our home. We have a kitchen and three bedrooms, a television set in our living room, a washer and dryer, and more. We're a couple. We obey the law. We don't go picket the city whenever something the city happens to do doesn't fit in with our lifestyle."

"You don't have to picket the city. You are the city, Chief Cosgrave."

"No you're wrong, I'm not the city. I don't even speak for the city. I only attempt to enforce its laws. Now our mayor, he speaks for the city of Ott. Do you want to know what he's been telling me? What the city of Ott has been telling me?"

The chief pushed his face out into the aisle. They might, by putting their heads together, through some telekinesis Flo could only hope for, lift Ray's school bus right out of the backyard, get the job done themselves, solve the problem. She was wondering who would take over the steering wheel, the chief or herself, if the bus did fly away.

"All right, you don't want to know. You don't care to know, I can understand that, but I'm going to tell you anyway. I've been in to talk to the mayor and believe me he isn't happy. He doesn't like this picketing going on all day in front of the city building. He can see it from his office. He tells me we have this weirdo out on the streets of Ott. I tell him he issued the permit, he didn't have to issue a permit. He tells me this has to stop. He tells me something has to be done."

Flo put on a smile she knew wouldn't work, "I wish I could help you, Chief Cosgrave, but Ray's going to do what he's going to do. Nothing I say will stop him."

The chief got up from his seat. "If you don't mind I'd like to ask you something. How can you live with a man like that?"

"Sometimes I don't know how I do it. But I'm doing it. That's all that matters."

Both of them knew there was nothing more she could say to Chief Cosgrave.

ONE CLOUDY AFTERNOON in late October while Ray was picketing in front of the city building a stoop-shouldered man with floury white hair stepped out from behind the water fountain, none other than Homer Brown, who did a column for *The Columbus Sentinel*, "Out and Around with Homer Brown." Homer Brown asked Ray to have a cup of coffee with him, across the street at the E-lite cafe.

After parking his sandwich boards outside the E-lite, Ray ordered apple pie a la mode and coffee. Like Ray, Homer Brown ordered the E-lite way, even though he lived in Columbus, Georgia, not Ott, Alabama. At the E-lite, people ordered by numbers and letters. Flo Mayfield thought the E-lite way was hilarious, this just couldn't happen anywhere else. Number one signified country fried steak, two, pork chops, and so on. The letters referred to side dishes. So country fried chicken, mashed potatoes, and slaw would go—I'll have a one, an A, and a C. The pies were from G to L, apple pie a la mode was L v, meaning ice cream, vanilla naturally. Coffee was X, iced tea was Y, diet Pepsi came last, a Z. Ray ordered an L v with X and Homer ordered an H for cherry pie and an X i for decaffeinated coffee. Homer's column had dealt with the E-lite's outmoded way of ordering food and drink, its hidebound waitresses who wouldn't put pencil to order pad unless you ordered your dinner the E-lite way. But with the waitress today, Homer Brown had on his best-behavior smile, his chin propped on one pudgy white hand, elbow on the checked oilcloth. He ordered an H, an X i. and got out his notebook and pencil.

Homer Brown asked Ray why he had to violate the law? Stirring sugar into his decaf, Ray said, "All you have to do is read my sandwich boards. A man's home is his castle."

"Most men don't live in a school bus, Ray. A school bus happens to be a vehicle. You know the law here, living in vehicles is prohibited within the city limits."

Ray's eyes narrowed. "A castle could just as well be a vehicle as not. At one time certain movable siege towers very similar to castles were used to assault castles and walled cities."

"I wouldn't call siege towers castles." Homer Brown scraped back unruly hair over his ears without stirring up a floury white dust. "If I were to write in my column 'a man's home is his siege tower' how long do you think I'd keep my job?"

"That depends on your readers. They might realize a man could live in a siege tower."

"Not my readers, not in a blue moon. I'll tell you what would happen. I'd be out on my ass. I mean pronto. So I don't write obvious falsehoods such as a man's home is his siege tower."

Ray tilted his eyes toward what the waitress was setting down on the oilcloth in front of Homer Brown, Homer Brown's cherry pie—that was an H. The cherries must have come out of a can. Ray's mother had no use for canned cherries, and since cherries weren't plentiful in Ott she drew the line at making cherry pies. Ray's apple pie tasted good to him. So did the apple pie filling. The pie crust, however, was hard to chew. His mother could bake a fine apple pie. Her pie crust would melt in your mouth, may the good Lord keep her wherever she was.

Homer Brown laid his pencil aside. "Let me ask you one thing, Ray. Some people might think you're crazy. I don't, but some people might. So let's not talk about castles. Let's talk about why you're doing this. Aren't you doing this because Chief Cosgrave is getting on your case? A man living in the city has every right to live in a school bus as long as it's on his property. It shouldn't matter to the community. He could be living in a dump truck and the city of Ott shouldn't interfere. But Chief Cosgrave, he's interfering. Am I making sense to you, Ray?"

"A man should be able to live where he wants, in the structure he wants to live in. I tried to tell Chief Cosgrave that."

Homer Brown looked down at the cherry pie he knew he was not going to eat.

After Homer Brown's story came out in *The Columbus Sentinel*, people showed up in front of city hall to cheer Ray on. They wrote letters to the *Ott Weekly Bulletin* defending Ray and excoriating Chief

Cosgrave. For the first time, Ray felt he wasn't alone. His sandwich boards felt light on him; he carried them up and down the long hill with the certainty that his cause would prevail. He'd take his sandwich boards to the police station. He was "standing tall" Homer Brown wrote of him in "Out and Around with Homer Brown." "Avoiding public scrutiny" was what Homer Brown said Chief Cosgrave was doing.

Early in November, waiting for Flo at the E-lite, Ray was reading what Homer Brown had written about him in his column. Ray had come in without his sandwich boards, parked outside like a miniature A-frame house. He had just ordered apple pie a la mode when Chief Cosgrave sat down across from him, belt and holster creaking. The chief pushed his craggy face at Ray.

"I'm only going to say this once, Rackstraw. You won't be seeing me again for awhile. But I'll be keeping an eye on you. From now on you'll be under twenty-four hour surveillance. That woman who's living with you, we will also be watching her closely."

That afternoon Ray went to his bandsaw and did a cutout of Chief Cosgrave. He set his chief cutout in the E-lite Cafe, did cutouts of columnist Homer Brown, the mayor, and Judge Popwell at the same table the chief was sitting at. Ray kept an eye out for unmarked police cars. Getting up at night while Flo was asleep, he'd go to the trailer and turn on the light. He'd turn the bandsaw on without using it.

He couldn't sleep much anymore. He had dreams about his mother and Flo. "I had a dream about you last night. You were wearing a beautiful wedding dress. This wedding was something special," Ray said to Flo one day. "You were kissing me in your wedding dress and you were everything that a man can desire. But my mother had run off again. She never did that when she was alive, but now that she's dead she does it. She runs off and comes back again and I never know where she's been."

In some of his dreams it was Flo who ran off. Flo ran off and had sex with other men. When Ray thought of his dreams about Flo, he couldn't eat his pie a la mode. He let it sit in front of him, on the plate.

"If you don't want to eat it, I'll eat it," Flo said.

In another dream, Ray was driving his first car, following his mother's school bus. It kept speeding up, so he had to too. He stayed behind it all the way through town and back again, back to his father's house. He saw the caution lights come on, then the red lights, the STOP arm shoot out.

IT WAS A cold night, the electric heater was on but it wasn't putting out much heat. Ray was sitting up on the mattress and box springs near the back end of the school bus, directly under the glass bubble overhead. Flo imagined Ray unbolting seats in the school bus. She saw a seat on his back as Ray staggered down the aisle toward the door, Ray having done that not for her but for his mother, so his mother could lie down in this bed. Flo pulled her side of the blanket up to her neck.

"I have a right to live," Ray was declaring to Flo, "wherever I choose. With whoever I choose. Don't you see, I can't run away from this."

The electric heater had a burnt toast smell. She should ask Ray to do something about it, but why do that, why bother? "We've had this conversation before and it always ends up getting nowhere."

"When this is over, I promise you, we'll leave. We'll shake the dust from Ott, Alabama. I'm only asking for my day in court."

"What you're asking for is a jail sentence. What you're asking for is losing me."

"Well you know I don't want that to happen." Ray pulled his side of the sheet up to his chest and turned his face up toward the bubble. Flo listened to him talk to the sky, not her. "You're wrong, Flo, dead wrong. I know I don't belong here in Ott. I belong in Portland, Oregon, with you. You know while I was with you out there I didn't think I would ever come back here."

The moon was moving overhead, Ray's full moon, for him only.

"But I did come back. I had to."

"She died on you, Ray. You can't bring her back."

"Not all of her died on me. Some of her is right here in this bus."

"I know you believe that, Ray. I couldn't feel that way about my mother." The moon moved on to the next panel. "When a woman dies, she dies."

"That's what I thought myself. I thought nothing of her would move again. I never thought she'd be with me again." Flo knew what was coming next, what had happened before the burial, on the way to the cemetery. The hearse had to stop for a school bus. It had held up a long line of cars. "It was what my mother would have wanted. She could have been driving that school bus herself."

"Well she wasn't. You told me a man was driving."

"It was a man driving the school bus. But my mother might have arranged for a man to be driving it. She would have if she'd been able to."

"Things like that can't be arranged. They are accidents, Ray. Just accidents."

"I know. But it made me feel better. I kept seeing her like I used to when she wasn't just my mother. She was who she was when she drove a school bus. Who she really was, not what she was to me."

Flo felt her stomach knot up. She didn't know what to say to Ray anymore. Ray had crossed some wide river, too wide for her to see him clearly. She saw a figure on the other shore, but it wasn't the Ray she had known. Yet she let Ray make love to her, tracing ovals on his chest afterwards until his eyes closed and he went to sleep.

She got up and smoothed out her skirt, draped a skimpy fringed scarf over her blouse. If Ray woke up he wouldn't look for her. He'd wait for her to come back even if he had to wait all night.

Flo parked the panel truck across the street from the E-lite Cafe, in front of Rusty's Oyster Bar. She went in and found a table. The men playing pool didn't stop their game, but she knew they were staring at her.

She was sitting with her back to the door, so she didn't see Chief Cosgrave come in. He was wearing his uniform. His holster creaked when he sat down. He offered to buy her a glass of white wine, and she accepted; she took what was offered her.

"We have things to talk about, Flo."

Chief Cosgrave pulled a newspaper clipping out of his wallet, "Out and Around with Homer Brown." Reading through it, she felt he must have been carrying it around for a week, for the print was creased where he'd folded it. She handed the clipping back without a word, and he put it back in his wallet. "This can't go on. I'm not putting up with anymore of this shit."

"I told you, Ray won't change his mind."

"Then we'll have to change it for him."

The chief's big thumb went into his shirt pocket. A small bag swayed on a drawstring. "If I find this in Ray Rackstraw's possession, he'll have to start seeing things my way."

The chief put the bag on the table, waiting for Flo to pick it up. She heard the crack of pool balls breaking. "I wouldn't ever do that to Ray. Not for you, not for anybody."

The chief's hands were heading her way, don't you force me, don't think you're scaring me because I'm not going to play your game. "You listen to me carefully. If Ray doesn't see things my way, there's a certain lady I know who might find herself in a lot of trouble. You're one of the little fish in my net. I can throw you back. Or I can keep you."

Chief Cosgrave took her by the wrists and laid her hands palms up on the table. She felt thumbs pinning her wrists flat. "I got news for you little missy. Where you're going, you won't wear your hair long. You'll be strip-searched, they'll give you a jumpsuit like all the others have, you won't be wearing any scarves, and you won't get no white wine to drink either." She felt the chief's thick thumbs boring into her wrists. "Where you're going, you won't be like you are now. So who's it going to be? You or Rackstraw?"

Flo gripped the bag in her hand. She was free to go now, because it's you chief, only you, and if you ask me nice I'll do my ovals on you, on your belly, wherever you want me to, just "please I have to be going now. You hear me, I've got things to do tonight."

Thumb and forefinger on his whistle, the chief raised it but didn't blow it at her. "You go on now, little missy," he said quietly. "I'll be talkin' to you. I'll be in touch."

A LIGHT WAS on in the bathroom window. Mason Rackstraw was brushing his teeth. What was on his mind Flo didn't want to know. He must have seen her drive into the backyard. He might be thinking she'd drive off in Ray's panel truck. Flo saw a cloudy water glass raised in the window to the toast of the town, Flo Mayfield. Flo wrapped her scarf around her shoulders tighter. Then getting out of the panel truck, she followed five extension cords to the trailer door.

The overhead light bulb had burned out so she had to find her way to the toilet in the dark. Once there she pulled the chain on another bulb that worked. The seat was loose but that wouldn't matter anymore. Ray could wiggle the seat with his skinny butt, or put in a new seat, or would that take up too much of his valuable time?

She set her handbag down and tinkled. She stood up and pulled her panties up, smoothed her skirt out, readjusted her scarf, dug deep into her handbag for the drawstring, pulled the small bag out like a tampon you need in a hurry, held the small bag over the toilet bowl, dropped it in. She flushed the toilet. She left the light bulb on so she could find her way out. She followed a trail of extension cords to the school bus, climbed in across from the driver's seat. Ray was sleeping like a baby in the back of the bus.

She packed her suitcase; some items she would have to leave behind. When she finished she bent down over Ray's closed eyelids and gave him one final kiss on his left eyelid. She couldn't risk kissing his right eyelid, or the lips she had kissed so many times. She left him a note. *Please don't wait for me to come back because I'm not coming back to this shit hole.*

The lights were off in Mason Rackstraw's windows as Flo drove away in Ray's panel truck.

SOME OF THE things Flo had left behind Ray took with him to the trailer. She had left a hairbrush beside the driver's seat, miscellaneous items in a seat near the back of the bus—Bic razors she shaved her legs with, a brass bracelet a little too large for her wrist, two photographs of them in Portland, in the rose gardens of Washington Park, holding hands on Pioneer Square. She left her thrift store shirt with its dirty beige diamond lettered WOMAN AT WORK. He would have kept these items in the school bus but he knew Flo wasn't coming back. So he moved himself and the bed out of the school bus and made room for the bed in the trailer workshop. He put the hairbrush, the bracelet, and the photographs in an empty shoebox without a lid, and set it at the foot of the bed. He left the razors on the seat near the back of the bus. The thrift store shirt he draped over the steering wheel of a school bus that wasn't going to run anymore.

Late one Sunday night Ray was cutting out school bus number twenty. His fingertips pushed the sheet of plywood into the blade of the saw. He had to concentrate, or lose a finger. When he finished, he turned off the bandsaw. Ray kept his eyes on the cutout. He would finish it, paint it, mount it. He would put it in with the other school buses, in the parking lot of his little school, at various points along the routes.

Mason Rackstraw had a bottle stashed somewhere in the house, but he hadn't brought it out here with him. He stepped over the shoebox at the foot of the bed and ran his fingers along the bandsaw's teeth. "I came out here to tell you I'm going to report a stolen vehicle."

"I don't want the police involved." Ray moved a schoolboy getting off of a bus outside the cone of the light on his father's bald head. "And I'd appreciate it if you stayed out of this."

"You can't collect on the policy on a vehicle that hasn't been stolen."

"That truck is just as much Flo's as mine."

"The title is in your name, Ray. That means you're the owner."

"Titles mean nothing to me. They're legal documents, nothing more."

"You're the one who should go to the police, but if you won't I will."

"That you're not going to do," Ray said.

"Don't be telling me what to do, little man." Mason Rackstraw was thumping his fist in his hand. "Let me tell you who's going to hear about this. My good friend Chief Cosgrave will hear about this because I'm going to tell him personally you know where your panel truck has gotten to."

"You do that. Oregon's one big place."

"Chief Cosgrave will know how to find that woman. He'll have her back here in no time. All I have to do is pick up the phone." Mason nudged Flo's shoebox with his foot, toed the bristles in Flo's hairbrush. "All I want is that truck back, son."

Ray picked up a claw hammer. A cutout of Homer Brown, his daddy Mason Rackstraw, there was the chief, don't forget Chief Cosgrave, they were all there where he'd put them. A school bus had its flat STOP arm out. Because the things he'd created wouldn't move Ray might have cracked his daddy's head like an egg. But he knew it was too late for that.

Once his daddy was out of the trailer, out of the trailer and out of his life, Ray finished the school bus he was working on. He painted it and set it up with the others. He cut out another school bus and he painted that one too. Then he went outside and put on his sandwich boards. He couldn't picket downtown on Sunday night, nobody would be there. So he'd do his picketing in his own backyard. From the Sno-Cone sign to the school bus, counting steps, one and two and three and four and five and six.

Chief Cosgrave was standing in front of the Sno-Cone sign.

"If I'm wrong, Chief, please set me straight, but I believe you are trespassing on my daddy's property."

Chief Cosgrave's flashlight beam cut a figure eight on the school bus windows. "It was your daddy who asked me to come here. He told me you threatened to bop him on the head with a claw hammer. And there's a matter of a missing panel truck. You wouldn't happen to know what happened to it?" The chief stopped wiggling the flashlight beam because he had to turn off his scanner.

"Anyone could have stolen it. I'm always leaving the keys in that truck."

Chief Cosgrave sidled along the Sno-Cone sign. He zigged the flashlight beam up and down, in Ray's face, at his feet. "All right, we'll forget about the truck. And what you nearly did to your daddy, I'm willing to overlook that too." Chief Cosgrave produced and lit up a cigar without interrupting his flashlight performance. "Let me tell you something, Ray. My daddy was like your daddy was once. He used to whale the living daylights out of me. Or he'd come up behind me and kick my ass if he even suspected I'd done something wrong. Hell, I even thought he was right. But if it had gone on, I might have done something drastic. I might have gotten myself in big trouble. But it didn't go on. Something happened." Chief Cosgrave took his cigar out of his mouth, put it in again, took it out, training the flashlight beam at Ray's feet. "My daddy, he got pissed off at me once because I wouldn't bring him the newspaper. He got out of the porch swing and tried to kick my ass one time too many. He was chasing me all over the front yard, and he skidded on one of my roller skates. Oh yes, I was to blame for that too, but it didn't matter who was to blame because my daddy, he broke his right leg in two places. All those weeks he was laid up, he thought about what had happened to him. After that, he didn't kick my ass. Not once did he kick my ass or lift a finger against me in anger. He was careful not to get near me after that."

Ray wished he had learned how to roller skate, but since he hadn't, what did Chief Cosgrave's story have to do with him? "I never hit my daddy with that hammer."

"You might have killed him. You know that, Ray. If you had, my problems would be over."

"Well I didn't and they aren't."

"Oh aren't they? I think they are. Because, you see, either you get your ass out of Ott or I run you in for disturbing the peace. I mean now. Right here in this backyard."

Ray couldn't believe that could happen, not in his daddy's own backyard. But the chief's glowing cigar said it could. So did the lights in the neighbors' windows, doors opening, people coming out of doors and hanging out of windows, including Mason Rackstraw brushing his teeth.

"You can see for yourself, you are disturbing the peace. I mean as long as you have a potential for disturbing the peace and folks are around to be disturbed, I can arrest you. I've talked to our mayor about this, and our mayor he talked to Judge Popwell. Judge Popwell construes disturbing the peace as potentially disturbing the peace, even if the accused is on his own property. And this backyard isn't even your property. So every time you turn on that bandsaw, well draw your own conclusions. You'll get six months in jail for sure. In my jail. How's that suit you?"

Ray saw what Chief Cosgrave was driving at, and he also saw him put out his cigar and unhitch the handcuffs on his belt.

"You coming quietly, or are you leaving this town?"

Chief Cosgrave kept the flashlight beam puddled at Ray's feet so Ray would be able to think about the choice he had. But Ray didn't want to think about anything. Instead he looked for a sign, in the sky, where else?

The sky looked like it usually looked when there was cloud cover, no stars visible. Then an old woman who had had a life once, a ghost woman coasted out from behind a cloud, her arms spread out like she was doing a swan dive from a very high diving board, dipping down over Ray's school bus, trailing flaky sparks like a comet, zooming up again, up up in the sky, into a cloud bank, gone forever.

THERE WERE DAYS when Flo Mayfield saw Ray all over Portland. Passing the Church of Elvis, Flo thought she had seen Ray entering. Flo had seen Ray wearing blue sunglasses in the Washington Park Rose Garden. Looking out over Portland from Washington Park, she saw Ray floating over Mount Hood.

Sitting quietly on her favorite bench on Pioneer Square, Flo was watching a woman with frowsy gray hair play "Blue Skies." The woman's music was attached to a music stand with a pretty pink plastic clothespin. The sky overhead was darkening. Not a chance, Flo thought, for the sky to be blue, not today, tomorrow, she would see. It hadn't started to rain yet. Two teen girls in red ponchos went by. "That's exactly what I said to him," one said, "what did you think I would say?"

When she saw Ray get off the trolley, Flo wouldn't go to him right away because a school bus on Pioneer Square had to stop in front of her. Its STOP arm shot out. Flo waited for it to fold in.

Kelp

Here is Carl doing his dance in the parking lot. Carl works for Florida Power, but he thinks of himself as a potter. He does pottery and takes it to arts and crafts fairs. Kathy told me they couldn't afford the trip out here, even though Carl wanted to see Oregon, so I offered to pay for his place on the coast. I didn't want them spending much time at home because Tony wouldn't go for that.

Tony has gone into his shell. This happened before, in Menlo Park. I could understand it then. His mother died of emphysema. Tony couldn't grieve and he couldn't forget, so our life went bad. In Oregon we started over. Tony got a good job with Hewlett-Packard, in Corvallis. We bought a nice house in a suburb. We'd had two good years together. Then Tony goes into his shell again. Lying in bed beside Tony, I think of us playing the alphabet game, the four of us driving to the coast. I see an A. I hear Holly say that's on a license plate. No license plates, I hear Tony say, that makes the alphabet game too easy gang.

Here is Carl in the parking lot, scuffed cowboy boots, black Levis, blue denim shirt with the sleeves hacked off, gray, black-beaded Stetson. I have all this on the camcorder. Carl picks up my daughter Holly and swings her up off her feet. Carl's big hands encircling her small hands, this big man towering over her, Carl swings her through whirling space. My turn! Now it's John's turn. Carl swings John out by the wrists. John yells but nothing will happen to him. I tighten my grip on the camcorder. What we did that night on the beach, yes pulling me out of myself. If I could take it back I would, I have this brass bell in my brain that deafens me with its nos. With Tony the nos are padded felt, of a piece with our way of life.

Here is one last shot of the Oregon coast. The lighthouse tipping the headland like a giant brow in a mountainous head, the endlessly incoming heaving waves, I get that all on tape. I put the camcorder back in its case, jauntily sling the strap over my bony shoulder, grope in my purse for my car keys, remember I gave them to Carl.

Carl tells Kathy, sit in the back seat with the kids. Carl will be the navigator. Kathy spreads out in the back seat. She has put on more weight since we went to the coast. She tears open a package of pretzels, gets settled for the ride to Corvallis. It's hard to believe she was thin once, really pretty. She didn't have to wear a bra when we were girls in Florida.

We can't do the alphabet game, for there aren't many road signs on this road. Kathy does whale riddles with the kids. What did the whale do when his piano sounded funny? Holly says he called the piano tuna. What did the whale do when he couldn't pay his bills? He called a loan shark, from Holly again. Two days ago we went whale watching. I have it on tape, the backs of the whales and their tail flukes sliding out of the sea. The swells were deep down, not choppy. That's how it felt up front on deck. I was keying in to deep-down swells. My turn! My turn!

Kathy hung over the stern rail, seasick, spitting, miserable. She wouldn't ask Carl to turn back. He'd rented the boat for two hours. Carl wasn't with either one of us. He was above us, on top of the cabin, up with our boatman who's letting Carl steer, his hands on the wheel, his face pushing into the wind.

There is an accident up ahead on the road. Cars are lined up ahead of us. No sign yet of an ambulance. Carl gets out with Holly and John. I tape Carl flapping his Stetson, whooping, going yi yi yi. Carl does what he feels like doing. The day I met their flight in Portland, we had a picnic lunch in Washington Park, in the rose gardens looking out at Mount Hood. I had to bat away the honeybees. Carl let a bee light on his ham and cheese sandwich and opened his mouth to eat it. Bee sandwich, he said, and snapped his teeth. It's on tape. Carl's bee sandwich, Kathy's submarine, my wispy watercress.

About an hour away from Corvallis we come to a railroad crossing sign. The sign is precautionary. Do not loiter on the tracks, it says, for the unwary. Kathy and Carl say the sign is a joke but for me it isn't that funny. People need to be told to look out for themselves. I say a child could get hit on his bicycle. Just waiting around for the train says Carl. Kathy says there are too many signs out here. She says no one in Florida would put signs in the fields, like rye grass, corn. I point out reddish brown from a field. When the rye grass is cut the fields are burned off—that isn't labeled, I say to Kathy. Kathy complains about no smoking signs, do this, do that signs. She says there are too many no-nos today. I let this pass, keep my eyes on the road.

We stop in Corvallis for groceries and beer. Carl buys a case of Oregon beer, microbrewed here in Oregon. I'm aware that he's picked out a cheaper brand. He carries the case of beer to the car. I look off at the hills, the Douglas firs, the hazed-over mountains behind the hills. Holly has to go to the bathroom. Kathy crosses the road with Holly to the convenience store's clean women's rest room. I have Holly on tape pulling Kathy's hand. Carl comes up behind me. He puts his hands on my hips. He takes the camcorder. He tells me he wants me on tape. You're doing all the taping. Know what that means. Means you're not here. So I pose for Carl as Miss Sultry Siren, hands on hips, come-hither smile. Then I thank Carl for going for beer. He doesn't have to know it isn't our brand.

Here we are at nine-o-one Spruce Lane. Carl's standing on his head, his long legs and back and buttocks reversed, elbows out, triceps on view. Kathy's outside on the patio. She's smoking another cigarette. I've lost track of how many she's smoked today. She smoked in the back seat coming back from the coast. My daughter Holly's opposed to smoking. She also keeps tabs on how much I drink. If I have more than two glasses of wine, I hear about it from Holly. I had my third glass during dinner. The children are watching Carl's headstand. Tony must be behind me for I feel his breath on the back of my neck. He wants me tonight, of that I am sure. But it won't be like it was once.

Here we are in the hot tub, Kathy, John, Holly, and me. Pools and streamers of churning suds circulate in our heated water. The tiles are blue, the rim is white, the boards are treated, resinous oak. A birdhouse hangs over Kathy's head, friendly, red pine fence colored. One of our Oregon finches tunes up.

Carl has the camcorder. The eye of the camcorder covers his eyes. I lower myself into the water, crossing my arms to conceal my breasts. Kathy cradles her breasts in her hands, stands up, sloshing water. She asks Carl to get her a cigarette. John and flat-chested Holly hop up and down like wary birds. Carl isn't going to get in the hot tub with us. He says he's allergic to hot tubs. They soften him up like too much sleep. Hot tubs are for softies, he says.

Here we are on the patio. Carl is wearing his netted shirt. Now I see the tattoo on his chest again—a hula girl and a mermaid in sun-slicked colored inks. Here's Tony doing yard work. It's Saturday, weeding and mulching day. Tony uncoils the garden hose, untangles a looped green snakelike snarl that has unaccountably configured. Kelp that night on the beach—feels like, looks like garden hose. Or swollen scallions, soggy, spongy leeks with yellow green leaves like artichoke leaves. K in the alphabet game. Now I try to reverse the comparison. A garden hose feels like kelp, even here in my own backyard.

Tony's weeder is kicking up dirt. Weeding goes on with him constantly.

— Any word on when Carl will stop being Carl?

— I haven't heard. Maybe after he leaves.

— Seems to me you left Carl's type in Florida.

I am holding the garden hose, watching Carl sweep off the patio with pronounced, exaggerated strokes of the broom.

— Things that get left can come back again.

— Like Carl and your sister. How many proms was she queen of?

— Two. One in high school. One in college.

— And the best she could come up with was Carl?

— Yes, the very best.

— Don't forget, she was also a cheerleader. Which you weren't.

— I didn't need to be, not for you.

But Tony knows I don't mean it, not in the way I would have once. Carl waves at me, and I try not to smile at him. Tony he goes on weeding. He's squatting, his knobby knees spread like a little man I could pick up and kiss, but not now, not how I am now.

Here are Tony and Carl watching a documentary about catching alligators that Tony's sister in Florida videotaped. The tape was run on Tampa TV and won a prize in a state competition. Tony and Carl drink our microbrewed beer. The fine points of catching alligators are demonstrated by an expert. You grip them firmly by the snout. There are classes, teachers, students. The teacher is showing his sweet young thing how to grip an alligator's snout.

I'm taping two men watching a videotape. Tony's never been close to an alligator. The tape ends where it began with a cracker woman who lost one hand to a gator she didn't spot in time. She got back to the road and flagged down a car and got to the emergency room in time.

The alligators are doped with a hypo, netted and taken to tourist traps where tourists with cameras take photographs of gators chomping raw chicken meat. Carl turns, gives me a wink.

Here we are having dinner. I did a meatless lasagna. Kathy did a spinach casserole. Carl says he will do the dishes. He does them at home but not all the time, only when Kathy lets them pile up. Carl does all the plumbing and wiring, and he carries the garbage out. Kathy does all the woman's work. Kathy tells us she'd rather have it that way. She'll do as she was brought up to do.

— I do like I was brought up to do. Carl does what he wants to do. If Carl wants to go fishing that's what he does. Kathy talks out of one side of her mouth when she's uncomfortable and doesn't want to show it.

— If there's something he wants that I don't want he goes after it without asking me.

— I don't just ask you, Kathy. I tell you what I want. If you don't like what I want to do, then I think twice about doing it.

Holly asks Carl what he does, what it is Carl thinks twice about? Carl says you wouldn't be interested. It is Kathy who cares what Carl does.

— I let Carl know what he can and can't do.

— You will do that, Carl says.

— Most of the time I let you know. And I draw the line on some things.

— Like what, Uncle Carl, from Holly.

Carl grins.

— Like sharing my secrets with little girls. That's one thing your aunt draws the line at.

— What secrets?

Holly, please don't ask, we don't want to know Carl's secrets.

Tony's salad fork stays close to his lips. I'm afraid he'll get up from the table. I might have to handle this by myself unless Tony takes the kids with him.

— Carl hasn't got any secrets. He has things he wants to keep quiet about.

Carl picks up the pepper shaker. He has this magical shrinking powder. It shrinks nosy children to the size of mice. I breathe easy. I see that Kathy is relieved. Tony doesn't get up from the table. Carl looks at Holly then at John. He shakes pepper out on the palm of one hand and rubs his hands together.

— Who wants pepper? Who's first?

Here we are playing volleyball at nine-o-one Spruce Lane. Our friends, the Lamars, are here, and our other friends, the Vanmeters. Carl's team is trailing by six points. It doesn't matter who wins, but I know Carl wants to win. I see Carl waving the Stetson going yi yi yi on the road coming back from the coast. He's wearing the Levi's, the netted shirt. His hula girl twists and his mermaid flops. By the time

Carl's breath slows down, they are in their usual dance and splash.

Our second game isn't on tape. I'm playing, Kathy's watching. Kathy smokes on the patio. Tony calls Carl's serve out of bounds, although even to me it looks on the line. But we don't have a line, just grass. It's hard to judge but Carl says no. Carl says the ball landed inside the line. Tony says the ball landed outside. See where the grass is matted. This is happening at nine-o-one.

— I say the serve was out of bounds.

— Come on, Carl, see for yourself.

Here we are after our guests have gone home, drinking microbrewed beer on the patio. Carl's ticked off about the volleyball game. Tony's not happy either. I say let's all take a walk. Kathy has to let her fingernails dry and she'd rather drink our Oregon beer than take a walk in our neighborhood. Tony says he'd rather do yard work. Holly and John want to take a walk, they want to show Carl the neighborhood. Carl says okay show me. They grab his hands and pull on his arms. Tony gets up, goes into the house. I talk to Tony inside the house. Can't you try to be sociable for a change. He says he's been doing that too long. He has yard work to do. So do it, I say.

I get a telephone call from a neighbor. He says this weirdo is with your kids, whooping and hollering. I put down the phone and run out to the street. I'm hearing them, all three of them. Holly and John are barefoot, and John is carrying their shoes and socks. Tony is right behind me in the station wagon. Tony's pissed but not showing it. You guys enjoy your walk, he says. Tony drives off with Holly and John. Maybe he's taking them to Jack Lamar's, or maybe he'll drive them around for awhile. I can look at Carl without Kathy because Kathy has gone to the guest bedroom. Kathy might take her shoes off, flop down on the bed.

I can't take my eyes off Carl's fishtail. The colors are clashing on Carl's chest. Things go on in my brain. Carl bares his teeth. Bee sandwich. Who cares who sees us together? Not Tony, he's in the station wagon working his way through damage control. Holly and John are with Tony. I touch Carl's chest through the netted shirt. His hands slide down my hips. I remember Carl slathered over with kelp, coming on and on like a god for me, the crash of the wave jolting through me. Carl takes me in his arms. We're turning, we're dancing. The summer foliage expands, compounds, and butterflies are going yi yi yi.

Here are photographs in an album. Here's where we live, Spruce Lane. Here's Kathy with Holly in her lap. Here's Holly. Here's Carl. Why are you wearing a netted shirt? But I don't care. You wear it Carl. And Tony, you keep on weeding the yard. You stay in your shell. In a photograph one is supposed to smile. Family photographs are usually cheery. Here's Carl and his bee sandwich. I'm wearing huge circular earrings like tiny inner tubes. I'm hoping they will keep me afloat.

Tony's had it with Carl so Carl has to go. I tell Tony all right, Carl has to go but not before their flight leaves Portland. I'm driving us to Portland today. We play the alphabet game three times on the trip. Kathy runs out of whale riddles.

Here we are at the terminal. I tell Kathy I'll come visit her. Kathy says she wants me to visit, but I know she doesn't mean it. I won't kiss Carl on the lips but I can, I will kiss Kathy. We pucker our lips, squinch up our eyes, we kiss each other goodbye.

It is Carl who has the camcorder. It is Carl who gets us on tape.

Mr. Hardcastle

After Katie and I called it quits, she took up with this ball bearing salesman, Freddie Snipes, and they got married and moved to Valdosta, Georgia. Freddie Snipes wanted to adopt my son Tommy, but I wasn't letting him do that, even though the child support was hurting me. In the last four months, I had only been to visit Tommy once, and that hadn't turned out well. I got into it with Freddie Snipes, over being behind on the child support. Katie had to pull me off of him.

Lately, I had been spending my Sunday afternoons fishing on the Alabama River with Cole Hoskins. He was a house painter at Dixie Paint. His trailer was down the road from mine, and if you kept on going down that road you got to the Alabama River. I still went fishing with Cole Sunday afternoons even though Cole's wife Charlene and I were seeing each other on Saturday afternoons. Cole made it easy for me to be with Charlene. On Saturday afternoon he took their daughter, Dyan, their little four-year-old, downtown with him; she was with him shaking a tambourine while he preached on a street corner half a block from the state liquor store.

One Sunday afternoon while we were fishing, Cole told me about his eye problem. He had trouble reading his Bible unless he kept his left eye closed. They came and went, these zigzagging motes in his eyes. He was afraid he might be going blind, and he didn't know what to do about it.

I was still doing odd jobs for my neighbor across the road, Elinor

Williams. I'd replaced I don't no how many thirty-amp fuses for Elinor. Elinor used to tell me the next time she married it wouldn't be for love or money. She'd marry a man who knew how to do the things she couldn't do for herself. After I put in a float in Elinor's toilet tank one Saturday afternoon, I brought up Cole's vision problem. Elinor looked up at me from a novel she was reading, sipped on her Canadian Mist and soda. I felt the sun's flat rays heat up my neck and moved my lawn chair in toward Elinor.

"Cole says he won't go to an eye doctor."

I knew Elinor would set me straight. "Who says he has to, Wesley." All my friends but her call me Wes. I'm just beginning to get used to Wesley from her. "Tell Cole he should go to a drugstore and buy a pair of readers. That would be a lot cheaper than going to an eye doctor." She took another big sip on her Canadian. I didn't know how she put so much away every day. Catch her early enough in the afternoon, what she said still made some kind of sense. "All Cole has to do is put his readers on and he can read his Bible to his heart's content. You tell Cole these drugstore glasses are cheap. He can get a pair for nine ninety-five. I'm sure that's what you must want to tell him so I won't say anymore about it now."

Elinor dipped down to her book, waiting for me to say something. Instead I asked myself just what had made her settle down in this trailer park. She liked it here by the river, with your kind of people, she told me once, because she was so far away from the people she'd known while she'd been married to Rutherford. She'd moved back here from Athens, Georgia, to not far from where she'd grown up, which was just this side of Wetumpka. Rutherford was a paleontologist at the University of Georgia. She had never had much in common with him, so their marriage hadn't lasted very long. Rutherford would talk your ear off about fossils, she'd say, but he didn't know beans about the human heart. She'd say the human heart, for Rutherford, was just a muscle.

The novels Elinor read meant nothing to Rutherford, less than nothing he used to tell her, because they weren't about people who did something in the real world. I didn't know Rutherford, didn't want to. But he might have been right about Elinor's novels. She kept them in her mother's bookcase, a golden-oak job with glass doors which she had with her now, in her trailer. The binding was loose on the novel she was reading—a long one with pen and ink illustrations, a Victorian novel, she'd told me once. I offered to slap some tape on it, but she knew I had this other thing on my mind. She was waiting for me to get to Charlene Hoskins.

Instead I asked her about Mr. Hardcastle, what was he up to today, in what looked like about two fingers worth of her novel.

"Is Mr. Hardcastle still blaming the wind for how he feels?" I asked her, swinging my foot up across my knee. Mr. Hardcastle blamed everything on the wind. If the wind was blowing from the north, he'd say that's why I'm pissed off today. From the south, hey man I feel just great. From the east he'd be crying a bucket. From the west he didn't give a shit about anybody. "I never knew a dude like Mr. Hardcastle," I told her.

"Well you see he's a little eccentric. That's how he's supposed to be. The wind can do Mr. Hardcastle that way because he's a character in a novel."

"You ask me, he's a weirdo."

"You, Wesley, might think so because you don't know what winds blow your life around."

"Are you telling me I'm not in control of my life?"

"I'm only saying you could be more in control. So for that matter could Mr. Hardcastle. That's why he's in this book, so the reader can judge for himself how wrong it is for Mr. Hardcastle to attribute everything he feels to the direction of the wind. His putting everything on the wind is irresponsible of him. If you read this book you would see that."

I sensed Elinor was floating up over the pines, above the trailers, way up over the river, and since I didn't want to pop her little balloon I said, "If you ever get finished with that novel, you lend it to me and I'll read it. I mean carefully."

"Yes, carefully, Wesley, that you should do."

I let the subject of Mr. Hardcastle alone because I had something else to talk to Elinor about. I told Elinor Charlene and I had had a fight last Saturday, last time I'd seen her. Instead of dragging her off downtown so she could shake that tambourine, Cole had taken Dyan to see Charlene's grandparents in Montgomery. I had to tell Charlene she should be the one to do that. That should be your job, not Cole's, I told her. Charlene told me to stay out of her life with Cole. I said I'd try to do that in the future, and she said we wouldn't have a future if I didn't give her and Cole some respect.

I got a strong beam of disapproval, not Elinor's usual fuzzy focusing. "Here you are sleeping with this woman and you think you should run her life. If Charlene stopped washing the dishes for Cole, you'd probably come down on her for that."

Reaching over to pick up her glass, she let her other hand run through her matted gray hair like she needed to loosen it up. "Let me tell you something, Wesley. I tried sleeping around for awhile. About a year after Rutherford left me I would go to the bar at the Holiday Inn. I'd go on weeknights, when men my age were there. They'd be moving on the next day, so both of us knew what the score was. But Charlene, she obviously doesn't know the score. She thinks she can keep Cole for a husband and have you on Saturday afternoons."

"Remind me to ask her what she thinks. I mean who knows what goes on in Charlene's head?"

"You don't know because you don't want to. You're only interested in yourself."

I saw a lizard crawling off the patio and thought of Cole going blind. He wouldn't be able to lace his boots or squint down the barrel of a shotgun. Charlene came out of their trailer and dropped a bag of garbage in the garbage can. She had on the tight cutoffs she was wearing the first time I knocked on her door. She waved at me from down the road, and I waved back, knowing I'd go to her unless Cole and Dyan came back from downtown while I was sitting here. If he did I'd tell him what Elinor told me, you get some readers and see if they don't help you see better.

COLE WASN'T WORRIED about going blind anymore. He had bought a pair of readers, and right away the zigzagging motes went away, and he was able to read his Bible again. He put them on while we were ordering our lunch at Burger King, reading off today's specials to me. He took them off while he ate his Whopper, wiping his fingers carefully once he'd popped the last fry into his mouth. He picked the readers up and carefully hooked the temples over his ears, just to make sure they were still working. Cole got to talking about Bible movies, what Hollywood did to the Bible, twisted and changed it, Cole said. I asked Cole why that mattered since some of the things in the Bible plain just didn't happen. I said no one Israelite could slay that many Philistines with the jawbone of an ass.

Cole's blue eyes never wavered. "What you don't understand when you say that, Wes, is what the good Lord is showing us. He's showing us He can intervene in our lives just like He did in their lives. He helped Samson smite his enemies, and then He punished Samson for sinning."

"So how would the Lord intervene in your life? What does Samson have to do with you?"

Cole spoke slowly, without raising his voice. "Samson's story has everything to do with me. It warns me to shun the harlot's bed. I'm a man. I can be tempted. I was tempted and I gave in. The Lord has seen fit to punish me."

I didn't want to ask how it happened. I made myself look at Cole's blue eyes, still set on the path he was following.

"Charlene had gone to the Gulf Coast with Dyan to see her mama. I was painting houses at the time. We had this woman in our crew. Rena Latham. Rena asked me to take her home one Friday night."

"That all you have to tell me, Cole?"

"No, that's just the beginning. Saturday morning, Rena Latham shows up at my house. She's all dressed up, ringing the doorbell on me. She's wearing this pretty flowered dress. I was hoping I had locked the door, but I hadn't. I didn't know what to do next."

"So you waited for her to come in. Or you went to the door and let her in?"

"She had walked from her house to my house. I went to the door and let her in."

A man and his wife and two teenage girls wearing shorts and not much on top came in, moved on to gawk at the specials. I heard something beep, the French fry machine, or maybe it was an oven somewhere, letting us know that its time was up, whatever was in the oven. We won't be letting you guys out alive, was what the beeper might have been saying.

"I knew right then I would pay for it, but for a long time nothing happened to me. Then one night in that same house Charlene and I were together in bed. We heard someone ring the doorbell. Charlene said I should answer it and I told her, Charlene it's midnight. I told her someone must have the wrong house, but that doorbell kept on ringing."

"And you answered it?"

"No way," Cole said. "I let the doorbell ring until it stopped."

"Are you saying that had something to do with the Lord?"

"I'm saying it did," Cole said. "I'm saying it was like the Bible says, when the Lord comes down on sinners. He was letting me know I'd done wrong before He came down on me for it."

I had to ask Cole how the Lord came down on him. Cole didn't hesitate to tell me how.

"The next time I tried to make love to Charlene, I couldn't do anything, Wes. It's been going on for a long time now, ever since I heard that doorbell ringing."

Coming back with their trays of fast food, this family had nothing to say to us, not the father with his tiny mustache or the mother with her big handbag swinging and swaying and bumping her hip, the girls with their acne and silly talk, they kept to themselves. Cole put his head in his hands. I looked at Cole's coffee getting cold, the slashed pink packets of Sweet'ner.

I HAD SEX with Charlene again while Cole was preaching downtown. There were the two of them on a street corner, Cole preaching, Dyan shaking the tambourine. I passed them on my way to the state liquor store for tequila and margarita mix. I thought of stopping and listening to Cole. He had a permit to use speakers, so his voice carried all the way to my car. He had to compete with the traffic, a burring monotone of passing vehicles. Cole was going on about Sodom. The Sodomites were hardened sinners. Lot never should have tried to reason with them. Nobody paid Cole any attention, not even when Cole brought in fire and brimstone.

COLE WOULDN'T BE fishing with me for awhile, not on his Sunday afternoons. He would be painting his church, working for the Lord, he told me at Burger King, the French fry machine dinging away. I told him he didn't have to sacrifice his Sunday afternoons, and he said since he'd talked to me he'd decided he had to serve the Lord first.

"Charlene says I should get paid for painting the church, that our church can afford to pay me. I've thought about that a lot, how much it means to me now not to get paid." Cole's simple blue eyes bored into mine. "I mean it's helping me accept the Lord's will," he said. "That's all that matters."

"For you. But what about Charlene? What about your little girl Dyan? Don't they matter?" I wanted to get across to him he'd better climb down off that church steeple.

"Of course they matter. Don't you understand, Wes, if I'm right with the Lord, then I'll be right with them too."

So I did my fishing by myself, and for awhile I felt that was the right thing to do. Cole would go his own way, and I would go mine. A crosswind was blowing my line around, so I had to shift my boat around so the stern was into the wind. I got to thinking about Mr. Hardcastle, would the wind have affected his fishing? What would it be like to be him, I thought. If the wind was right would I be a good man and give up this thing with Charlene? Would a north wind make me blow my top and a south wind cause me to laugh like hell or like

Mr. Hardcastle ride my good steed over the moors, and let no one get in my way? Would a west wind send me back to my bed with the drapes pulled and the lights out?

It was time to get back to fishing. I had the idea of trying it close to the shore, so I took off my beetle spin lure. I worked the tail of my worm lure into the shank of the hook, about to snug it up to the eye of the hook. I stuck myself with the eye of the hook, something I almost never do. I slashed the ball of my thumb working the barb loose. I had the anchor down and the river was calm, nothing stronger than slow-moving wavelets.

Out here on this aluminum boat with no one, entirely on my own—what if I had a heart attack? Bad things I had done came back to me, back when I was married to Katie. One time Katie showed me a letter from an old boyfriend she had before she had Freddie Snipes, and I hit her; I slapped her hard. The river glittering with sunspots, it brought back the sweep of my open hand, the flat pop, Katie's face jerking.

It wasn't long before I hauled up the anchor and dropped the bass I'd caught back in the water. I took the boat back in to the boat dock, and hitched it to the boat trailer. I got in my car and drove to Cole's trailer. Charlene was outside getting her mail. She was flipping through a stack of junk mail. I could tell she wasn't happy to see me show up. She bit her lower lip, turned, and made the strip of carpeting outside the front door. I had to go to her, that's how she wanted it. She set the junk mail on the gas grill, pulled her hip huggers up. Dyan, she told me, was inside watching TV so I couldn't come in.

Right away she had to talk about Cole. "I see you been fishing without Cole?"

"That's right. He says he'd rather paint the church steeple."

"I think it's better that way," she said. Charlene put her hands on her hips, her eyes narrowing like she was going to lecture me, like it was my fault Cole was painting the church. The sun blazed on the blue carpeting. I heard the window unit rumbling, thought it's cool inside but I knew I wouldn't be going inside. Charlene wiggled her toenails, patted one sandal on the carpeting. Her voice, when it came, was distant.

"Look there's something I ought to tell you. About how Cole came to find the Lord."

I slid my feet away, looked at Charlene. "Okay," I said to her, "tell me how Cole came to find the Lord."

Through a gap in the legs of the gas grill, a green lizard crawled past Charlene's toenails, without her seeing it since she was staring at me, crawling inch by inch along the carpeting Cole had tacked down, a cheery sky-blue surface for lizards. I was about to stomp on it, would have if it hadn't melted into a shimmying blob.

"Cole's first wife ran off from him. He couldn't get over losing her. He wanted to throw his life away." What Charlene was saying, dwelling on, I knew it meant something to her, but it didn't mean anything to me. "Cole told me he got in his car one day and drove out on County Road 179. He was going to drive his car into the first big truck he came across. It would have happened, but something else happened instead. Cole saw a little girl on a tricycle, and he forgot about ending his life. He stopped the car right away, and got out—she couldn't have been more than three years old. He asked her where she lived, and she told him. Cole put the tricycle in the back seat and took this little girl home. It was this little girl that saved Cole's life."

It took a lot of concentration, but I made those tufts of blue carpeting come back again, Cole's well-spaced carpet tacks showing forth for me. The lizard had gone its own way. So it was easy for me to say something Charlene would want to hear. "That little girl, who was she?"

"It was the preacher's little girl, at this country church."

"The preacher's little girl. If that isn't something."

"You ask me it was a miracle, Wes."

I thought of Cole up on a ladder, slapping paint on the boards of the squat little steeple that seemed stuck on, not actually nailed down or in some way built, the sun beating down on the back of his neck, Cole painting his way down from the steeple because he thought the

Lord wanted him to. I would have said it, where does that leave you and me, Charlene, just to get started again with Charlene, make her feel like having sex with me was okay, but I couldn't speak, I couldn't even move. Sunspots flashed on the gas grill. I couldn't blink the green blob away.

I didn't have sex with Charlene that afternoon. I spent the afternoon in my trailer with a cold wash rag on my forehead. I watched the Braves lose to the Marlins. In the seventh inning I remembered the date, July twenty-fifth. Today not tomorrow, was my son Tommy's birthday. I had sent him a present, a Tinkertoy set, and a birthday card in time for both to get there. He was four years old but I had forgotten, not that he would soon be four years old, I had forgotten today was the twenty-fifth, not the twenty-fourth.

I turned off the TV and picked up the telephone and called Katie, but all I got was a busy signal. An hour later I called again. All I got was the answering machine. I told myself I would call later. I told myself I would get in my car and drive down to Valdosta tonight.

Once the sun went down and it cooled off outside, I left my place and walked over to Elinor's. I knocked but she didn't come to the door. I heard her tell me to come on in. She was sitting in her favorite chair, by the bookcase in front of the television set. She was listening to the radio. The radio was turned down low, and the music was soft, music for dancing I said to myself, only I didn't feel like dancing. She had the lights off, her book in her lap. A mug of black coffee sat close at hand, on a low wicker table in front of her. She had positioned a chair beside her, for me.

"There's a can of beer in the fridge if you want one."

I didn't want one, not tonight.

There wasn't much light in the trailer. A moth lit on Elinor's novel, then spiraled on up to the ceiling light as if it had been caught in a tornado. Mr. Hardcastle, I got to thinking of him again. Had the same wind that blew him around blown the moth up to the ceiling light? But that couldn't be, except in my mind. I remembered this old man I used to see when I lived in Birmingham. This old man was vigorous for his age. He turned up all over the city. That's how this old man spent his life, moving from one public place to another, hospitals, the public library, city parks. He had a bald head and a gray beard, and in warm weather he wore his shirtsleeves rolled up.

The books in the bookcase, the bindings were running together so I had to look back at Elinor. I saw her clearly for a little while, closing her book, marking her place with a bookmark. She picked the mug up with both hands, sipped on the coffee, set the mug back down, her hands jittering from the effort.

"This thing with Charlene, it's doing things to my eyesight."

"Your eyesight isn't your problem." Elinor turned off the radio. She moved her chair close to mine. "Your shiftless way of life, that's your problem."

"Shiftless is how I have to live."

"You have to do better than that."

Fork tines, I felt them scratching my eyes. My left eye was burning, specks jittering, zigzagging floaters speeding up. Floaters, that's all they were, no way I would go blind.

"You can change, Wesley. You can be a new man."

A new man, like Cole Hoskins on Highway 179, saving that little girl on a tricycle? I'd just as soon stay like I was, but that wasn't helping any. Sooner or later tonight I'd have to go back to my place. I might go in the other direction first, go past Cole's trailer and on to the river. I'd take off my clothes and jump in, swim upstream, against the current, let the current carry me back. I felt the floaters settle like sand in a pool; they would go away pretty soon. All I had to do was get out of Elinor's chair, do something, keep on the move.

Elinor took my hands in hers. This woman half again my age, I didn't want her to let go of my hands. That's when I got down on my knees and thanked her for believing I could change. That's how the wind was blowing for me.

Remission

The sun was out, but it was windy and cold. My wife Dorinda was spraying her plants with water and concentrated dish liquid. She was dressed to go to Atlanta. Her high heels clicked on the screen porch floor as she moved from one plant to the next.

The plants were standing on the screen porch. She had watered the plants this morning, with the garden hose before she got dressed. Diagonal roof beam shadows crossed a translucent sheet of plastic—only last month ineptly staple-gunned to the two-by-fours of the screen porch. What we actually had was a deck that we had converted into a screen porch, after much hard labor and many harsh words. Dorinda moved from this Japanese tree with its jade-green leaves like glossy tongues to (my nemesis now for many months) a plant that would prick and gouge my hands whenever we moved the plants inside, into our dining room, on cold nights. I had a name for this plant, crown of thorns. Leaf-flecked, with clusters of flowers, its tentacles bristled with thorns. I watched Dorinda spraying this plant, standing just a little away from it, her hand an inch or so from the thorns. The leaves, the tiny vermilion flowers, even the steely thorns themselves were soaked in the hissing spray. I watched her moving pots around, sliding them across the floor of the porch. It wasn't long before she was sweeping up, leaving mounds of refuse for me to scoop up, then inside again, having left the broom, the dish liquid back in its cabinet, its underworld cleanser-choked cave. She sat down across from the breakfast plates, across the kitchen table from me. I asked her if she was up to the trip.

"You're staying right here," Dorinda said. "Today, I'm on my own."

She told me she would be okay. She was getting used to the nausea; she had been on chemotherapy for months. I wanted to go with her, but I had to work at the station today. I watched her carry her plate to the sink, douse it thoroughly in hot water. I was expected to do the same whenever I got around to it. She put her plate in the dishwasher, just to be doing something. It wasn't time yet for her to go.

"You're sure you're going to be okay?"

"Of course I'll be okay," she said, leaving the racks in the dishwasher out. She scrubbed egg out of the frying pan. She would be in the car for two hours, in the hospital for another three hours. I had been with her before she had surgery. I still thought of her wheeled down corridors, her eyes tilted up from the gurney at blocks of lights, smoke sensors.

Our alley cat, Singalong with Mitch, lowered his whiskered, coal-black face to the leavings of my breakfast—dried egg yolk, bits of sausage, an egg-clotted crust of toast. Singalong had come in from the bedroom, having spent the night with us in our bed. Now Dorinda came back to the table, watching Singalong lick at his egg yolk.

"I notice he hasn't been fed," she said.

"I haven't gotten around to it yet. But I will. As soon as you're on your way."

I watched her pick up Singalong and set him carefully on the floor. "I think you'd better feed him now," she said.

"Singalong can wait," I said. "I'll feed him after you go."

"Promise?"

"Yes, I promise."

Dorinda kissed me on the mouth. Her slender legs were between my thighs, now over the hill and much slowed down. I held her close, I stroked her hair, but that didn't keep her from going.

When I got back from the station that night, Dorinda was feeding Singalong filet of sole from a doggie bag. She had news for me. She'd seen Zack again. Zack had met her at the hospital because Dorinda had called him on the road. I moved to my console piano, sat down, put my hands on the keys without moving them, without making a sound. I saw Dorinda laying out change, pumping in nickels and quarters in some Huddle House off of I-85. Zack would answer in his hot tub. He had cordless and cellular telephones and could be reached anytime, anywhere.

"You told me you were on your own today."

"I was until the traffic got bad." Dorinda put the doggie bag in the garbage can, clamped the lid on tight, watching Singalong eat. "I mean I wanted you to be with me, but you weren't so I had to call Zack."

"You told me you didn't want me along."

"Okay, so I wanted to see Zack," she said. "I wanted him to be waiting. I wanted him to spend money on me. That way, I thought, I'd get through it." Singalong finished, bowl licked clean. "We can't afford to go out in Atlanta," she said. "You know that as well as I do."

"We can afford to go out in Atlanta," I said. "What we can't afford is Zack's lifestyle."

Dorinda looked out at the screen porch. Just checking. The plants were all okay. Even the crown of thorns was okay. She sat next to me on the piano bench and put her arms around my waist.

"Zack was trying to be nice to me. He tried to act like we were having fun. I was watching Zack eating his escargot, and I thought—we're having a real good time." She arrested my silently chording hand the way she would do when I played for her. Then she lifted her hand and touched my face. "Not the kind of good time I have with you."

I lifted my hands and clasped hers. "I want you to know I'm glad you're back. And I'm glad you enjoyed your lunch."

We embraced, as we had so many times.

So Zack took Dorinda out to lunch on those days I couldn't go with her. She continued to have chemotherapy. I kept on spraying the crown of thorns, its little red flowers coming back with zest. I knew Zack still cared for Dorinda. He was a fervent lover in Oaxaca. His heart had kept an undying flame, to refer to a line from one of his songs, the song he called "Undying Flame." None of Zack's songs were ever recorded, although he badly wanted a record contract. He used to sidle up to me in Oaxaca and ask me to take him to Nashville. He thought I really knew my way around in the music business.

Most days I worked at the station here, and on certain nights, until midnight. I kept on being a D.J. and a sports announcer for high school football games. I played keyboard one night a week in the Carriage House; it brought in some extra money. Even though I was not playing my best, I could forget about how it was at home.

It was a beautiful spring, no denying that. The dogwoods and redwoods were blossoming; the azaleas were blooming all over the block. There was a radio on the bed table, and an ashtray brimming with cigarette butts. Dorinda had laid out a cigarette. Sunlight speared the venetian blinds and liquified on the pillow. Her blue eyes widened in her face, and she laid cold hands on my body. Quick like a bunny, she told me.

I got up and went to the bathroom for the pills that had been prescribed for her. I splashed water into a paper cup and was quickly back at her bedside. Now I was helping her hold the paper cup, my hand on the cup, my steady hand. My elbow bumped into the catheter tube, and she moved it away from her exposed flesh. "Okay," she said when the nausea went, or started to, "that's better."

Dorinda sat up in bed and lit a cigarette. Palm cupping her dorsal elbow, she took a long drag on the cigarette. She studied my face for second thoughts. Pretty soon I would be going to work. The things I had said last night, I was hoping none of that still showed, but the tight lines around Dorinda's lips showed me she had not changed her mind. She was going to spend the weekend with Zack.

Dorinda put out the cigarette. "So you're on your way to the station."

"I'm not rushing off. As long as you're here I'll be here."

Dorinda asked for the ashtray, which I was emptying into the wastepaper basket. Singalong was on top of the bookcase, those plywood boards and concrete blocks housing paperbacks and audiotapes. Wanting his breakfast, he rattled his dish. But I couldn't really say he rattled the dish, for this cat could eat deftly and quietly. Dorinda was putting the coffee on. It was my job to feed Singalong. I was spooning wet cat food ahead of his tongue. Dorinda had something to say about this.

"I thought we agreed on dry food?"

We had, but I wouldn't admit it. I told her we had agreed in principle. "We agreed we would go to dry food as soon as we ran out of wet food."

"Is that right?"

"Yes, that's right."

"I don't want to make an issue of this, but this is not what we agreed on."

"Okay, what did we agree on?"

"We agreed on using up what we had, what we had in the refrigerator."

She was nit-picking and I thought I knew why. She knew I didn't go along with her plans this time.

"Okay, so I opened another can. Now what? Any suggestions?"

I was not going to get an answer, for, having finished his hasty breakfast, Singalong wanted to go out. Dorinda followed him out the kitchen door, through the screen porch, to the backyard, pausing on the screen porch to put on the Oaxacan hat. It was a sombrero she'd picked up in Oaxaca. It was getting a little too large for her, now that her hair was almost gone. She had put on her Oaxacan hat to remind me of Oaxaca. The screen door was reverberating. There was another way to say this. She was not talking to me this morning. She'd rather lean on the picket fence and watch our neighbor mowing his lawn. She wore the hat whenever she left the house, regardless of what it reminded me of.

Azaleas rippled in the breeze, white dogwood, yellow forsythia. There was a brown thrasher in the birdbath, across the fence in our neighbor's backyard. Singalong joined us at the fence. Dorinda was in her nightgown, wearing the Oaxacan hat. We rubbed shoulders under her hat's brim while our neighbor, Mr. Seymour Smith, drove his mower ahead of flying grass. Later he would rake up the grass. He had refused to purchase a grass catcher. Now Singalong was across the fence, stalking the unwary thrasher. I watched him leap for the thrasher, already high in the Georgia pines as again the Oaxacan hat reminded me of days in Mexico when I sat with my tequila and salt looking out at eyes that were hurting me.

At last I got down to it. "Why don't you wait until Monday? That way you wouldn't have to drive. I could drive you. How does that sound?"

"I've already made arrangements with Zack."

I knew all about the arrangements. Zack had a friend who did acupuncture and another friend who was adept at Zen. He was also giving a party, and taking Dorinda to a Braves game. Dorinda crossed her arms on the picket fence, looking out at the swatches of grass, at Seymour pushing his power mower. I was thinking of Zack's latest girl, of Tami with the long black hair, whom I'd only seen in a photograph of the two of them in Zack's hot tub. Tami was smiling out at me next to Dorinda's thumb and forefinger. I thought of Zack in a comic book, like a rubber man or a plastic man, stretching and coiling all over the yard.

"Why can't Zack make arrangements? Why can't he come to see you?"

Seymour Smith turned off the mower. He hobbled across the patio to his back door, which he firmly closed.

"You're making too much out of this. It's been over for years," Dorinda replied.

"Then why are you spending the weekend with him?" This was the sort of husband I was, racked with longing and possessiveness. "I'm thinking there's something between you now."

To this my wife said nothing. I was hoping nothing must have meant no. I stared at the Oaxacan hat. I thought of it sailing over the fence, clearing the rooftops, the pines.

"What was between us, was," she said. "I'm only interested in what happens now."

We stayed out in the backyard awhile. I looked at the dogwood next door, thickly blossoming in radiant white. Zack's white hair didn't match up to it; his needed another coat of paint. It had turned white during a hurricane was what Zack had told us in Oaxaca. Dorinda tilted the Oaxacan hat the way she would do in Oaxaca, at the zocalo where we would go some nights to listen to the mariachi band. Now she seemed to be breathing in Mexican air. Her breasts were rising and falling, no longer slack in her nightgown. She smiled at Singalong pacing the picket fence, at our neighbor's lime green lawn. I realized she was feeling good and said nothing more about Zack. If she could feel good wearing her nightgown she could spend more weekends with Zack. If her lips would stay closed I would welcome him, with open arms and broadmindedness, but not even his acupuncture friend could stop the pulley lines spreading her lips, or the spasm twisting her face and neck. She pulled the hat off, let it drop. I looked away from her baldness.

"Quick like a bunny," she said.

Was Zack quick like a bunny?—my peripheral thought as I made a dash, for the nausea pills in the medicine cabinet. I was back in half a minute or so, sloshing water in the usual paper cup. Dorinda stayed out in the backyard with the pulley line working her upper lip and her teeth sinking into her lower lip. It took awhile for her to feel better. She told me I should wear the hat but for the time being I left it where it was. We moved on back to the screen porch. We sat down; we took our time.

"Can this really go on?" I asked my wife, with a glance at the flowering crown of thorns. "Do you think we can really continue this way?"

"I have to continue some way," she said. The Oaxacan hat blew about the backyard but neither one of us went out to get it. "All I can do is continue. When I look inside I see nothing. Zack is helping me look outside."

"Outside," I asked. "What is outside?"

"I got the sun in the morning and the moon at night." Dorinda smiled. "I know, you think that song stinks."

"I think Zack's songs lack something too," I said.

"I want more than the sun in the morning," she said. Singalong scratched on the screen door. He wanted in. Dorinda got up. "You're not the one," she said, "who has to choose a life."

"I'm choosing a life just by being here. Here for you," I said. "That's choosing."

"I think you believe you are here for me." Singalong sat on our back steps. I was watching Dorinda approaching Singalong. "But you aren't, you're here, that's all."

"I agree one hundred per cent," I said. "So I'm here and Zack's out there."

"That's right. And sometimes I like it out there."

Dorinda opened the screen door. Singalong eased in silently like the interloper he could be sometimes. Dorinda moved a fern to catch more light, looking too thin in her nightgown. I saw her again in a hospital, on a gurney pushed down corridors. The lights overhead, in fluorescent squares, then rectangles, were passing over her. It shouldn't come down to this arrangement, her life coming down to this—why certain rectangles were longitudinal; others, in sections, lateral. Something she had to avoid thinking about, the arrangement of fluorescent lights on the ceilings of hospital corridors.

It was only a matter of time before Zack and Tami came down to see us. Dorinda asked them to come for the Fourth of July. They pulled in on the third of July, before I got back from the station. When I saw Zack's white convertible occupying my spot in the carport, I let my hatchback idle awhile. I turned on the air while the motor ran, but the compressor had not been miraculously restored. In July the car was an oven, but today the humidity was down. I turned everything off and got out of the car. Singalong came out to greet me.

Zack and Tami were with Dorinda. Tami sat on one side of the bed, her long legs crossed, looking beautiful. Zack was standing in front of a window, adjusting a venetian blind. In the slatted gloom of the bedroom, his hair seemed two-toned, gray and white. He said

Dorinda was looking better. Singalong hopped up on the bed and dug his claws in Dorinda's nightgown.

That night we ate out, at the Carriage House. Zack had gifts for us, from Paris, cheap medallions and overpriced T-shirts from the Porte de Cligancourt flea market, a gilt Eiffel Tower from the Monoprix. He had a story about the Eiffel Tower.

"Up there it's all second-class. Rich and poor, on this creaking elevator. The cable has never been changed. All this for one hundred francs." He sat with his fingers touching, his hands arched, eyes set deep in thought. "If you wanted to take it to the top you had to wait in line for a while," Zack said. "It was the same way going down. People were jammed against the doors." He paused, his fingers still touching. Dorinda put a hand on my knee. She was liking Zack's Paris story.

"There were people from all over, just hanging up there in the wind. Someone asked if we were going up. Some guy from North Africa or somewhere had an answer. What he said was don't you wish we could. Go up. Up in the sky," he said.

"Up, up, and away," Tami said.

"The point is we were together," Zack said. "Our little group on the Eiffel tower was meant to go down, not up. But remember we were up in one sense. All of us had one hundred francs. The North African must have had a lot more than that. So why worry?"

"He was worried about eternity," was what Tami said, not Dorinda.

"He must not have been a Muslim," I said. "If he had been he wouldn't have said what he said."

"He wouldn't have been there at all," Zack said. "Muslims all know they're going up. And when they get there," Zack grinned at Tami, "when they're rolling around in Paradise, guess what happens to the men. These Muslims have virgins begging for it."

Tami was not a Muslim, she said. She would not qualify for Paradise.

We had our dinner and I got down to the gig. I played "Undying Flame of My Heart," with straight-up, two-five-one chords. I wasn't about to stretch. I saw Dorinda only had eyes for Zack. Since the candle's flame didn't block his view, he could keep his eyes on Dorinda. She looked like she did when I met her, casual and sure of herself, in a bar with a man at her side. Her eyes moved left of the candle flame, then right as she turned from Tami to Zack. I kept the keyboard on organ, and turned my face away from our table.

They left before I finished the gig. I was putting the keyboard back in its case, unplugging the speakers, packing up. Zack came back in, through the doors up front. He offered to give me a hand, and I said he could carry the speakers. I knew he had something to say to me, but he would want me to feel comfortable before he actually got down to it. We finished loading the hatchback. It was hot; we were both sweating. He told me he thought I played well tonight. A few couples were still in the Carriage House, watching the baseball scores come in on TV. Others were getting into their cars.

The darkness was lanced by headlights, throwing Zack's face into sharp relief. "With me she'll have all that she can ever want." Men were joking, women were laughing. One couple was having an argument over which of them would drive the other home.

"All she wants right now is to live," I said.

Zack moved a little closer. "The question is how well will she live. I can give her so much more."

I looked at him and quietly said, "I want her with me."

"I know that. I can understand that. I'm only asking you to think of her."

The next day was the Fourth of July. The sun was shining on the patio. Zack and Tami came back from the picket fence, holding hands, a loving couple. Dorinda joined them on the patio, after spooning out wet cat food for Singalong in the kitchen. She was wearing the Oaxacan hat. She sat down next to Tami, on one end of the patio. Zack crossed his legs on the other end. Singalong scarfed up the cat food. I mixed a stiff gin and tonic.

From the kitchen I watched what was going on out there. Dorinda lifted the hat from her head and handed it over to Tami. Tami handed the hat to Zack. Zack was getting to his feet now. He lowered the hat on Tami's head. Tami pulled on the brim but the hat didn't fit. Zack held out the hat to Dorinda. Dorinda shook her sun-soaked pale bald head, nothing doing. So Zack lowered the hat on his own head. He turned the brim up in front of his face; then he stooped to receive Dorinda's kiss. Then, taking Dorinda by the hand, he lifted her out of her lawn chair. Again she kissed him. This time they embraced.

Barreling out to the patio, I left the French doors open. It was the humiliation that got to me, Dorinda playing Zack's game, one of many, liking it, letting me know she did, stroking Zack's face, the back of his neck. Finally, Dorinda slipped out of Zack's embrace. She took possession of the hat, came to me, gazed up at me, lifted the hat up over my head.

"Nothing doing," I said. "I'm not playing Zack's game."

"All right, then don't," Dorinda said, and put the hat back on her head. That ended the hat-passing game.

That night I did barbecued chicken on the grill. We stayed out in the backyard drinking Zack's cognac. Firecrackers were going off up and down the block. Zack had picked up bottle rockets. They were lined up on the patio, trained on Seymour Smith's backyard. Dorinda and Tami twirled sparklers.

It was Zack who lit the first fuse. I heard the hiss and flitter of the rocket launching, the lift off, the sputtering arc. Zack looked pleased with himself. He must have known I'd grown up with bottle rockets. Getting down on his hands and knees with his skinny butt in the air, he was sighting, measuring along the fuse. This one made a beautiful arc and detonated high over Seymour Smith's house.

Dorinda got up and went to Zack. She said she wanted to go out for cigarettes. Zack said he would drive her. He suggested we all do a tour of the town, watch the fireworks display at the city park. No thanks, Tami said; she'd rather stay here with me. I said I'd keep Tami company. That's how Dorinda wanted it. Before she left with Zack she handed me the Oxacan hat, with a faint smile of culpability.

"You keep it for me. Where I'm going I won't need it."

Tami said she wanted to wear it, which was all right with me, why not? She kept it on over drinks in the kitchen, slow dancing in the living room. In the guest bedroom she took it off, arranged it over her naked navel, the plaited straw of the crown poking up. She asked me to tell her a story, a bedtime story, just for her. Zack never told her stories. I couldn't think of any stories but the ones I told Dorinda.

There was this grasshopper on casters. He really thought he was hell on wheels. There was this butterfly girl with gossamer wings who was kind to this foolish grasshopper, who got him out of all kind of scrapes, saved him from cats and marauding birds, literally lifted him up sometimes. Tami put my hand on her tummy, but I couldn't tell Tami this story. I left Tami hugging her beautiful legs. Singalong was in the kitchen. He was waiting for me to feed him so I filled his bowl with dry cat food. Then I went to the medicine cabinet, in the bathroom, to look for Dorinda's nausea pills. They were missing, as I had expected.

I stayed up, playing some tapes. I played John Coltrane and Thelonious Monk, a little Miles, some Bill Evans. I wouldn't be able to sleep tonight. The sky lightened over the rooftops. Singalong paced on the screen porch, unable to push through the screen door. I let him out and went outside. I thought of turning on the lawn sprinkler.

I heard a monoplane, like an outboard on a windy lake. The monoplane flew in out of the east and started circling high overhead. A second plane circled around the first. I saw a pink rectangular parachute, all the beauty of it flying open, then Zack's wind-surfing raucous blue parachute flapping open in witless mimicry. A man and a woman in gliding descent, still a long way above the pines. The parachutes scudded in billowing flight, the pink one moving below the blue, the lines taut, harnesses snugly in place.

Tami pulled on my shirtsleeve. The egg white of her eyes stood out. "You want to know how it's done? You have to climb out of the airplane. You have to work your way up the strut. Your instructor will give you the go sign and then you let go of the strut."

Tami was wearing the Oxacan hat.

It has gone into remission.

Singalong wants to stay where he is, curled up in Dorinda's lap. Sing isn't happy when she asks him to move. His ears are set back when I pick him up, when I set him down on the floor of the porch. He goes to the screen door and waits. Let Singalong stalk the unwary bird, the chipmunk that forgets to look.

"You might have a lot of time left," I said, thinking medicine cabinet, pills. I wouldn't be doing that for awhile. "What is it? What do you really want?"

Dorinda gets up and goes to the door. She looks out at the backyard as if she might really hate to leave it. But when she turns to me, she has gone far away.

"I know you care for me," she says. "But you're not connected to me anymore. You haven't been since I became ill. Everything that is you is inside you."

"That's where you are, Dorinda," I said, knowing she already knew that and that it wouldn't help for me to say it. "You're the one who's not connected."

Dorinda tilts the Oaxacan hat. "I'm connected to Zack for the present," she says. She asks me to look after Singalong. "You'll feed him. Change his litter?"

I say I will look after Singalong. And her plants, I say I will look after them.

It has been turning cold again, at night. Most of the plants I have moved inside—the potted palms, the bougainvillea, the little Japanese tree with its jade-green leaves, the plant with the thorns, a scattering of tiny red flowers. I have been making up new bedtime stories. I've changed the grasshopper to a cricket on wheels. Something new, a cricket on wheels.

Singalong is on the bed table, his tail wrapped around his forepaws. Dorinda has put down her water cup. I think of Dorinda with Singalong, imagine a summer day, and begin.

White Orchid

Lorna Wiggins had taken to sitting out on the back porch, leafing through real estate brochures, woolgathering. She might meet a man on Destin Beach, win the Georgia lottery. Someone solid but fun to be with. And if she won the lottery she could say goodbye to handing out license plates, sitting in front of a computer screen.

It was time to move the sprinkler. Tendonitis clawed at her ankles as she forced herself to her feet. She ducked under the arcing spray, catching drops in her hair. Traced the sinuous hose to a leaky spigot. Stooping, she turned off the water, unscrewed the hose. She dragged hose and sprinkler to the front yard, found another spigot behind dense spirea bushes. She heard her sprinkler harmonizing with her neighbor's across Shelton Mill Road. Mr. Kayline, his wife had left him a year ago, not long after Brad left Lorna.

She turned the lights on in the living room. Found a magazine that had come in the mail. Smoked a cigarette, suddenly realizing it was the next to last one in the pack. Braxton came out of his room, trousers puffing over Reeboks she had given up on urging him to tie. A sweatshirt lumped over his belly.

"I won't be having dinner at home tonight," Braxton informed her in a snooty English accent he'd picked up from Monty Python reruns.

"And tomorrow night and the night after that?"

"Depends on what happens tonight. Tonight is very important to me. I have a date with a chahming young lady."

He didn't ask her for money.

"You could get me a pack of cigarettes?"

"With what, pray tell. I'm nearly broke." Braxton smoothed out his hair. His pale blue eyes begged her to see things his way.

She handed him a twenty. "Never mind about the cigarettes. And I expect you back here tonight."

"I'll be back at the stroke of midnight." She felt Braxton's hands on her shoulders. "Don't worry about me, Mom. You need to worry about yourself. Smoking two packs a day, I'd say that was something to worry about."

"Really."

"Really and truly."

"I'll keep that in mind."

"You won't so what can I do?"

"You can get a job. You can consider graduating from high school. You can do anything but what you're doing."

"What I'm doing? I'm improving my mind."

"How does doing nothing improve your mind?"

"It opens it up to what really matters."

She didn't ask like what. She knew what. Meditation. Letting out all the bad air. Being in tune with the grass and the trees.

"This girl I met. She likes what I like."

"So if all you're going to do is meditate, what do you need money for?"

"For sushi. There's this Japanese sushi bar where we hang out a lot. And gas for my car."

"And car insurance, which I'm paying for. And your Reeboks, and your iPod."

"That's entertainment, Mom. It's the icing on the cake."

He seemed so sure of himself. And if whoever this girl was dumped him? He'd be back in his room or they'd be watching television and he'd take over the remote for the night.

LORNA PICKED UP chicken, potato salad, coleslaw at the Lazy Bee.

Josh was clerking tonight. He had graduated from Beauregard High yet here he was working in his father's convenience store. Someday Braxton might graduate, and if that day ever came find a decent job. But finding a wife, what woman would want a man looking and acting like Braxton? Brad used to say he'll grow out of it. Brad did what he could to make a man of him. Took him quail hunting, but Braxton refused to kill a bird. Took him fishing, but Braxton snarled up his fish line, and when he did catch a fish he threw it back in.

She asked Josh for a carton of cigarettes. She handed Josh her Mastercard and he ran it through, and she signed the receipt. Jack Lazenby's boy, his bright blue eyes would melt snow. She'd been to his baptizing, on the same day Braxton, howling, was baptized in the creek behind the church. Brad tried to shush Braxton up. And Reverend Willoughby lifting Braxton up, managed to get out—"in the name of the Father, the Son, and the Holy Ghost I baptize thee" . . . then broke into a fit of coughing. A doubleheader, Brad's not-so-funny joke concerning Josh and Braxton's immersion.

Driving back she crossed the millrace, its lacy pool sapphire-sheathed. Passed trailers, cabins set back in the woods, stands of pine inching upward, close to topping the power lines.

Ranch houses strung out on either side of Beauregard High greeted her, as they usually did, with what she suspected was disapproval, their lawn systems twitching out spray. Her front yard would soon need mowing. The gutters were choked with last winter's leaves. Braxton's dirt bike lying on its side in her marigold bed, she thought of having it taken away to Goodwill.

She heated the chicken in the microwave, a breast and wing for her. The leg and thigh she saved for Braxton. And some potato salad and slaw. She had her dinner off a TV tray, sat up watching television, smoking, drinking decaffeinated iced tea with sweetener.

BRAXTON DIDN'T COME home that night. Or the next night. He came home on Sunday morning. She heard church bells ringing. She heard Braxton honking his horn. She wouldn't open the door, go to him, he could come to her. She pulled her bathrobe over her nightgown, went to a front window. Her neighbors, on her right, on her left were backing out of their carports, church bells ringing hurry up hurry up you might not get here in time.

Braxton opened the door on the passenger side and out stepped a girl wearing a dress Lorna wouldn't be seen dead in, more a gunny sack than a dress.

All she could say was come in.

Inside, insulated from Mr. Kayline, who had come out of his house with a Polaroid camera, crossed Shelton Mill Road and asked them to pose—all three of you—she felt calm settle over her like mist over a field.

"I want you to meet Eenonee. Eenonee this is Lorna."

Eenonee hiked her granny glasses up from her nose. "I feel like I know you already, Lorna. Like I've known you all my life."

Lovey-dovey—you'd think their hands were glued together.

"I've got news for you, Mom. Last night we were out in Eenonee's backyard. These lights in the sky seemed to be dancing just for us."

"Just for us," Eenonee echoed, squeezing Braxton's big hand in her little hand.

"What else could they be but UFO's? Right over our heads."

Braxton had been down this road before, the extraterrestrial express he called it.

"So where did they come from? Mars? Venus?"

"Does that matter? Would I ask you where the sun came from? The important thing is it's where it is. The same goes for the stars." Braxton seemed to be pondering an algebra problem Lorna knew he'd never solve. "Last night there weren't many stars in the sky. Like they got the word somehow. Via Morse code or telepathy, them thar stars got the message and moved out for the night. Move out!"—reminding Lorna of every John Wayne movie Brad ever watched.

"And the message?"

"Them thar lights"—*please stop*—"hoppin' and skippin' you shoulda seen 'em Mom"—*I've had enough*—"know what they was a telling' us you an' Eenonee go out and get hitched. So we did." Braxton put his arm around Eenonee and hugged her tight.

SHE HAD TO talk to Eenonee's mama. Eenonee—that's how she'd taken to spelling her made up name so everyone she knew could pronounce it. The name Braxton had given her, a mythical name, Braxton explained—how he knew that he didn't disclose. Oenone was a Greek nymph abandoned by Paris for Helen of Troy. Nymph and Greek, that didn't sit well with Lorna.

So much you keep from me. Lorna took her eyes off a giant red rocket up ahead, primed for liftoff.

From Brad—hugging Eenonee in the back seat. "We should stop for firecrackers, Mom."

"This isn't the Fourth of July."

"I know. It's the third. But on an occasion like this I think a celebration is called for."

"I think not."

Eenonee said, "Lorna's right. Firecrackers, who needs them?"

Silence. Lorna drove on. Abandoned cabins she passed, a rusty harrow, sheep grazing, a sign to the right saying FELICITY ACRES, a road she knew was circular because she had already been down it with Brad. The last time she had heard from Brad he had sold one lot in Felicity. Not enough to pay her back alimony. But if she took Brad to court it would cost her.

How many more miles would she have to drive to do something about this situation? She had a few words for Eenonee's mama. *How could you bring up a girl to do such a thing? Run off with my boy? How could you?*

She hadn't been down this road for awhile. She took Lee County 29 to town, where she spent her day behind a counter in the Probate Office, taking in checks, handing out Georgia license plates. On her computer screen love bugs with smiling faces.

From the back seat, "Pull over, Mom."

A barbed wire fence, the sign on the gate, NO TRESPASSING. Braxton got out of the car, swung the gate open, Eenonee scooting after him. They skipped down a rutted clay road. *If they can't read I can.* Daylight was on its way out in here, first thing she realized following them. Not them, the trail they left, what Eenonee must have stored in that gunny sack she was wearing, candy corn, one every ten yards. She should go back and unlock the car and drive off. Let them go their way. But what if at the end of the road there was a cottage, there was an oven?

She followed their trail to a clearing, a picnic bench, a cabin, a huge cedar tree, a barbecue pit silted in ashes. Out in front of the cabin, a NO SMOKING sign. Lorna lit one last cigarette. Took her time, inhaling luxuriantly, allowing nicotine to caress her lungs, exhaling streams of smoke. From inside she heard Eenonee giggling.

Inside—no one should have to live here—it was musty and hot. Cobwebs everywhere. Climb a ladder to get to the loft, that she definitely wasn't going to do.

Don't you realize what you're doing? You don't belong here.

Coming down the ladder a pair of legs in panty hose, a waist you could put your arm around and have some arm left over. Bangled wrists, pointy breasts—lipstick, rouge, eye shadow. Descending behind her Braxton's big can, his torso, his straw-thatched head. Braxton took Eenone's hand. "Mom," his voice resonating the way it did when he came home from school with C's, not D's, on his report card. "Meet Rona Beth."

Rona Beth smoothed out her miniskirt.

Lorna called 911 on her cell phone. Asked for the sheriff's office. Two deputies, one she used to date, Buddy Bolton, before Brad came along, spotted her car and after closing the gate took the road to the cabin. Buddy Bolton had put on a beer belly and his gun belt creaked from too much fat and the arm he felt he had to put around her and the hand he gripped Braxton's arm with wasn't exactly welcome.

They would take Rona Beth to her place, Buddy Bolton reassured her, before pulling the gate open. Behind him the patrol car came to a stop. Scratchy voices on the radio. "If this happens again, we'll have to take both of them in."

"I know. Trespassing is trespassing."

"Lucky you didn't get shot."

"I know. I know."

"Next time you call me first."

"There won't be a next time, Buddy."

It took Buddy to get Braxton in the car.

SHE HAD HIDDEN Braxton's car keys. Asked him not to see Rona Beth again. "Don't you get it? She isn't in her right mind."

"That's what you say."

"That's what I know."

Braxton still had Rona Beth's granny glasses. He would put them on when they watched television, his TV tray junked with food he hadn't eaten. One night she asked him, "Who do you like better? Eenonee or Rona Beth?"

"I like them both the same. Having two personalities, maybe more, isn't that what we all have? You too, Mom. You're one person at the Probate Office and another when you come home. With me, I mean."

"I'm your mother. I'm trying to do what's best for you."

Braxton's blue eyes filmed over with hurt. "Only I know what's best for me."

THE DAY SHIFT was just letting out at the mill—automobiles, pickup trucks, none of them new like her Saturn, were backed up at the traffic light. That was bad enough, but where Rona Beth lived must be worse. But Rona Beth didn't live near the mill. Just Braxton's way of letting you know what *you* didn't have to contend with. An auto graveyard. Trailer parks. Mill houses with 110-volt air conditioners humming in the windows.

"Taking the long way can be the best way. So you won't say it's Eenonee's background that's made her the way she is. She doesn't have to escape from anything. She's exploring what might be possible for her."

Granny glasses, miniskirts? Braxton drove past the courthouse, closed for the day. Crossing the tracks, Braxton pulled into a motel. A bricked-up pool. Weekly and monthly rates. "Right now Eenonee's living here." Next to Wendy's and an Exxon station. "She grew up in the last antebellum home in Calhoun County. Her grandmama's still living there. Lucky for her she hasn't cut off her allowance. I wanted her to check into the Holiday Inn but Eenonee wasn't having any of that."

"How did you know she was here?"

"We kept in touch. By cell phone."

Which Lorna could confiscate but what was the use?

Eenonee had checked out. Left a note in a sealed envelope at the front desk. Braxton tore open the envelope. Read from lined yellow note paper.

> Braxton—
>
> A sad occasion has called me home. Please don't try to see me.
>
> Rona Beth

Lorna followed Braxton to room fourteen. Braxton pounded on the door, pulled on the knob. She waited for him to calm down—how many times had she waited for Braxton to clean up his room, do his homework, participate in at least one team sport? Steaming off what was once a swimming pool, heat from the low-hanging sun in the murky sky. She couldn't walk home. She had to let Braxton take her arm and escort her to the car.

"Take me home."

"I'm afraid I can't do that."

"You can't go on acting crazy."

"Why not? The whole world's crazy."

What was the point in sitting here listening to Braxton go on, parked in front of a motel no one in his right mind would stay in for more than one night?

"We deny it, we build more prisons, we put people in funny farms, go to church, read our magazines and newspapers thinking they must know what's going on."

And—"You want to renovate our house. Put tile floors in the kitchen, in the bathroom, repaint the living room. A bird is satisfied with a nest. But not you, Mom, not Dad either. He thinks he's buying lots to make money. He thinks Lu Ann will get her dream house if he socks enough money in the bank."

The motor on and the windows rolled up—if Braxton didn't drive off they would both die of carbon monoxide poisoning.

Eenonee's grandmother's house sat on a low hill. It had a portico, columns, a porte cochere, ivy crawling up dingy brick. Behind the house the overseer's cottage, on the front door a sign, WET PAINT. And from Braxton—"You ask me this place should be torn down." Braxton took her arm, guiding her to the front door. "Best thing that could happen, wipe it *all* out of our minds. I've been after Eenonee to sell the property." Knocking, getting no answer, pushing open the door. "Eenonee should talk to her grandmama. Sell the land off to developers. Cut up the land into lots. Give Dad a chance to buy a few."

Lorna followed him inside through the parlor, chairs covered with sheets, a grandfather clock, its hands stopped at 11:55. At the foot of the stairs Braxton hollered—"Eenonee?"

Lorna gripped the bannister, needles of tendonitis pain tattooing her ankles and calves. *You did this to us, Brad. You and Lu Ann.* The clock on the landing was ticking. She followed Braxton into the bedroom.

The grandmother lay on a double bed, a sheet pulled up to her neck. Her fingers kneaded the sheet. Hooked into an oxygen tank, a nasal canula looped over her ears, pronged into her nostrils, her mouth, she seemed to be waiting for something that wasn't going to happen. Her eyes moved from Braxton to Lorna, and when she opened her mouth she showed gum. In a glass jar on the bed table false teeth submerged in cloudy water.

Rona Beth stared at Braxton as if she'd never seen him before. On a chest in the bay window, a potted white orchid. Somebody ought to move it. Orchids couldn't stand direct sunlight.

Braxton would be home any minute now, with Eenonee, Rona Beth. They had the back bedroom all to themselves. Eenonee's string of Christmas lights lit up the headboard—up to you to replace the bad bulbs. Up to you to take care of both of them.

She had gone to the grandmother's funeral. Braxton wanted her with him. The burial was in Pine Hills. She'd been there before, with Brad, years ago early in the fall, for Lanterns in the Cemetery Eve. Townspeople dressed up like dead and buried former citizens paraded around the tombstones. The mayor dressed up as a dead mayor and Colonel Obediah Lewis rode again on his white horse, right here in the cemetery, a horse turd steaming on a marble slab, Brad had to point out, for he hadn't wanted to go, she had nagged at him until he took her. Lanterns swaying on the cedar trees, she'd felt Brad's hand slip down to her bottom, how could he do that, ruin all this, just to show her she was his for the taking?

She moved the sprinkler to the front yard. She heard a limb fall off the pecan tree. Crepe myrtles, once pink and lavender snow cones, most of them shriveled by the drought. Mimosa pods too. Brad used to say mimosa pods poisoned horses. If pecan trees couldn't get enough water, they'd sacrifice one of their limbs.

She went inside to fix dinner. She turned the oven on. She took two chicken breasts out of the refrigerator, chopped up potatoes, carrots, onions. Rubbed them with garlic, olive oil, sprinkled on pepper and paprika, set them in a casserole lined with aluminum foil. Eenonee was a vegetarian—she liked broccoli, eggplant, Brussels sprouts—but the potatoes, the onions, the carrots she'd eat and the salad you'd make just for her.

She opened a bottle of Chardonnay—chilled not iced, Brad would tell her—poured out half a glass, the oven on, chicken breasts beginning to brown. The orchid shouldn't be in the kitchen window. How many times had she told Braxton that? *But that's where Eenonee wants it, Mom.* She would move it and Braxton would put it back. Well that wasn't going to happen again.

She found a place for it on the island. So she could look at it while she was boiling eggs, slicing onions, green peppers. What didn't belong on the island, draped over one of the burners, were Eenonee's granny glasses.

She poured out more wine. Picked up the granny grasses by one temple, put them on.

She might just keep them on. Show Eenonee how silly they looked. The temples pinched her behind the ears. She pulled them down over her nose. Pulled up her skirt and did a dance. With Brad she'd danced. And he'd gotten ideas. Still wearing Eenonee's granny glasses, she let her skirt fall, felt its hem slip over her knees.

Pagoda

Today I received a reply to my first application for a job. My resume has been put on file.

Loraine's back from town, in the station wagon. She gets out from behind the driver's seat, swings the door shut, announces herself. Charlie gets out on the other side. He waits for Loraine to unlock the tailgate, thumbs hooked in the pockets of his jeans. The back seat of our station wagon has been lowered to make room for fiberglass. There is also a bag of birdseed, which is not large, and not heavy. It is sitting in front of the fiberglass, easy for me to get to. Charlie will haul in the fiberglass. The birdseed is easy to carry. I can support it on one shoulder, without any strain or dizziness. I don't have to worry about my heart, which can go out at any moment.

I set the bag of seed down on the screen porch. Charlie shoulders the fiberglass. Charlie is wearing a red muscle shirt. His sinewy arms and chest are tanned. His sweat-streaked hair is pulled back tight, in what Charlie called a rat tail. Loraine tells Charlie where the fiberglass goes, beside the sheetrock inside the garage. Charlie will put up the feeder, under Loraine's supervision, of course. She knows just how the feeder should hang.

I go back inside to do some work. I have some changes to make on my resume. When I come out, the feeder is up, between the screen porch and the tulip tree.

Loraine and Charlie go off again, this time for peat moss and potting soil, for the garden, beyond the tulip tree. While they're gone I look at the feeder. Two walls of the upper section have windows in front and back. I can look right through these windows at the foliage behind the feeder, through the upper sections of the panes. Through the lower sections of the panes I can look at a column of birdseed. Circumscribing the upper section's base is a deck, or porch, or balcony. In actuality, it is a feeding trough. Its dimensions match those of the trough below, circumscribing the base of the feeder.

From a projecting beam of the screen porch to a lower branch of the tulip tree runs a clothesline, from which the feeder hangs. A copper wire falls from the clothesline, through the roof and on through the feeder. The copper wire is wrapped around a nail, a two-inch, monstrous nail inset in the flat-bottomed base. The lower section could be a ship, with windows and a flat-bottomed hull. The ship resembles a Chinese junk, without the high poop and battened sails. From the center point of the flat-bottomed hull, this copper wire makes a curlicue, resembling some kind of pigtail, resembling, perhaps, a Chinese queue.

The birds, too, have my attention. Some of them I will learn to identify, with the help of a manual on birds. The birds are a pleasure to look at, and, in the evening, a pleasure to listen to. But when they wake me up in the morning, it seems that all the birds in the neighborhood are in league to grate on my nerves. The little bastards just won't stop; the tweets and twitters and chirrups and caws roll over me like an avalanche.

If I hold the feeder in place—already the stepladder is in place—Loraine can pour seed straight from the bag, a plastic bag half-filled with birdseed, yet unwieldy, difficult to manipulate in the process of lifting the lid on the wire. But she does it, does it easily. The feeder is filled to the brim. We put the stepladder in the laundry room, and, comfortable now on the screen porch, the mail all in for today at least, the letters ready to go out tomorrow, we talk some about the feeder. In steadying it while Loraine filled it, I noticed the wire wrapped around the nail. I bring up this matter to Loraine—why the wire, why the nail?

"I assumed," I say, "the nail was there from the start."

"Let me explain," Loraine tells me.

The nail didn't come with the feeder. The wire from which the feeder hangs runs vertically down the center, along which one raises and lowers the roof in order to introduce the seed. It was a knot at the end of a cord that was the sole support of the feeder once. The problem was that the cord was too long; the feeder hung too close to the ground; it was necessary to shorten it. It was Charlie who came up with the idea of using a wire instead of the cord. He wrapped the wire around the nail so the nail would provide support. There was no need for him to snip off the wire. That's what happened. We had to shorten the wire."

"But you didn't tell me who thought of it."

"No, I told you Charlie thought of it."

"You told me you raised the feeder," I said. "But it doesn't matter who thought of it. What matters is I didn't know." I was angry for not having figured out why the nail was there for myself.

I see Loraine with a roll of fiberglass, beside the ladder to the attic. She has Charlie insulating the attic now. Why do I have to see her there, instead of with me, close to me?

The weeks pass, lengthen into months. Other applications are put on file. It is time to think of what to do next, how to put my abilities to use. Not that we can't make ends meet here. Money continues to come in. When our expenses exceed our income from the land and securities I own, I have only to pick up the telephone, call my broker in Atlanta. Only yesterday I had him sell off a hundred shares of Georgia Power and Light. He informed me I'd take a capital loss, which would help on my income tax.

I usually get up early, on edge from the chattering birds and the prospect of nowhere to go. I have a way of getting through mornings. I watch the nostalgia channel, with my orange juice, my cinnamon toast. I watch old movies, "Movietone News," the big bands of the swing era. What I like best is "The March of Time." Only yesterday I saw the Hindenburg go, a climbing, spiraling column of flame, then tiny moth-like crumpling steel still hopelessly trailing mooring lines. I think of the people on the ground, just footage now from the

"March of Time." I too might soon be footage, assuming we made home movies here.

I still have the feeder to contemplate. The windows are turned away from me, an upper and lower sliver of glass, in perspective, turned away from me. The walls are protected from the rain by the overhanging roof. Droplets are beading the edge of the roof. I hear raindrops on the shingled roof that Charlie put in when he built the screen porch. Charlie is down by the river. Loraine has him painting the boathouse. Some termite-infested boards on the pier also need to be replaced. Since Loraine had already pointed them out, I will have no trouble avoiding them on my way to take the boat out, to take a spin on the river.

We are sitting out on our screened-in porch while Charlie paints the boathouse. A squirrel leaps from the roof of the porch. He is swinging the structure like a trapeze. His bushy tail flaps on a window; his head comes around the other side, and he buries his head in the trough. I find myself looking at the squirrel, not the rocking, gyrating feeder. Loraine hasn't really noticed the squirrel.

"I'm willing to move if you are."

"I know. That isn't news to me. The point is I don't have a job yet."

"You'll get a job, " Loraine tells me. She strokes my hand, my right hand, along and around the palm and on up the ball of the thumb. "I know someday you'll get one. And if you don't, you'll find something here. Until something better comes along."

The squirrels are becoming a problem. They are coming on board from the screen porch, making giant leaps, happy landings. The level of seed is going down, below the level of the feeding trough. The upper windows are unobstructed by seed. In a bend of the river not far from the house, the large-mouthed bass are feeding.

Loraine has an idea to foil the squirrels. There is a certain netted shield, or hood, that can cover the roof of the feeder. Charlie knows where to pick one up. A squirrel is sitting on the roof, large-eyed, with lots of time on his hands, his tail overhanging the edge of the roof.

The level of seed in the lower windows is still at the top of these windows. The reason for this is simple; the squirrels haven't room to operate in the feeder's lower section. The seed that spills out of the lower vents, due to the pressure from above, is available only for birds. The squirrels having frightened the birds away, the level of seed remains the same in the windows of the lower part. We wouldn't need any netted shield if our birds had a little gumption. Charlie wouldn't have had to pick one up, at the pet store, where these things are sold.

We discuss it, on the screen porch. I tell Loraine the birds should fend for themselves.

Loraine—she still looks good to me, although her hair is gray and her legs are thin—is about to place her hand in mine. What she says I am willing to accept, for what else can I do now?

"Charlie will come up with something," she says. "He'll find a way to keep off the squirrels."

"Charlie will show them who's boss," I say.

We play Ping-Pong in the basement. Just before Charlie starts his serve, he holds the ball flat on the paddle. He serves a high, bouncing, easy ball, but that doesn't keep him from winning the point.

I still send out applications. The boathouse has been painted, and the rotten boards on the pier replaced. We are about to put in a redwood fence. Charlie is unloading the boards from the back of the station wagon. I hear the boards slap and clatter, thinking Charlie has found a home here. We have taken him in. We like him. We have accepted him as our man of all work. When I go, Charlie will still be here for whatever Lorraine has to have done. So it doesn't matter so much when I go. And now that I have accepted this truth, I can see the feeder differently. I see it as image, as metaphor. It's a temple, a kind of pagoda, in a garden where there are exotic birds. So one roof isn't set on another, each section and roof a bit smaller in diminishing tiers that thrust at the sky. It isn't literally a pagoda, but it could be where pagodas are found. Seed flows into the feeder. Loraine is pouring in the seed. I steady the feeder, holding the lid. There is a lump in the surface of the roof, a palpable bulge for the fingertips.

Another squirrel makes a leap. It is amazing how agile these squirrels are. Charlie is putting the fence up.

A blue jay is causing the feeder to tip. It is pecking birdseed out of the trough, its head down, tail extended straight. It looks around before flying off. Next a pair of purple finches show up. The carmine breast and head of the male make me think of when I was a child and my mother—warning me this will hurt—put Mercurochrome on a cut. The female finch is a grayish brown, and she doesn't have a crest. Her tail shoots up while she eats. The male finch stands guard on the upper trough while the female feeds from the lower trough. This, I tell myself, is chivalry.

In a heavy flap of beating wings, a grackle slams into the feeder. Its eyes are yellow thumbtacks. Its beak is a cruel, curving blade that punches and hammers the glittering glass. The finches, they panic, screeching. These finches, streaking across the yard, I follow their flight to the river.

Treasure Hunt

How my mother persuaded her big sister to keep us boys is still a mystery to me. Uncle Amber and Aunt Edna would be spending two weeks at their cottage on Lake Lagoda. Uncle Amber had two weeks off from Apperson Finance, where I used to see him behind his desk, in shirtsleeves, wearing suspenders and a floral four-in-hand tie. He had been a staff sergeant in World War One, seen combat at Chateau Thierry and Belleau Wood. Yet Aunt Edna could wind him around her little finger.

Aunt Edna at one time had been a looker. She'd had lots of beaux before she married Uncle Amber. She had the figure of a Gibson girl on a bicycle built for two. Aunt Edna, Mom used to say, wouldn't ride tandem with anybody, not even Clark Gable.

We would stay for ten days, Mom told us. Ten long days, while Mom and our stepfather, Horace Fridlin, vacationed in Cape Cod. Dad would pick us up on his way back to Indianapolis. He couldn't keep us because he would be pushing Bond and Lillard bourbon in southern Indiana and eastern Ohio. Since his insurance agency had gone down the tubes, not long before his marriage did the same, Dad had been working out of Indianapolis, "On the road," he used to tell us, "the open road for big boys like you two will be when you get to be my age." I put down *The Open Road for Boys* when I heard that, his eyes engaging ours like semaphore flags wigwagging from one foundered ship to another—don't abandon ship, help is on the way.

On our way to Lake Lagoda my little brother, Rex, fizzed up his Coca-Cola, took a swig. I knew he shouldn't be doing that in the car. My

Coca-Cola stayed between my knees, where it was supposed to be.

Aunt Edna turned toward Uncle Amber, her thin lips edged with pink lipstick, powder caking her sallow profile. "Amber," she said, "you're driving too fast."

Uncle Amber slowed down to thirty-five. When Aunt Edna turned to us to make sure we were on her side, a belch came from Rex. Aunt Edna's powder-caked face returned to profile. "Amber?"

Uncle Amber kept his eyes on the road, the back of his head tilted toward Rex. "You apologize to your aunt," he said, meaning business.

His Coca-Cola stashed between his knees, Rex swiped off his beanie and said, "I'm sorry I upset you, Aunt Edna."

Aunt Edna directed her sour smile over the passenger seat toward Rex. "I'm not upset but I am concerned. Drinking Coca-Cola in the car, from now on that has to stop."

A Studebaker chugged past us. What if, I thought, Dad passed us gunning his Buick Roadmaster, on his way to the lake, honking his horn to let us know he would be waiting for us, he hadn't forgotten us, he would drive us back to his apartment in Indianapolis, take us to the ballpark to watch the Indians play, buy us hot dogs, all the Coca-Cola we wanted. But he didn't pass us. Other cars did. I didn't count how many.

Uncle Amber stopped for fresh eggs at a farmhouse about half a mile from the cottage—and for tomatoes in wicker baskets, tomatoes almost the size of softballs, and a carton of strawberries. He parked the car by the mailbox, waded through goldenrod and sawgrass to the front porch, where a woman with a goiter the size of a lemon rocked on a porch swing until he climbed the front steps. She got up, smoothed out her flower-print dress. He followed her into the house. Aunt Edna powdered her face in the rearview mirror until Uncle Amber came out the front door, a basket of tomatoes in one hand, a carton of strawberries in the other. The goiter lady carried the basket of eggs.

We passed a row of poplar trees, fresh eggs pillowed in Aunt Edna's lap. We were getting close to Pioneer Cottage. Through the gaps between the cottages, patches of glistening lake water cheered us up, all of us, including Aunt Edna. Her voice, usually abrasive, perked up, as if she felt she had at last glimpsed an end to her innumerable discontents. She turned to Uncle Amber and said, "We'll have strawberry shortcake for dessert tonight," and to us boys, "How does strawberry shortcake sound to you?" Rex said, aware that the shortcake was stored in one of several paper bags in the trunk and the whipped cream was packed with ice in the cooler, "Sounds like a winner to me," and I said, "I'm with Rex."

Uncle Amber parked the car beside the outhouse, and we all got out. Rex and I followed him around the cottage to the lakefront, into the front porch, the screen door unhooked, on to the locked front door. Uncle Amber fitted the key into the keyhole, and the door swung open. He had us unlocking the windows, opening them to cool the cottage off. A musty smell trailed us as we moved through the living room and the narrow dining room to the cramped kitchen and on to the back porch. Uncle Amber unhooked the screen door and in came Aunt Edna. She opened the refrigerator door. There were cubes in the ice tray and half a pitcher of iced tea. The first thing she did was fix four glasses of iced tea, one for each of us. Rex and I helped Uncle Amber bring in the sacks of groceries. He hauled the cooler to the back porch.

WHEN REX GRIPED about the outhouse, our stepfather, Horace Fridlin, had this to say: "You boys should consider it a privilege to use the last outhouse in Indiana." Horace had used an outhouse on his grandfather's farm outside of Marion. "What is good for your aunt and uncle should be good enough for you."

Our stepfather, Horace Fridlin, owned and managed Fridlin's Laundry and Dry Cleaning—a loaf-shaped structure sandwiched between the plate glass factory and the gravel pit on South Buckeye Street. Horace lifted weights, worked out with dumbbells. He'd tell us, "If you boys aren't careful you'll turn out to be ninety-eight-pound weaklings." Horace had Mom working out with dumbbells. He gave up playing golf on Sunday afternoon so he could take us to the country club pool. He would swan dive off the high dive. His legs churning water, he'd swim to our end of the pool, wade out, pectorals thatched with sodden black hairs, booming "Come on in, the water's fine."

DURING OUR STAY at Pioneer, the one thing we took pleasure in was fishing with Uncle Amber. We fished with cane poles for bluegills and perch. Uncle Amber would row out to the southern end of the lake. I remember him feathering the oars, water trickling off the oar blades, the boat docks, piers, trees, and flagpoles getting smaller and smaller. I remember him saying when the fishing was good, "Boys, they're biting today," with an excitement we shared with him, when all you had to do was throw your line into the lake and before you knew it your bobber took a nosedive and you pulled and felt the line yank taut and you hauled in a writhing bluegill.

We were up at six and out on the lake by seven. Around eleven we quit fishing. Uncle Amber rowed us back to Pioneer. Sometimes Aunt Edna was waiting for us at the top of the steep front steps leading from the pier to the front porch. I can picture her standing pigeon-toed, her frizzy red hair catching snippets of a breeze off the lake, her lips, one corner twisted slantwise, pressed together in what for her was a smile. Rex held one of the pier posts and I held the other while Uncle Amber set his tackle box and rod and reel on the pier. Then he looped a line over one post and then the other and only after he had done that could we get out of the boat with the cane poles. If it was Rex's turn to carry the fish net, he'd hold it up and holler at Aunt Edna, "Looks like you'll have a lot of fish to fry." If it was my turn, I didn't hold up the fish net and I didn't say anything. And if we hadn't caught any fish or had to throw the undersized ones back in the lake—the ones, Uncle Amber would say, that weren't keepers—we still waited for Uncle Amber to get out of the boat, with his rod and reel and tackle box, before we got out and clumped up the steps behind him with the cane poles. It was our job to prop them against the roof of the porch, the lines wrapped around the poles. We wrapped while Uncle Amber was rowing us in, turning a pole with the right hand, the line held out and taut with the left, taking care to make sure the hook was snagged in the line.

Something Uncle Amber made clear—we were not to play our radio after nine o'clock because that would upset Aunt Edna. We had brought along our radio, a pink Bakelite that Horace had purchased for us, so we could listen to Jack Armstrong and Captain Midnight and the Lone Ranger late in the afternoon and after dinner in the evening. At the cottage we could only listen to the radio in our room up over the living room. Its one window let in a little breeze at night. After our radio curfew but before lights out, we were permitted to read comic books, which were to be kept upstairs, a stack of them we had packed with the radio, our clothes, Citronella to ward off mosquitoes.

We would roam around the lake in the afternoon. We slurped on Popsicles, licked Brown Giants, swilled Coca-Colas, taking care to bring the empty bottles back to the cottage. The Popsicle sticks we dropped on the road.

One afternoon toward the end of our stay, I thought up a game I would play with Rex. Something we could do while we were supposed to be on our afternoon walks. Supposing, I said to myself, I told Rex there was treasure buried along the lakefront or next to the road behind the cottages or in the peony bushes next to the bedroom window, or in the phlox bed behind the outhouse. I would draw a treasure map. This I would find in the attic one night. As for what the treasure was, the map didn't have to say. Then it came to me, it would be one of the bloody handkerchiefs dipped in John Dillinger's blood, after he was gunned down by G-men coming out of the Biograph Theater. Whoever buried the handkerchief might have also buried his share of the swag from Dillinger's last bank robbery—right here, near Pioneer Cottage, on Lake Lagoda. This unknown gangster had intended to spend a weekend with his latest gun moll in the Palmer House in Chicago, where Mom and Dad had spent their honeymoon. On his way to dig up the swag, he had a heart attack and keeled over.

X marks the spot. Where would that be? And where would I find a bloody handkerchief, a bag of big bills? On the eighth day of our stay, sitting out on the front porch playing Go Fish with Rex, raindrops plunking on the roof, lacing the lake, pooling in Uncle Amber's rowboat (we would have to take turns bailing it out with an empty worm can), a light bulb lit up in my head and I came up with a masterpiece of wily subterfuge. The next morning, bright and early, I told Rex I had a terrible headache. It was up to Rex to tell Uncle Amber I would not be able to go fishing today.

With his back to me, pulling on his blue jeans, Rex said, "Then I won't be able to either."

"You don't have a headache."

"I can fake it."

"I'm thinking you don't want to bail out the boat."

Rex turned around and stuffed his T-shirt into his blue jeans. "That's a big job. It will take two of us." He picked his beanie up off the goosenecked lamp and, with both hands, as if he were trying on a hat, fitted it on his head. Picked at a pimple, waiting for me to say something. Which I did.

"If we both have headaches Uncle Amber will have to bail out the boat."

"So?"

"So we're in the doghouse. No more Popsicles for us, Rex. Or Cokes."

So Rex agreed to sacrifice himself so I could lie in bed with a damp washrag on my head and two aspirin dissolving in my stomach. I asked him who was making the bigger sacrifice, him or me. I'd have Aunt Edna to contend with. All he had to do was bail out the boat.

Rex went downstairs and notified Uncle Amber. Uncle Amber sent Rex back up with aspirin and a glass of water. He stood over the bed looking down at me like I was a mummy he'd come upon in an Egyptian pharaoh's tomb. Then he went back downstairs. I heard him say to Uncle Amber, "It's Max's turn to empty the chamber pot," and Uncle Amber, "Max isn't up to it today," and Rex, "You mean I have to do it?" and Uncle Amber, "You heard what I said, Rex." And then they were out to the front porch, and I got out of bed, still pressing the washrag to my forehead, went to the open window and watched them descend the front steps to the pier, Uncle Amber with his rod and reel and tackle box, Rex with the cane poles. I watched Rex bail out the boat, scooping up water with the worm can—that was the hard part, when the water level sank and you could only scoop up a little at a time. I should be helping him, but it was too late for that.

I waited for them to shove off. Then I got dressed, tiptoed downstairs, padded through the living room, pausing at the bedroom door to make sure Aunt Edna was asleep. I took one of Rex's two handkerchiefs with me. From the fridge I took a bottle of ketchup. I soaked half of Rex's handkerchief in ketchup in the kitchen sink, put the ketchup back in the fridge. Squeezed ketchup out of the handkerchief, leaving a ketchup stain that might pass for John Dillinger's blood. I turned on the cold water, washed ketchup down the drain.

I found Aunt Edna's garden trowel on the back porch, went out behind the outhouse, and buried the handkerchief in the phlox bed. Back in the kitchen, I stole Aunt Edna's grocery list. I erased her list of items, penciled in what was to be discovered by us, along with the treasure map. WHOEVER FINDS THIS TAKE HEED, I wrote, in meticulous block letters. Treasure map and warning note I would hide in the steamer trunk between the chamber pot and a hall tree hung with Uncle Amber's winter overcoat and his rubber overshoes, each occupying a hook. I opened the trunk and breathed in mothballs. The mothballs were sprinkled over garters, a ruby-red camisole, sketchy skirt, high-heel shoes, over Aunt Edna's college yearbook, opened to a photograph of her with three other lookers, each with one hand on one hip, big smiles. I closed the trunk right away, snuffing out the odor of mothballs. It occurred to me I could improve on the treasure hunt by leaving clues along the way. I went downstairs again, snuck out the back porch door with four notes, notepaper torn from Aunt Edna's grocery pad. I was sure she was still asleep. I buried three clues. Clue number one beside the dam, clue number two in an inlet near the fish hatchery. Clue number three across the road from the goiter lady. X marks the spot, in the phlox bed behind the outhouse.

"LOOK HERE, REX." I extracted the note I'd printed, WHOEVER FINDS THIS TAKE HEED, and handed it to Rex.

Rex took in what else was in the steamer trunk.

"So what is a treasure map doing in Aunt Edna's trunk?"

"How do I know?" I lied. "What if Aunt Edna's trunk has been sitting here just waiting for us to open it? So we'd find the map."

Rex grunted. "I'm on to your little game, Max."

"That doesn't mean you can't play it."

Rex looked up at me like I had grown a foot right in front of his eyes. "You mean *we* can't play it, Max."

AUNT EDNA WAVED goodbye at the back door, Uncle Amber behind her. Passing the outhouse on the way to the back road, I felt both of them were watching us. Once we came to a bend in the road, I looked back. The back door was closed.

Rex followed me around the bend and down the road to the dam, creek water slopping over it, a few cottages spaced out along the creek. He skipped stones off the lake, skipping three, sometimes four times. He handed me a flat stone.

"Your turn, Max."

I did a wind up, cocked my left leg, blazed a hardball across an invisible plate. Not even one skip.

"Could I have another look at the map?"

"Here, take a look," I said. "X marks the spot. Right over there by the dam."

Which provided enough gurgly background music while Rex and I, taking turns, scooped up mud with Aunt Edna's garden trowel.

My first clue, GO TO CLUE #2, was mud-smudged but still readable. We veered away from the lake to the fish hatchery, passing a weedy inlet seething with cruising gar, sunlight silvering their snouts. Rex turned up a lichened rock, grub worms wiggling. He handed me the trowel.

"It's your turn, Max."

"Whose idea was it to play this game?"

Scooping up grub worms, I uncovered CLUE #3. GO TO GOITER LADY'S MAILBOX.

"You go, Max."

"We're both going."

"I don't want to go there, Max."

"You scared of her? You think she'll bite you. It says here go to her mailbox. She won't even know we're there."

"She'll be sitting out on her porch."

"So what? Her mailbox is across the road. And she can't sit out on her porch all the time."

We took the back way, down a blacktop road away from the lake. When we got to the access road, Rex took it. I knew I had to follow him.

Up ahead of us, next to the goiter lady's mailbox, to our left a head-high cornfield, tassels shushing in a cooling breeze that rippled the goldenrod to our right, fluffed the spirea bushes beside the front porch. The goiter lady sat in the porch swing where she had been sitting nine days ago, stilling her palmetto fan, slowing the swing to quietude.

Rex squatted beside a clump of Queen Anne's lace, and with Aunt Edna's garden trowel unearthed clue number three, IN THE PHLOX BED BEHIND THE OUTHOUSE X MARKS THE SPOT.

Rex got to his feet and tore clue number three into four strips, held them high up over his head, let them spiral down. One clung to the clump of Queen Anne's lace; the others drifted into the hole. Then he handed me Aunt Edna's garden trowel. "From now on you do the digging. And the walking. I'm staying right here."

To do what, ogle the goiter lady? "You're coming with me."

"Why? What for?" Rex asked. He swiped off his beanie and, balancing it on his right forefinger, twirled it slowly. Across the road the goiter lady pushed off, swung in the squeaky porch swing up up up and away, landing on both feet, kerplop, without toppling into the spirea bushes. Beanie-twirling, Rex asked me. "Is she nuts or something?"

Galumphing through sawgrass and goldenrod, on came the goiter lady, yelling "Get away from my mailbox!" Rex took off first. When I caught up with him he was breathing hard. The first of the row of poplars chuffed and shuffled in the breeze off the lake.

"We aren't going to find any treasure, Max."

"We'll find it. It's where the treasure map says it is."

Rex grabbed the treasure map out of my hand. "X marks the spot, my foot," he said.

"You'll see," I said, wishing he wouldn't see.

How did our treasure hunt end? As we turned the last bend in the road, robins in the pecan tree flurried off in a cloud of flapping wings. X marks the spot, buried in the phlox bed behind the outhouse, had obviously been tampered with. A gaping hole confronted us, minus Rex's ketchup-encrusted handkerchief but containing a note from Aunt Edna—WOULD YOU PLEASE RETURN MY GARDEN TROWEL!!!!

Rex turned to me and grabbed the garden trowel. He started digging, flinging out dirt, yanking phlox stalks out by the roots. He must have dug two feet down. I knew then that he had known all along what I had done. And I knew Aunt Edna hadn't been asleep, had known I would use her bottle of ketchup to further my ends, not hers. Uncle Amber must have dug up the handkerchief and left the note.

The back porch door was locked. We got in through the front porch screen door. Since the night latch was on in the door to the living room, we sat in the glider and looked out at cruising speedboats, girls water-skiing in their wake. Uncle Amber came to the front door, unlatched it and let us in. The first thing he did was ask me for the garden trowel. I handed it over. Then—"From now on you boys will stay in the cottage."

Aunt Edna came in from the bedroom, her sunflower-emblazoned kimono closed tight on her throat. "No more treasure hunts for you two." She dabbed at her mascara with a wad of Kleenex. "And don't you ever steal my garden trowel again!"

Rex stared at her like she was the lady with a beard or the fat lady in a sideshow. Uncle Amber scanned the ceiling like he thought it might fall down on him. Then, his eyes dropping, clamping on us—"Go to your room, both of you, 'til supper time."

Rex asked if we could play our radio. The answer, from Uncle Amber, was no. From Aunt Edna, "Amber?"

"What is it, Edna?"

"It's all right if they play their radio."

Aunt Edna gave us her sour smile. Then she went back in the bedroom and closed the door.

Up in our room, I opened the trunk and realized certain items had been taken out and later put back in—Aunt Edna's garters, her camisole, her skirt, her high-heel shoes. Had Aunt Edna put them on, put on a show for Uncle Amber? Had Uncle Amber put them back, re-sprinkled the mothballs? Rex went to the chamber pot in one corner. He picked up a mothball, squinted at it, put it back in the trunk. He sat down on my side of his bed, turned on the radio. He pulled off his beanie and twisted it.

Without taking his eyes off me—"Who's been up here messing around with Aunt Edna's clothes?"

I had to tell him. "Must have been Uncle Amber."

"Why would he do that?"

"How do I know, Rex?"

Rex put his beanie back on, flattened it over his ears. "When are we going home, Max?"

"When Dad comes to get us," I said.

"You hope," Rex said.

"He'll be here, Rex."

"He better be," Rex said.

We took a last look at the mothballs in Aunt Edna's trunk. Then Rex got up and closed it.

Our father did come for us. He drove us to Indianapolis, passing car after car on the road. He took us to an Indians baseball game. He bought us hot dogs, all the Cokes we could drink; he did everything he could to show us a good time. We soon forgot all about our treasure hunt. But Aunt Edna in her bedroom, her sour smile stitched into her vanity mirror, or stretched out in her bed, her face turned to the wallpaper, waiting for Uncle Amber to bring her her garters, her skirt, her camisole, left an imprint I couldn't wipe away.

www.ingramcontent.com/pod-product-compliance
Lightning Source LLC
Chambersburg PA
CBHW020611310726
48979CB00008B/1433/J

* 9 7 8 1 6 0 3 0 6 1 1 2 4 *